You Didn't Know Me Then

A Riviera View Novel

Lily Baines

ISBN: 9798426931961

Chapter 1

Hope shifted uncomfortably on the high barstool, feeling the beads of sweat slithering down the center of her back, under her sage green, chiffon dress. The Californian summer sun hit her freckled skin through the gaps in the shade that the large oak tree supplied. The ocean breeze was too light to be of any help, and she hoped she didn't have wet circles showing under her arms. Her cheeks flushed deeper as she looked at the bartender.

His toothpaste ad smile made him look approachable, yet she could almost feel him eye roll when her mouth kept going all by itself, as if she had lost control over her tongue, despite having only one drink.

"You can also try reverse spherification. The long molecules in the surfactants won't be attracted by the water, so they'll ..." *Shut up*, she rebuked herself, but her mouth kept going. "You'll get a really nice, festive foam sitting on top of the cocktail." *Shut. Up.* "It's not as pretty as the spheres I told you about, but ... Of course, you don't have to use either; these cocktails are really good as they are. It's just that spherification, or any chemical … Anyway … yeah …" She finally managed to stop.

"Interesting. Thanks. I might try it," Josh said with another smile while smoothing a cloth over the bar's spotless, shiny surface.

Hope could tell it was a fake one.

She didn't know if he had even heard her over the music that played in the background and the chatter of the wedding guests that accumulated on the lawn. What she knew for sure was that, by now, Josh, who had given her a cute smirk when she had first sat down at this long beach bar built especially for the Delaneys' backyard wedding, reacted to her as if she was the water and he the molecules that would never be attracted to it.

She shifted on her seat again, feeling the weight of another set of eyes—those of the man two bar stools to her left. She had side-eyed him a couple of times before and had noticed the amused little grin on his face as he eavesdropped on her one-sided flirt with the bartender while pretending to be engulfed in his phone.

If one could call her going on endlessly about chemistry "flirting."

She slid off the chair to stand up, the heels of her beige pumps penetrating the flawless lawn. "Anyway, thanks for the mimosa. If you ever do want to try it, surfactants can be produced from egg whites, or soy lecithin, if you're worried about vegans or aftertaste, and you can also—"

"Can I get another one, please?" the man to her left cut her off, addressing Josh and pointing at his empty glass.

Hope used the opportunity to look at him and wished she hadn't. Catching the full sight of him made her swallow.

He returned her gaze with a little smirk. His light brown hair was short on the sides and slightly wavier on top, making him look like a Hemsworth sibling. From where she stood, his eyes were the color of bourbon, and his white, button-down shirt, that was cuffed at his elbows, accentuated his tan, as well as the broad shoulders and biceps that filled it and seemed to cord under the fabric. Even sitting down, he looked tall, big.

"Sure thing," Josh replied, grabbing an amber bottle. "Have a good one," he addressed her nonchalantly with a half-hearted nod.

"Thanks," she mumbled, turning to leave and go look for Libby, surreptitiously pulling her heels out of the grass.

What was she thinking? First of all, Josh was probably ten years younger than her. And she wasn't keen anymore, as her younger self used to be, on that hot, surfer look of his with that long, sandy blond hair. Reluctantly, she had to admit that that other man, who looked about her age—she could tell from the lines around his eyes—was even hotter.

Secondly, she had always been flirting-illiterate, and now especially. She hadn't gone out or flirted with anyone in years. Even with Eric, he had done all the flirting, and that had been over a decade ago. He was remarried now, and here she was, trying to flex a muscle that she rarely practiced.

Hope tugged at the waistline of her dress, pretty sure the liner of her body shaper, which felt more like sausage casing in this heat, was detectable through the fabric.

A few steps away from the bar, she felt a soft hand on her arm and lifted her head.

"Libby!"

"Hey, sweetie. Having a good time?"

"Lib, do you think virginity can just grow back after you haven't … you know?"

Libby laughed as they crossed the lawn. "Why? What happened?"

Hope sighed, relieved to be with her best friend. "It's all your fault, really. You got that idea into my head that Josh was cute and single, and there he was, tending bar, and I went to get a drink, and … you know how you know you should shut up, but you just can't stop yourself from speaking, because you're already embarrassed about talking so much, so you try to cover it up by talking even more? Yeah, that was me now. And the worst part was that this guy was sitting there, looking all amused about it. It made me go on and on even more."

"Oh no. I'm so sorry. Luke's family kept me and since it's his sister's wedding—"

"No, no, don't be. I'm so happy for you!" They were heading toward the rows of white wooden chairs that were facing the flower-covered canopy, and Hope stopped and turned to face Libby. "Luke is amazing and, of course, the Delaneys wanted to welcome you after all this time apart. I'm so happy for you!"

They hugged, careful not to smudge their dresses with makeup.

"Don't mind me," Hope continued when they let go of each other. "I was just kidding when I said it was your fault. I'm just not ready yet."

Libby smiled. "I think you're more ready now than you've been in the last two years. So, baby steps?"

"Baby steps, hoping I won't crash on my ass."

The music in the background changed all of a sudden into something more melodic, then the D.J. announced that the ceremony was about to begin. Luke Delaney's younger sister, Ava, was about to tie the knot, and despite what had just happened, Hope was still excited she had been invited as Libby's friend.

"Here's my mom and David," Libby said, waving at the two.

Rows were filling up with people taking a seat for the ceremony. Hope sat next to Libby's mother, Connie Latimer, and her partner, David. Libby remained standing next to them, and Hope couldn't help but smile, knowing just from the expression on Libby's face that she had spotted Luke.

Hope followed Libby's gaze and, sure enough, it was Luke who Libby had locked gazes with. The expression on *his* face clearly indicated he was melting on the inside.

Hope shifted her eyes to the man who stood next to Luke, and her stomach dropped two floors. It was the grinner she had entertained at the bar.

Her stomach plummeted another floor when she realized that he and Luke looked incredibly alike.

He wasn't looking in her direction, busy pointing people to what empty chairs were left, as the music ceased and the murmurs of the crowd were being hushed.

Coldplay's "A Sky Full Of Stars" began playing, and the man, who she now figured was Luke's and the bride's brother, straightened up and looked over at the far end of the aisle, between the two blocks of chairs. He was an inch taller than Luke, and his shirt fit him in an unholy way, especially given the minister who had just passed him on his way to the flowery altar.

When even Luke and Libby tore their eyes off each other, Hope swung her head along with everyone else to watch first the groom, then the bride, make their way down the aisle, each escorted by their parents.

She didn't know Ava Delaney, but based on the choices that she had made for her wedding, she liked her already. She knew from Libby how amazing Luke was, so that left what looked like another sibling of theirs as the douche sheep of the family. A man who sneered at women who didn't know how to flirt.

"It's Luke's brother," she said urgently to Libby as soon as the ceremony was over, pointing at the at least six-foot-tall man. "Now that I see them next to each other, they even look alike."

"Jordan? That's the guy who listened to you talking to Josh?"

"Talking to Josh! Making a fool of myself, you mean." Hope's cheeks reddened again at the memory. "It's even more embarrassing now. I wanted to make a good impression on your boyfriend's family."

"Don't worry about it. So he saw you trying to flirt with someone. Big deal. It's a wedding—everybody does that. And I don't think Jordan's the kind of guy who would ... Please don't feel bad about this. If anything, it's my fault for leaving you alone."

Hope smoothed a hand over her dress and averted her gaze. "No, I wanted to ... you know"—she lowered her voice—"get away, be all sexy and flirty, and sitting alone at a bar, and ... Ugh ... I'm so not made for this."

"It takes practice to get back in the game, and you haven't had that in a long time, so don't worry about it. It's good that you practiced on Josh. He's too young, anyway. The next guy you talk to, you'll do better." Libby rubbed her palm over Hope's arm. "And trust me; no one who knows you will have a bad impression of you. You're the sweetest person I know."

Sweet. She wanted to be spicy. Maybe Libby was right and all she needed was practice.

"Okay, but I'm not showing my face again at Life's A Beach until Josh forgets what I look like." She gave Libby an effortful smile.

"Plenty of other places we can go to for you to hit on their bartenders." Libby chuckled. "Come on; let's find our seats."

Two hours and two phone calls later—one to the babysitter and one with her nine-year-old daughter—Hope zig-zagged her way through the wedding tent, from the table she was seated at to the dance floor. She tapped on Libby's shoulder.

Libby and Luke turned to face her.

"Hey, sorry to interrupt, but I have to go. Your mom and David are leaving, so I'll get a ride back to Riviera View with them."

"Are you sure you don't want to stay?" Libby asked, signaling to Luke that she would be right back and stepping aside with Hope.

"Yeah, Hannah and the babysitter are not getting along. They both called me."

"Can't Eric's parents stop by or something?"

"You'd think, right? No, they're in Nevada, visiting the prince himself."

Eric was an only child and the center of his parents', her former in-laws, existence. Remarried and living in Nevada, the old couple traveled there almost every other weekend instead of enjoying the company of their granddaughters, who lived in the same town as them.

"Oh, honey, you wanted this to be your grownup fun. If you stay longer, I'll find you a ride back to Riviera View, if you don't want to wait for us. Hannah will survive. Come on; dance some more."

Hope had joined the dancing before and had even danced two couples' dances; one with David and one with Luke, who had managed to leave Libby's side long enough to dance with others. While she had been on the dance floor, she had spotted Jordan Delaney dancing with his sister in her beautiful, vintage wedding dress, and with his mother and an older aunt. Some of the untouchable sophistication was gone from his face when he chatted with them. It was rather sweet and weakened her resentment. Now, from the corner of her eye, she could see him standing and talking to two younger men.

She put her hand on Libby's arm. "I had a great time. This *was* the grownup fun I wanted. But this Cinderella has to march her glass slippers home now. Thanks so much for making me your plus-one, Lib. Although, I have to tell you, Luke is everything you said and more. He's your plus-one forever."

Libby's face brightened further, though she was already glowing. "He is," she said, turning her head to look at Luke, who was laughing with the newlyweds. "Will I see you on Monday, as usual?"

"If you manage to leave bed." Hope grinned, biting her lower lip and winking at Libby.

"Mmm ... You have a point." Libby laughed. She and Luke were so new together, although they had known each other all their lives, and they were so much in love. Hope couldn't remember what that felt like.

They hugged. "Tell Luke I said bye and that I hope to meet him again."

"You're gonna!" Libby said enthusiastically, and it dawned on Hope just then that she would probably meet the other Delaneys, as well, including Luke's older brother with his confusing presence, and smirk, and that tendency to be amused at others' expense.

Oh no.

She went back to her table and picked up her purse.

Just as she turned to tell Connie and David that she was ready to leave, she saw Jordan Delaney approaching them with a smile. He had dimples, and not the cute kind, but the sexy kind, like Bradley Cooper's.

"Connie," he said. "Can I call you Connie instead of Mrs. Latimer?" The Latimers and the Delaneys had lived next door to each other for years before the Delaneys had moved from Riviera View to the much better off Wayford.

"Jordan! Of course you can," Connie responded smilingly, shaking his hand and fondly placing her palm on his forearm. Hope wondered what that felt like. It looked so strong with those visible veins running under the skin. "How you've been?" Connie asked.

"Good. Been good," he said, but his smile slightly faded and the spark ebbed in his eyes. Hope's curiosity was piqued. "I was hoping to catch you before, but it's been so hectic here," he continued. "How are you? How's Gabe doing?"

"He's great. He has two daughters, and Tammy, his wife, is lovely," Connie said proudly. Gabe was Libby's older brother who lived in L.A. Hope figured that, if Jordan was Gabe's age, that made him forty-one. Five years older than her.

"Tell him I said hi. I'd be happy to see him next time he comes to Riviera View."

Connie grinned. "He will … for the holidays. And with these two being like this"—she gestured with her head toward Luke and Libby, who didn't even have a centimeter between them on the dance floor—"I hope we'll see a lot of all you Delaneys."

Jordan shifted to look at his brother and Libby. "I've never seen him like this," he said, returning his gaze to Connie.

"Your mother tells me that you're doing wonders in D.C. You work with that congresswoman …

What's her name? Patty told me, but I forgot. Sorry." Connie tapped on his arm fondly.

"Rush. Sharon Rush. I don't work for her anymore. I'm ... I finished that project and took time off. So, tell me more about Gabe."

Hope tried to seem uninterested, standing next to David, a few steps away from Connie and Jordan, pretending to be busy with her phone. Well, she was, because another text from the babysitter had arrived, asking her when she would be back.

"Oh, Jordan, excuse me. I'm being rude," she suddenly heard Connie say. "This is my partner, David." Connie pivoted abruptly toward David and Hope.

Hope jerked her head up, and her gaze met with that of Jordan's. For a single, drawn-out moment, she was a deer caught in headlights.

Jordan stepped forward and reached out his hand to David. "Jordan Delaney, pleasure to meet you, David."

Hope gazed at the strong palm that covered David's, hoping he wasn't crushing the older and smaller man's hand with his strong shake.

"And that's Hope, one of Libby's best friends. You didn't know her then. She moved here from Minnesota only about ten years ago," Connie continued.

Coming from a tiny town herself, Hope wasn't surprised that, despite her years in Riviera View, she wasn't considered a local in the eyes of those born there, like Connie.

The deep, umber eyes and the dimples on the otherwise rough edges of Jordan's face and jaw were now turned toward her. He was so tall and his shoulders so wide that Hope was sure she was screened from view if someone were to look over at them.

She hoped her palm wasn't sweaty in his when he gripped it and shook it.

His smile, directed at her, was a warm smirk. "Nice to meet you, Hope." It was obvious they both recognized the other from the bar before. "We hope to see more of Libby's friends. We're trying to make a good impression on her, for Luke's sake." He held her gaze and her palm, and although he spoke in plural, she felt a heatwave rushing through her body, as if she was standing under the blazing sunlight with no wedding tent over her head.

"Nice to meet you, too."

He released her palm. "You're a teacher, I hear."

"Um, yes. I teach chemistry." She felt idiotic. Had he heard it from Libby or inferred it from her silly chatter at the bar earlier? And, why did he have such an effect on her? He was attractive, but so what?

He made a single slow nod of *now it makes sense.* "There's chemistry in everything," he said, still holding her gaze. Yes, there was no mistaking he had heard her one-sided conversation with Josh.

"Jordan and Luke's mother was a teacher in your school," Connie chimed in, addressing Hope.

"Yes, Libby told me," Hope said, glad to have someone else to avert her gaze to.

"Riviera View's school … Can't say I miss it. It wasn't fun being a teacher's son."

Hope had to revert her eyes back to him. "My daughters go there."

She noticed his gaze drop to her left hand that was void of a wedding ring. He then looked back up at her.

"There's someone here you know," he said. "Avery Miles, she's the vice principal there, I believe."

"Yes, we met." She had been surprised to come across Avery at the wedding and found out through Libby that Luke's mom had kept in touch with the school after her retirement. The few words she had exchanged with Avery had been mostly her answering Avery's questions as to how she knew the bride and groom and about the school's summer program, which Hope was teaching in for extra income while Avery and others were on summer break.

"Didn't you use to go out with her, Jordan?" Connie asked with a playful grin. "You seemed to be surrounded by all the pretty girls from your class back then."

Jordan just smirked again. "Connie, it was wonderful meeting you again. I hope we get to see a lot more of you all. Don't forget to tell Gabe hi for me."

Hope hoped that her surprise at Connie's question wasn't written all over her face, especially since Jordan seemed to have deflected answering it.

"I sure will. Take care, Jordan. I hope you stop by Riviera View."

"You bet. Unlike Wayford, Riviera View has a pulse. I miss it." He nodded once with a smile toward her and David then left.

She watched his broad back as he walked away.

"He hasn't changed," Connie remarked to David as they turned to leave. "He's always been charming and had a way with words. I wasn't surprised he became involved in politics."

"He's a politician?" David asked, hooking Connie's elbow in his.

"A political advisor. He works with them, but it rubs off on you, you know?"

A way with words. No wonder her incoherent mumbles to Josh had amused him. He was used to the sleek and smooth, to those who made speeches for a living.

"From what I could see, if he got it from anyone, it's from his father," David commented dryly. "The rest of them seem very down to earth."

"Could be. Joe Delaney has always been a bit of a stuck-up, but his wife and kids aren't. Gabe was friends with Jordan and liked him," Connie replied.

They were just exiting the well-kempt garden out to the street. "I wonder if they employ someone to keep it this way. Patty used to have a little herb garden when they lived next to us. It was nothing this grand. Our kids were small, the houses were small. It's so strange to see her living out in Wayford."

"Being a stuck-up paid off for Joe." David laughed.

"As long as he's nice to my Libby ..." Connie remarked.

Hope looked around as they climbed into the car, wondering which of the elements in the periodic table Jordan Delaney resembled the most. She detected some detached outer shell that wouldn't bond with other elements. On the other hand, he seemed capable of creating explosions, even with the slightest contact, if her reaction to him was any indication.

Chapter 2

Fuck. The brunette wore a determined expression as she beelined her way toward him through the thinning crowd. He had hoped that their little reunion conversation earlier had been enough. He had let her keep talking about herself and all the fun they used to have in high school. All he could remember was that they had *been* to high school together.

"So, Jordan, will I get to see more of you?" She brazenly placed her palm on his chest and cast her eyes down his body.

"Avery, how d'you like the wedding?"

"It was great. Even better was meeting an old friend. Glad you're paying us a visit."

"I visit every year."

"So, how come you never get in touch?" She patted his chest.

He was beginning to wonder how much she'd had to drink.

Why would he keep in touch? He had hardly remembered who she was when she had approached him earlier.

He went out on a limb. "I knew you'd be busy—marriage, kids, work. Right, Avery? You're a busy vice-principal now. You wouldn't have had the time for me." He tried to keep it gallant and hoped that mentioning her position would make her cease what she was now doing—smoothing her palm over his chest, down to the part just above his midsection.

Looking around, Jordan hoped to find some excuse to get away.

"Well, like I told you, I'm divorced." She grinned. "We could recreate the old days before you go back to D.C. Life's A Beach is still operating. We could get together for a drink." Avery now dragged her palm up his abdomen.

How different from Libby's friend, who he had seen trying to hit on Josh at the bar. Maybe if she had tried *that* on Josh ... But since it wasn't working on him, maybe it wouldn't work on Josh, either.

"One of your teachers is here," he said, removing Avery's hand from his body. The redheaded chemistry teacher had already left but mentioning her might help Avery get a grip. She seemed to be slightly swaying on her feet.

His mother had told him that Avery had pretty much invited herself to the wedding. "*But I didn't mind to have more Riviera View people to balance all the Wayforders your father invited,*" his mother had said.

Avery dropped her hand to her side. "Yes. Hope Hays. We talked. She's sweet, unlike her ex-husband. You might remember him. He was in your brother's class. Eric Hays."

"Oh yeah," he said, recalling a fluffy sort of guy with all the snazzy surfers' gear, minus the talent. "Had a new BMW the moment he got his license? That guy? The first PlayStation in all Riviera View? I think I remember him. Luke wasn't a fan."

Avery giggled. "Yeah, him. My ex may be guilty of a lot of things, but at least we share raising our son." She brought her hand up to coquettishly touch his chest again. "Speaking of ... he's over at his dad's now. So, how about you drive me and my car back to Riviera or ... d'you stay here while you're in Wayford?" She looked over at the upper windows of his parents' house.

Jordan rubbed the back of his neck. "Yeah, I do. Let me find you a ride back." He wasn't sure she should be getting behind a wheel, and he had no intention of taking her up on the offer.

"If I leave my car here, I'll have to get it tomorrow. Will I see you then, Jordan Delaney?"

"Busy tomorrow. Post-wedding stuff."

Spotting his aunt passing by, he called out, "Sylvia, do you have room in your car for one more? Avery here needs a ride back to Riviera."

"Sure. We'll be leaving soon. I'll come get you, Avery dear."

That was the great thing about these small towns—everyone knew everyone.

When he had first left for Cornell then to D.C., he had been relieved to get away from it, but at the age of forty-one, and after years in the dog-eat-dog, steel-cold of the capital's politics, he appreciated the warmth, familiarity, and sense of belonging.

"Thanks, I guess?" Avery half-slurred.

"Take care, Avery. See you around." He patted her arm then left, looking for his brother.

Spotting Luke with Libby sitting close together on one of the white patio sofas at the impromptu beach bar that had been erected by Life's A Beach's staff, Jordan marched over to join them.

Slouching on the soft cushions, he breathed out, "How are you two holding up?"

"Great, as long as Ava's having fun, but I think she's ready for this to be over, too," Luke replied.

"Liberty, I spoke to your mom and friend before they left," he addressed Libby, using her full name, as Luke did. Running a hand through his hair, he added, "I hope we made a good impression on you, for this guy's sake." He angled his head toward his younger brother.

He remembered Luke and Libby as teenagers, always together, before he had left for college then Washington. Luke, too, had left to later become an air marshal and spent fifteen years away from home. Ava was the only one of the three of them who had remained close to home, while he and Luke had pursued careers far from their father's onerous presence.

"No need to impress me. I've known you all forever," Libby replied, leaning her head on Luke's shoulder.

Jordan smiled when Luke leaned his head against hers.

Speaking with her earlier, he had liked Libby immediately, much more than he had ever liked Luke's former girlfriend. He hoped to be as lucky as his brother one day.

When Libby got up to speak with a lingering guest, Luke turned to him. "Tell me you didn't say anything to Hope about, you know, the funny/sad bar scene," he said, quoting Jordan's own words.

"I didn't know who she was until you figured it out when I told you about it. And, of course I didn't say anything, but she recognized me. She must have noticed that I … Anyway, I tried to be friendly." He felt bad, remembering his amused conversation with Luke before the ceremony.

"Like watching a train wreck," he had referred to it. *"She realized she was blabbering, but was embarrassed, so she blabbered even more. Like she hasn't been in the game for a while. I felt sorry for her. I'd give her a few pointers if she didn't talk so much,"* he had told Luke. *"I wanted to interfere and help her; at least grab the bartender's attention so she'd be able to shut up, but your girlfriend arrived. I heard her asking Libby if she thought you can grow your virginity back."* That last sentence had made Luke realize whom he had overheard. And now that he had spoken to her, seen the embarrassed yet determined look in her eyes, and knew that Hope had been married to Eric "The Douche" Hays, it all made sense, and he felt like an asshole.

"Okay. Don't get too friendly, though," Luke said now, just as he had when they had spoken about it before.

"I told you already, I'm not like that. Trust me; if I wanted to get friendly with anyone, I just received a very open invite from Avery Miles. Remember her?"

"No."

"Never mind. I didn't remember her, either. She was in my class, and she's here because, apparently, Mom invited random people who work at the school."

"Oh, now I know who you mean. Yeah, Liberty told me she worked with Hope. You passed up on it?"

"Yep. You don't believe me, do you? Told you I've been celibate since I got here."

"Figured it's temporary. Hasn't been that long since you came back," Luke commented as he stretched his legs.

Jordan scoffed. "Whatever it is, I'm not planning on fucking around. Haven't done that in a long while." Except for that stupid mistake that made him put three thousand miles between him and D.C. and still haunted him with its potential consequences.

"What happened in D.C., Jordan?" Luke suddenly asked, as if something in Jordan's expression had given him away. "Why don't you have plans of going back? You came here weeks before the wedding."

It was the first time Luke had touched that point since picking him up from the San Francisco airport. He had evaded answering back then, and their bro code ensured Luke didn't push.

Jordan breathed out. He wasn't sure he could explain. "It wasn't one thing. It was … things piled up like dog shit. And the stench rubbed on me and wouldn't come off."

"Work or …?"

"Both." He had tried not to think about it since his return.

They were both slumped on the sofa, watching the wedding pavilion emptying and returning a few goodbye waves.

"Did you quit or …?"

"Not exactly." He had left overnight after texting his former employer the last open details of his project. Not that Sharon minded. Getting back with her husband after several months of separation which, thanks to Jordan's professional advice, they had succeeded in hiding from the public eye, she had been relieved to see him go.

"If you're staying, you can move into the beach house. I'm over at Liberty's most days," Luke said, turning his head toward him.

Jordan looked back at him. "Thanks, man. I was going to ask. If you're not using it as much … Mom and Dad are driving me crazy." After living on his own since he had been eighteen, as much as he loved them, he couldn't bear his mother's coddling nor the not-so-subtle hints that his father dropped, concerning his job, which Joe Delaney had been using as lever, as if his political advisor son could, or would, do something to further his attorney business.

Libby was approaching them again.

"Listen, if she says something about her friend, don't tell her I even told you about it," Jordan said. "That way, it would seem as if I didn't notice or just forgot about it. You know, like it made no impression on me either way."

Luke nodded. "Yeah, that'd be best."

But it *had* made an impression on him. A strange one. After years of being around people who controlled and calculated every word that came out of their mouths, it was refreshing to see someone who seemed incapable of it.

Jordan noticed the ocean breeze for the first time since he had gotten back. It was refreshing after the musty Potomac he had left behind.

Chapter 3

"I don't want to tell you, and you can't make me."

Hope stroked her daughter's shoulder over the blue pineapples T-shirt. "Hannah, sweetie," she said softly, "I won't make you. I want you to feel like you can tell me. I'm not mad at you, because I don't really know what happened. And I won't believe anything until I hear it from you first."

"I didn't mean to kick her." Hannah's voice was muffled by the unicorns bedcover she was burying her face in. She had thrown herself on it and hidden her face the moment Hope had arrived. "It was just a little kick. And I said sorry."

"I know you didn't mean to hurt her, and it's good that you apologized." Hope smoothed a hand over Hannah's more strawberry than blonde curls—a combination of hers and Eric's hair colors—that splayed around her, further concealing her face from view. They were somewhat knotted at the back because she refused to brush them or let Hope brush them for her more than twice a week.

"I didn't even know why I did it, but now I do. Ainsley is annoying. She thinks she's so smart just because she's older and gets to watch over us. And she said I talked too much."

Hope's heart clenched in her chest. She could imagine Hannah, her bright and clever-beyond-her-nine-years daughter rambling on and on about something she read, or watched, or thought, or dreamed, and Ainsley, just sixteen and busy also with seven-year-old Naomi, losing patience. It wouldn't be the first time. Whenever Hannah had a friend over, Hope would hint to her in advance, or while the friend was there to watch, for the signals of the other person regarding their level of interest in the topic. Not everybody was interested in history, the environment, and current global affairs like Hannah, who loved watching the news and read everything she could get her hands on.

It stung extra especially today because she, herself, had failed in it miserably, so how could she expect a socially awkward nine-year-old to avoid it?

She had failed Hannah.

Any social anxiety must have come from her and not Eric. If anything, society was made anxious *by* him and not the other way around. And though she would take social awkwardness over his puffed-up confidence any given day, today wasn't a great day for such comparisons.

Hope controlled the constriction in her throat so her voice wouldn't sound choked. "It's very mature of you, Hannah, to say this—that you didn't know what was happening to you then but that you now understand yourself. I won't ask Ainsley back. We have other options." The options were limited, but she didn't say that, and she also made sure not to use the word "babysit," because Hannah had said she wasn't a baby. "Now, come here, sweetie, let me hug you."

She tried pulling Hannah up, tickling her, all the while feeling the rock of guilt in her chest. Feeling shackled by routine, she had jumped at Libby's offer to join her at the wedding instead of being satisfied with the pottery classes that she was taking and the almost-weekly Monday night outings she, Libby, and Roni had. Why did she have to go to that wedding, too? Nothing good came out of it.

Hannah giggled and squirmed into the blanket. She was somewhat tall for her age, probably got it from her father, because Hope wasn't on the taller end of the scale. Hannah's long limbs still had that childish roundness, and Hope feared the day all this would be replaced by a grumpy teenager who she could already discern glimpses of.

"You look pretty, Mom," Hannah said when she finally raised her face, creases from the cover adorning her sweet, freckled cheeks. "You should always wear dresses like that and do your hair like this." She raised a hand and played with Hope's copper hair.

While Naomi was still at an age where she thought her mommy was the most beautiful woman, Hannah had reached the age where she began criticizing her fashion choices and comparing her to other moms, real or TV ones.

"Thanks, baby. Sorry! Not baby. You're a big girl." Hope chuckled. "Now, let me tell you about the

plans I made for us now that summer school is over."
She wrapped her arm around Hannah.

"Naomi, sweetie, come here please, I want to tell
you something," she called out to her sever-year-old
from the next room.

When the blonde-haired, blue-eyed Naomi
sauntered into the room with her latest rainbow
unicorn in tow, Hope cuddled with them on Hannah's
bed and told them about the fun they would have
before the school year started.

Later, when she poured herself a cup of coffee in
the kitchen, she thought of Avery and the
conversation they'd had on the last day of the
previous school year.

*"I filled in for Hannah's homeroom teacher for a
week, and I think you should get her diagnosed,"
Avery said. "Maybe it's your divorce. She's very
intelligent, uses vocabulary that leaves her friends
wondering what she's talking about, but she answers
back without thinking, her handwriting is barely
legible, and she gets herself into corners she can't
back out of, both with staff and peers. I could be
wrong, but I'm thinking ADHD or some sort of
emotional regulation disorder."*

She had simply thanked Avery back then, biting
back a comment about Avery's completion of a one-
week counseling course that was part of her
promotion from administrator to vice-principal, with
minimum teaching experience over the years. Though
she didn't exactly like Avery and could never pin
down why—except that Avery had a way of making
things sound unnerving—she had touched a sensitive
point, something that Hope had noticed, too.

She didn't know why, but hearing earlier that Avery might have gone out with Jordan Delaney coiled her stomach inexplicably.

~~~~~~~~~~~~~~~~~

"After that, she was fine. She doesn't have a high threshold for frustration, but we're working on it." Hope sighed. It helped to talk to Libby about it. As a social worker, she was familiar with these things. That was how they had met six years ago, when Hope had thought one of her student's family should be looked into and had consulted with Social Services. She and Libby had hit it off, and she had found her first best friend in Riviera View. The second was Libby's childhood friend, Roni, who she had met shortly after.

"How was the rest of the wedding?" Hope asked, shifting the phone to her other ear. The girls were asleep in their rooms, and she was folding laundry on the couch with the TV on.

"I wish you didn't have to leave early, but you didn't miss much after," Libby replied.

"Did Josh or Luke's brother say anything?"

"Nothing. I think you're making more of it than either one of them noticed. And about Hannah, you and the school counselor are aligned. You spoke to a therapist. They both said it's normal for gifted children, so I wouldn't worry. She's an amazing kid, and with a mom like you, she'll be fine!"

Hope couldn't answer immediately, her throat choked.

"And I can ask Aunt Sarah if she could sometimes help with babysitting," Libby continued.

"Thanks, Libby, for everything. And it'd be great! If Sarah has time, I'd be so relieved." Sarah was Libby's aunt and owned a pharmacy in town. A colorful, local persona with even more colorful hairstyles, which she changed every three months. Single at the age of sixty, she gave free relationship advice to her niece and anyone who would listen. "I had my little share of romance, but observing everyone else's mistakes has made me an expert," she often said.

"I'll talk to her and let you know."

Hope placed a pair of folded pink pants on top of a similarly pinkish pile. "Are we meeting tomorrow?" Their Mondays' start-the-week-on-the-right-foot evenings were a lifeline.

"Don't kill me, but everything has been so crazy until now, and Luke and I have hardly had a chance to spend time together."

"I won't kill you, and neither will Roni. We totally get it! You two should take the time to be with each other after all these years. I'm kinda relieved, because I don't think I can leave the girls with a babysitter again tomorrow evening."

She was genuinely thrilled for Libby, though she couldn't help but notice that, for the first time since the divorce two years ago, being the single one in their trio bothered her. Up until now, just the thought of a relationship was repugnant to her. It was funny, if an alien had met the three of them, they would probably think that Roni, with her flighty attitude, was the single one. But Roni was the constant one, despite having a mini marital crisis a few years back.

Libby had had a few and far between short relationships, but Luke was her endgame.

As for herself, for four years out of the six that she had known her friends, she had been in a marriage whose crumbling she had first refused to admit, and then she had become a two-year divorcee, licking the wounds of failure. Although her wounds didn't hurt as much anymore, her taste in men required a serious reevaluation.

Only after the divorce had become final, her friends had dared to reveal that Eric had been nicknamed "Eric the Douche" in high school. Meeting him when he had attended college in her home state of Minnesota, she hadn't known that. She had found out the hard way.

Recently, the craving for a relationship began taking more headspace, which could explain Josh. Or maybe it wasn't headspace as much as it was further south than her head, which could explain her reaction to the eldest Delaney sibling.

Chapter 4

"Will you let me know?" Jordan cast his eyes over his parents' meticulously groomed backyard. Just a day after the wedding, it looked unscathed.

The silence on the other end of the line churned his stomach. "Sharon?"

"I will. I hired someone to cover my PR and she thinks that, however this turns out, we shouldn't be in any kind of contact. But I promised to let you know, and I will. To be honest, mostly because I'm pretty sure that—"

"Dana Brin, is it? That's who you hired and you disclosed this to her?"

"I didn't have to. She put two and two together. You're not the only one in this city who's capable of sniffing shitstorms before they occur and take preventive actions."

He wasn't the only one, but he was one of the best. So sought after that he could afford not to be a regular member on anyone's staff and have the luxury of choosing his projects and legislators. He strove to take on those whose goals somehow reminded him of why he had entered this game in the first place—to do good. Or, at least try to in a system that hid cynicism under every stone and favored personal agendas over most things. Too many years in, he ceased to believe there was anything genuinely good left anymore. In anyone. Including himself.

He expelled a breath. "Preventive actions? Like spreading the word that you fired me because I under-delivered? I quit, Sharon. You didn't fire me. I got you every vote you needed to pass your bill because I believed in it. And, although it wasn't part of my job description, my work is the only reason the media still has no inkling that you and Phil were separated."

"I know all that, Jordan, and I thank you for everything. That rumor, I believe, is of Dana's doing; it didn't come from me."

"Don't try that on me. Dana wouldn't have done it without your blessing." There were no colleagues in that city. Only competitors. And he had known Dana Brin years ago … in every sense.

"Jordan, if either one of us wants a future here, then …"

Then we shouldn't have had that one-night stand when you were separated, he wanted to say but didn't. It hadn't even been a one-night. Ten minutes was more like it. Brief and hollow. Zero feelings. He didn't say that, either.

"Don't invent lies. Say nothing if you don't have anything better to say," he said, instead. "That's my professional advice."

"Anyway, I'll let you know, because I know you won't use it against me, however this turns out. I trust you. I wouldn't be holding this conversation otherwise, knowing you could record it. I know it's not your style. You don't operate like that. Hell, this is why I hired you in the first place. I wanted fair and clean." She snickered at her own words. "Jordan, I wouldn't worry if I were you. I don't think that it's really ... and if it is, then it's my problem. Dana thinks I can use it as leverage—garner sympathy and affiliation with working mothers. It's our best shot."

Jordan took a deep breath as he strolled to the end of the backyard and stopped by the large oak tree that had served as a canopy over a bar just the day before. The sun rays infiltrated through the foliage and warmed his skin while the words chilled his blood.

He should be used to this. He had heard such words, such calculated motives before. Hell, he had *advised* for or against the utilization of things that shouldn't be part of the political game yet had been cynically capitalized on, nonetheless. He had become one of *those* people—the type he had sworn he would never be.

He looked over at the house where his parents, and Luke and Libby, and his sister and her husband were having wedding leftovers for lunch. "Does Phil know?"

"Of course not."

Of course not. The spouse, married or separated, was always last to know. Too many times he had been the one guarding the truth so it wouldn't harm the professional aspirations of the people he advised. He had known everyone's dirtiest secrets—what they did, who they did—and now he was someone's dirty secret.

His years in D.C. felt like a landslide, and this was a new low.

"Just let me know. And, Sharon, if it is, I'll decide if it's a problem for me or not, okay?" When no reply came, he muttered, "Take care," then hung up.

His cell phone buzzed in his hand.

"*Came with an Uber to pick up my car. You here?*"

He didn't recognize the number, but the text clarified who it was.

Jordan rubbed a hand over his nape. He didn't mind meeting old friends. He remained in touch with most of them, the very few who were still in Riviera View and those who had left. Avery Miles was not one of them. None of the girls whom he might have hooked up with in high school were among his friends. In fact, he hadn't thought that those girls, now women in their early forties, would remember him.

"*If you're ignoring me, it's rude. I'm an old friend*," another text appeared.

Sighing, he circled the house to the front. Avery stood next to her car beyond the lawn.

She waved. "Hey."

"Hey. I have to head back inside," he said as soon as he reached her. "We're having a post-wedding family lunch."

"My son's still over at my ex's."

"Gonna be tied up here all day."

"Tied up? I like the sound of that."

Not a muscle moved in his face. That kind of crafty sass passed right over his head on any given day, and especially today. He didn't find it cute, sexy, or remotely enticing. He would much rather have a green-eyed redhead blabber chemistry facts to him over this. At least it would be genuine.

Avery must have sensed it, since she opened her car's door. "I remember you as more fun, Jordan," she muttered.

"I don't think we knew each other very well, Avery. And, in any case, people change."

"We didn't, but we can get to know each other now. Maybe have a drink some time? Your mom said you're staying here for the time being. She had this idea that you could judge at our Model UN at school and gave me your number."

"She did, did she?" He should really talk to his mother about this.

Jordan put a hand on the car's roof, and as if she took the hint, Avery climbed in.

"I thought we could discuss it," she said. "Not every elementary school has it. And we do the real stuff, not Burgerland versus Candyland."

"I'll think about it. Drive safe." He helped close the door then tapped once on the car's roof. When she drove off, he turned toward the house and went back inside.

"Hey Luke," he said as soon as he saw his brother in the kitchen. "About the beach house. Can I move in next week?"

"Sure."

"Just until I figure some things out."

Chapter 5

Hope hugged Libby and Roni as if she hadn't seen them for two years instead of two weeks.

"Is this you being excited over the school year starting, Hope? Because I can't wait to ship my kids there tomorrow morning." Roni flicked back her raven-black, smooth hair.

They perused the menus of The Mean Bean, as if those ever changed, and caught up on the last two weeks of the summer vacation.

"So, besides Six Flags, two movies, and the baking, crafts, and beach days I organized, they also spent two days with Eric's parents. The prince himself was too busy but promised to come and get them on Labor Day." Though she had her own issues with him, the girls loved spending time with their dad, and his new wife was kind to them. She stopped trying to understand how he could have moved away from them and focused on maintaining their positive connection with him.

"We had fun on the beach with you," Roni said. "I wish Hannah was in Lulu's class. They got along so well. Well, until it ended in tears. But it always does with kids."

Louise, Roni's eldest, was Hannah's age. They clicked but never became besties.

"And this one over here"—Roni gestured with her head toward Libby—"looks like she had all kinds of fun with Luke."

Libby glowed.

Hope wondered if over two years without sex and intimacy had dulled *her* into the opposite of radiant. That thought, and the mention of Luke, brought his brother's image into her mind.

"How about that brother of his? Any hope for our Hope?" Roni suddenly asked, causing Hope's heart to skip a beat. Was she a mind reader?

"Don't remind me," she muttered, trying her best to look unconcerned by concentrating on the menu, though she knew it by heart. She hoped the red heat that coursed through her at the mention of him didn't show on her face.

"We'll have to go back to Life's A Beach at some point," Roni said, "even with Josh there."

Thankfully, it seemed that Roni had attributed her embarrassment only to Josh. Maybe because, when she had told her about it, she had minimized the mention of Jordan Delaney.

"Jordan said you were cute," Libby said.

Hope hated that her heart skipped yet another beat. Why on earth would it?

"He did?"

Libby nodded.

Knowing her friend's kind heart, Hope figured she was probably stretching the truth a bit for her. "He hasn't seen my stretch marks," she muttered, playing with the handle of her fork. "Besides, doesn't he live in D.C. or something?"

"It's uncertain when he'll go back. He's taking over Luke's lease at the house in Wayford."

"Go for it, Hope. Let him detonate you," Roni encouraged in her usual nonchalance, citing the expression Hope had once used to describe her lack of sex life. "If I remember him, and I think I do, he looks the type. Then get back to the dating world with a bang."

Hope blushed. Encountering him only once, she suspected that Roni was right. Jordan Delaney looked exactly the type. The type that the single Ronis of the world could probably handle, not her. The type that wouldn't notice her, anyway.

"Nah. I'm not the type. And who said he'd be interested?"

~~~~~~~~~~~~~~~~

"Crappiest coffee ever. You'd think the note I put in the suggestion box would help by now."

Hope laughed. "You put a note, too? So did I! I guess they don't take us seriously around here." She faked a baffled expression, casting her glance over the other occupants of the teachers' lounge who seemed preoccupied with their phones. No one paid attention to the two of them by the coffee corner.

Chris laughed, bumping his shoulder against hers. "Great minds …"

"I'm in charge of the science fair. I'll make sure we have good coffee there, and I need volunteers," she said. *Why was it so easy to talk to someone you work with?*

"Happy to. Avery put me in charge of the Model UN because she thought I could help with correcting their grammar, but since she's micro-managing it, I have plenty of spare time, especially when Mason is with ..." Chris stammered toward the end.

"I understand." Smiling softly, Hope briefly touched his forearm in commiseration. She knew what being newly divorced was like, and Chris was an involved dad to his four-year-old.

"How was your vacation with the girls?" he asked, as if trying to get a grip.

"We went to Six Flags and the science museum. Half the time, they just wanted my phone to watch cat videos, toys unboxing, and doll houses on YouTube."

"And, how's Hannah doing in Debra's class?"

"It's been only a few days, but it seems to be going well. She did say she liked you better as her English teacher." Hope smiled and lowered her voice at the second part, though the lounge was half-deserted by now.

"A clever student like her would do great everywhere. I know who she took that from."

"Who or whom?" she quipped at his comment. They had been bantering like that since working together during summer school. It was collegial banter, though her instincts about these things were not to be trusted.

"Pretty sure it's *who*, but I'll have to check my notes," Chris said almost right into her ear. It sent a nice, little shiver down her body. It had been ages since a man had gotten this close to her. Okay, maybe it wasn't only collegial.

"I have to go. Naomi brought a lemon volcano experiment to class, and I want to peek when she presents it." Naomi's science class was under a fellow teacher.

"Have fun!" He touched her arm before she turned and left.

Was she spreading pheromones around for the first time since her divorce? She was pretty sure that Blake, from her pottery class that had resumed the evening before, after the summer hiatus, showed interest in her, too. She and Blake had exchanged looks before, but he had never made a move. She hadn't been interested in a move, anyway, until recently.

~~~~~~~~~~~~~~~~~

"Good girl! Finally! A date!" Roni said when the three of them met the following Monday.

"He just said coffee, so …"

"We're the only ones you've been having coffee with, so don't underestimate it," Libby chimed in with a pat on the back of her hand. They were just finishing the little quiches and pastries that Libby had brought from her mother's bakery, making use of the fact that Luke was on a shift at the San Francisco airport.

"Second piece of great news I've heard tonight," Roni said, raising her half-empty sparkling wine glass.

"It's just coffee. We didn't get engaged." Hope smiled at Libby, who was beaming two feet from her on the couch. "I still can't get over the fact that you and Luke are engaged! You'll be Libby Latimer-Delaney." Was it bad that the second thought that came to her mind after Libby's revelation earlier that evening was that Libby would now be Jordan's sister-in-law?

"Me, neither," Libby replied. "It was spur of the moment, but feels so right."

"So, after pottery class this week?" Roni splayed her long body across Libby's armchair, her knees cradling one armrest, her feet dangling toward the floor.

"Yes. It was cute that he found my number through the class participants list, right?"

"Very cute." Libby gave her a lopsided smile.

"You know what just occurred to me?" Roni muttered, throwing her head back against the backrest and closing her eyes. "That scene in *Ghost*. Maybe you two will stay after class and make a vase together or something, sink your palms in the wet clay, then rub it all over each other."

"Are you sure we're still talking about me, Roni?"

~~~~~~~~~~~~~~~~~~~~~

Maybe her car breaking down the morning of the class should have been warning enough, or maybe Blake showing up in old-fashioned mandals should have done the trick. But she had ignored both signs and now she was sitting across the table from him and repressing an overpowering need to yawn.

"So, I beat him again in the numbers game, and that's the only game that counts, especially in a supermarket chain. Next time a regional position opens up, guess who's gonna be spearheading that line?"

Though she was slowly dying inside, Hope stretched her smile as far as she could, mainly because she empathized with him. Maybe, like her, he couldn't stop talking about a subject that he was passionate about when he was embarrassed or nervous. She was nervous, too. This was her first date in nearly fifteen years.

"And, what do you like to do after work? Pottery, I know, but what else?" She tried yet again.

"I used to like hiking. Do you hike?"

"Sometimes with my daughters. Do you have a favorite place?"

"Oh, right. You have kids. I forgot."

She pressed her lips together.

"That reminds me," he went on. "We had a big recall of one of our most popular hiking gear and I was in charge of that. But there are branch managers who wouldn't do as they're told because they don't like one of theirs telling them what to do. You know those types?"

She nodded then tuned out when he went on and on about it.

Blake hadn't been chatty during their joint classes, so she had thought he was cute and mysterious. That had been proven wrong soon after they had reached Fred's Bar just outside of Wayford. So much for coffee ...

At least the place was nice. Facing the room, she skimmed it while he spoke. The music was classic 80's and 90's rock, the crowd fit the music's bill, and the beer was unpretentious. She hoped she wouldn't stumble across people she knew.

"It hangs in my office. Recall Manager of the Year." He smiled proudly then downed the remainder of his second beer.

Pity that the lady who she had taken a ride with to class had already left. She would have to take an Uber back to Riviera View, because there was no chance she would let him drive her, even if he hadn't turned out to be so tiring.

"Retail is not dying," she caught the tail of another long speech. Was that how she had sounded to Josh and Jordan Delaney? *Oh no*.

"So, what made you join pottery?" she tried again.

Blake giggled. "To be honest, my mother and sister thought I'd meet women there. You see, the women at work aren't really my type. Plus, I'm their boss, so ..."

Oh God.

"And I met you," he added.

She managed to hear it, though her eyes were drawn to a couple who had entered through the front door. Her heart flipped when she first noticed the man—no one who had seen Jordan Delaney could mistake him for someone else. He towered above most people as he sailed farther into the room, and there was something about his presence that was so unlike the graphic-tee-wearing guys there, regardless of the fact that his grey button-down shirt, with its sleeves folded and its collar opened, looked effortless yet oh-so-befitting.

Her heart plummeted when she recognized the woman he was with—Avery Miles.

As they took a seat in the next booth, Avery sat with her back to Hope without noticing her. But right before he sat down, facing Avery, Jordan caught Hope staring at him.

She was about to duck her head so he wouldn't notice her, but surprise at their appearance delayed her reaction.

His lips curled up into a smile of recognition, deepening the two clefts that bracketed his mouth and somewhat broke the harsh edges of his stubbled jaw. His eyes sparkled in that Bradley Cooper way, though they were light brown.

Now she had to smile back, figuring that Avery would become aware of her presence there, too. She wouldn't have minded if she wasn't there with someone like Blake, who was still speaking.

Hope swung her eyes back to him. He seemed to be on a new soapbox regarding his manager, who was being a bitch for not letting him do something.

In her peripheral view, she noticed that Avery didn't turn and was thankful to Jordan for not giving her presence away.

"Have you ever given any of the things you made in class as gifts? I made a set of cake plates for my former in-laws," she hurriedly said. "They didn't come out as pretty as I hoped, but still, it's a nice gift." She would have loved to talk about something else but couldn't think of anything they had in common.

"I made two large serving bowls. Maybe I'll give them to my manager, show her some attention, you know. Took me time to get the right shape, but I think my bowls are ready to be glazed."

Trying to bottle it in only made it worse, and the chuckle that burst out of Hope's throat was somewhat loud. The whole situation she found herself in and that last piece … she couldn't wait to tell Libby and Roni about it. That would be the only silver lining.

Realizing she was loud, her eyes were drawn again to the table ahead, and her gaze met with that of Jordan's. He was looking at her with a little, lopsided smirk. Thankfully, Avery's head was craned toward the menu that she was holding, and she still didn't seem aware of Hope's presence two tables behind her.

Hope quickly averted her gaze back to Blake.

"Oh, bowls, glazed, ha-ha," he said stiffly.

"Sorry, I didn't mean to laugh."

"No, that's okay. I have a sense of humor, too." The veins in his forehead and temples were visible all of a sudden.

"That's good to know." If she needed more proof to the fact that her taste in men sucked, then this guy, her first date since her divorce, her first date since college, was beyond a reasonable doubt.

"Excuse me," Blake suddenly called loudly and waved at a passing waitress. "Hey, excuse me. We want more drinks here and the menu."

Hope leaned forward, lowering her voice as if she was trying to soothe a fourth-grader who was about to cry. "Um … I think you need to—"

"No. They serve to the table if you order food," he cut her off sharply. "Hey, are you avoiding me on purpose?" he called toward another staff member.

People were turning their heads to look at them.

"One menu is still here," Hope hurriedly said, pushing it toward him and dying inside from embarrassment. Her joke and laughter hadn't flown with him, apparently. And, of course, this had to happen when Jordan Delaney was there to enjoy the spectacle.

"At least something good came out of their poor service, leaving the menu here," Blake began a new rant.

She put her phone in her bag and prepared an excuse to leave, knowing she would quit the pottery class, too. It wasn't that great, anyway.

From the corner of her eye, she noticed movement, then a whiff of aftershave and soap reached her just as a shadow fell over their table. Hope raised her eyes, and her breath nearly caught.

"Hi, Hope. Great meeting you here. How are you?"

Jordan Delaney, with that breathtaking intense gaze.

"Hi." She forced a smile, swallowing.

Blake stopped speaking and looked up.

Jordan turned to him. "Jordan Delaney. A pleasure to meet you," he said with a hint of a question at the end of his sentence and stretched his arm, almost forcing Blake to shake his hand.

She could see that Jordan squeezed his palm hard.

Blake tore his eyes from Jordan and looked at her. She wondered if he, too, noticed the strong abs and arms that delineated under Jordan's grey shirt and took it as a warning, along with the strong handshake.

"Jordan, this is Blake Burnes," she mumbled.

"Why don't you two join us?" Jordan smiled at her. It was a soft smile, the kind she gave students when she wanted to assist them before they even noticed they needed help. "You know Avery, right?" He slightly pivoted toward his table, and she noticed Avery now looking at them. Their eyes met, and Avery gave her a quick smile.

Oh, the humiliation. "Thanks. We're good." It wasn't good, far from it, but the last thing she wanted was this.

"Okay. If you change your mind, we'll be right there," he stressed. "And we can give you a ride back to Riviera View."

"Thanks, but there's no need." *Thank God for Uber.*

Jordan nodded and returned to his place, sending a glare in Blake's direction before he sat down. Avery spun back, and Hope averted her eyes as soon as she saw Avery whispering to Jordan. She could just imagine what those two had to say about her.

"Who's that?" Blake asked.

"Listen, Blake, I need to get back. My babysitter has to go soon. Thanks for the cider." She got up. Her daughters were with their grandmother, but this was as good excuse as any.

"I'll drive you. I can get something to eat in Riviera View."

"No, that's okay. I'll take an Uber." She took a step farther from the table.

"But—"

"I don't think I'm ready to date yet. See you around." *Not really.*

She turned and left before he could say another word.

Passing by Jordan and Avery's table, she threw a quick gaze and a half-smile at both, then hurried out, hoping the clay stains on her clothes weren't too prominent.

As soon as they were behind her, she closed her eyes under the weight of mortification at the fact that there were witnesses to yet another man-related catastrophe of hers.

Taking a deep breath outside, Hope opened the Uber app.

Seventeen minutes. This meant forever right now. If Blake came out, she would hide around the corner. Though Fred's was at the side of the road that led from Wayford to the highway, people here weren't creeps and no one approached the woman who stood alone, waiting for long minutes in the early dusk.

"Hope."

She spun around to the sound of the woman's voice. Avery and Jordan were strutting toward her.

"Avery."

"Your friend is still inside. Do you need a ride?" Avery seemed to recite the words.

"I don't—"

"Come on; my car is over there," Jordan said while passing by her, heading toward the parking area without stopping.

Avery followed him and signaled Hope to join them.

She hesitated for a second then followed, mumbling, "Thanks." She could imagine the awkward conversation that would follow the next day at school.

Buckling up in the back seat, Hope's stomach was like dead weight. "Thanks," she mumbled again, knowing that, like her seven-year-old daughter, her wish to be invisible would never be granted.

Neither of the front-seat passengers spoke as Jordan turned on the ignition, shifted into gear, and the wheels scraped the asphalt as they drove out of the lot.

Would this heavy silence continue the entire ride?

Hope glanced through the window, but in her periphery, she could see them. Avery was looking through the window, and Jordan was focused on the road ahead, his shoulders wide enough to stretch above and across the driver's seat of the sedan.

Withering with shame in the back seat, she found herself speaking before she realized it. "I was in a pottery class earlier. I joined several months ago, but my car broke down this morning, so I got a ride with Lydia Cortez. You know her, Avery, right? She's in my pottery class." *Now's the time to shut up. You've explained enough. The stifling silence of before was much better than this. Shut up*!

But her mouth disobeyed.

"Blake is in my pottery class, too. I wouldn't say I really know him. I'm working on a cake stand for my mother. The girls and I spent a few days with her a few weeks back, and Naomi broke her cake stand, so I promised I'd make her a new one." Her voice came out hoarse, her throat croaked, and her cheeks almost hurt with the red glow that spread on them. "I wish I took it with me today and didn't leave it in the studio, because I don't think I'll ..." *Oh, great.* Her self-operating mouth trailed off just at the most awkward part, where it was obvious she was referring to why she couldn't go back to class now. "I could probably go get it when—"

"I love that they opened this new exit between Wayford and Riviera View," Jordan suddenly cut in, bending his head slightly as he gazed through his side window at the exit they were passing, as if it were riveting. He then moved his eyes to the rearview mirror, and his gaze met hers.

"Yes, that was, like, three years ago. You must have seen it before," Avery took it up.

A combination of relief and deeper agitation raced over Hope. It was apparent that he was trying to save her from herself.

She peered out the window to her left and bit her bottom lip, something she should have done when silly, unwarranted explanations had rolled off her tongue.

"I saw it but never really paid attention," Jordan said. "It's interesting, the things you notice when you really look."

Hope's glance flickered back to his in the rearview mirror.

"Now that you're back, maybe you'll pay more attention to Riviera View," Avery said, and Hope was sure that even Naomi could decode that meaning.

"Given that this is my mother's car and that I'm temporarily living at my brother's, I'm not sure I'm really *back* or how long I'll stay."

Avery didn't reply. Her gaze was fixed on Jordan's profile. Not a muscle moved in his face that Hope sneaked a peek at. Avery then moved to gaze again through the side window, and Hope did the same.

The houses of Riviera View came into view as Jordan entered the town.

Finally. Hope took a deep breath. She was almost home. Ocean Avenue, the town's main street, stretched toward the beach. Ever since she had moved here, getting quickly used to the mild California weather, this street had signified home. Its beautiful, colorful façades containing locally-owned shops that were now brightly lit brought memories of the town parades and weekend ice cream jaunts with her daughters at Cone Inside. Libby's apartment was also there, a bit farther toward the beach.

Thinking of her best friend and feeling alone in this car, despite the presence of her colleague-turned-sort-of-boss, as well as Libby's fiancé's brother, Hope yearned to see her now.

"You're on Maple, right?" Avery asked.

"Yes, but you don't have to go all the way in. You can drop me off at—"

"Home," Jordan interrupted yet again.

He took a left turn and, a moment later, pulled over next to a pale-gray painted house. He turned to look at Avery.

"Shouldn't we …?" Avery didn't complete the question.

"You're closer," he said with a shrug. "We're right here."

Avery nodded slowly, narrowing her eyes and spearing his, her jaw muscle twitching. She then pivoted with a smile toward Hope. "See you at school tomorrow."

"Yes. Thanks." Hope had no idea what she was thanking her for, but it was the next best thing to apologizing for involuntarily intruding on what looked like a date between them.

Avery opened the door and climbed out without a word. As soon as she slammed it and turned around, Jordan pulled away.

"You should turn right over there," she commented, pointing from her place in the back seat.

"I know. I grew up here."

"Oh, right." It was strange to think he had grown up here like Eric, like Libby, Roni, and Luke.

"What? I don't look like a small-town native?" He smiled at her through the rearview mirror.

He didn't, but she didn't say it.

"Our old house is over there." He gestured with his head toward Avalon Street, which they had just passed by.

"You think this is a small town? You should see the town I came from in Minnesota." She chuckled.

"How small?" His golden-brown eyes flicked a smile through the mirror.

"Three hundred. If I stayed there, I probably would have married my second cousin."

Jordan laughed.

Oh God, it had a husky edge, and combined with those Bradley Cooper dimples that she wanted to stick her fingers into, her insides clenched.

Roni's words—*Let him detonate you. He's the type*—rang in her head. Yes, he seemed the type. The type every fiber of her being told her she wasn't cut out for, although all those fibers now rebelled against her and yearned to touch those broad shoulders of his that were a mere few inches away.

"So you married Eric Hayes, instead?"

Talk about a reality check. Of course he knew Eric. Everyone knew Douchebag Eric.

"I didn't mean it to sound rude. I'm sorry," he suddenly said, his eyes connecting with hers through the rearview mirror. "Trust me; I have no right to ..." He trailed off.

This took her by surprise. Wasn't he one of those who always knew what and when to say? A political advisor?

He had just reached her house, and before she was able to utter a word, as soon as the wheels of the car came to a stop, the front door was thrown open, as if her daughters had been waiting by the window the whole time.

Naomi ran outside, followed by Lucile, Eric's mother, who stopped in the middle of the lane, watching her granddaughter welcoming a strange car that had brought her mother home.

"Thanks so much for the ride. I'd better ..." she said, opening the door and getting out before Naomi could reach the car.

"Anytime," she heard Jordan say.

As soon as she stepped onto the sidewalk, Naomi threw herself at her and wrapped her small arms around her, as if she hadn't seen her in ages.

"She missed you," Lucile called, tightening her salmon-colored cardigan, though the evening was still warm.

"Who's that?" Naomi asked, pointing at the car.

Hope turned to look at the vehicle. Jordan's face was directed at the road as his blinker signaled his intention to pull away. She began walking toward the house with Naomi wrapping herself around her waist.

Lucile followed them. "Was that one of the Delaney boys?" she asked.

"Yes."

"Luke or Jordan?"

"Jordan."

"What's he doing here? I thought it was Luke who moved back to Riviera View. Isn't he a hotshot in D.C. or something like that?"

"I don't know. He gave me and Avery Miles a ride." She hoped this would close the subject. She hadn't told her ex-mother-in-law why she had to stay after class, not wanting to disclose she'd had a date. Good thing she hadn't after that disaster.

"Luke was in Eric's class. I hope you're making sure your daughters also get preferential treatment at school, like their mother did for them. I don't think they would have reached those universities if she hadn't."

Hope kept her eyes on Naomi and tried not to laugh. She knew from Libby what universities those were. Jordan in Cornell and Luke in Penn State, because their teacher mother got them "special treatment" in elementary school.

"I give them all the preferential treatment in the world," she said, fondly kissing the head of her youngest. She then closed the front door, but not before sending another look at Jordan Delaney's taillights.

Chapter 6

When Avery called, insisting he meet her at Fred's because, "You absolutely have to judge at the school's Model UN, and I have to provide the details," Jordan was at his brother's rented beach house, having moved in the week before.

The ocean breeze and late August afternoon sun washed into the living room. His phone, which used to ring at every hour of the day, including the middle of the night, had been silent on his brother's wooden coffee table. Therefore, when it had chirped, Jordan had nearly jumped.

"I'm at a friend's near Wayford," Avery said after unsuccessfully trying to induce guilt in him for not keeping in touch—he had never promised or even hinted he would. In fact, he thought he had done the opposite. "Wanna meet me at Fred's so I can walk you through our Model's details?"

"It's elementary school level; can't you email it to me?" he asked.

"Come on; it's five minutes from you," she insisted.

He liked Fred's and had been there with Luke and a few old friends over the past several weeks. If he'd had to drive more than five minutes to meet her, he would have declined. And maybe because she had managed to make him feel a little guilty for being a dick, he agreed.

What he hadn't expected was seeing her climb out of the passenger seat of her friend's car and wave goodbye to her once he got there.

"How do you plan on getting back to Riviera View?" he asked when she reached him at the bar's entrance.

"I could stay in Wayford, or you could drive me," Avery replied with a wink, pushing open the door to Fred's bar.

He smacked himself internally but didn't say anything.

"I saw Belinda Soto—she's Belinda Tuffin now, by the way—in town yesterday," Avery said as they walked in. "She said she bumped into you outside Books And More."

Luke and Libby lived above the bookstore. Jordan had encountered Belinda when he had visited them. Belinda had been his girlfriend in their sophomore year at Riviera View's high school. Unlike Avery, seeing her hadn't included hints or invitations to hook up. She was happily married and had introduced him to her teenage kids. Looking at them, it had been strange to realize that people his age had kids the age that he and Belinda had been when they had lost their virginities to each other.

"I forget how small these towns are," he muttered just when another proof of the smallness of their area caught his eyes.

Libby's redheaded friend was in the booth furthest in from the table that he and Avery were approaching. His heart lurched at the sight of her. Then, just as unexpectedly, it plunged when he noticed a man sitting with her.

He smiled at her and noticed she had gone red in the face.

The moment they sat down, Avery opened again about how shitty it was of him to not keep in touch, but his attention was elsewhere.

There it was again—Hope's plain-to-read face that expressed everything she felt. It somehow defrosted the edges of his heart that had been invariably cooled by the poker faces that he had encountered in D.C.

She seemed uneasy, and he tried not to look in her direction, thinking that Avery's and his presence had probably contributed to it. But the redness soon cleared when the guy she was with became loud, bordering on aggressive, and her face went from flushed to pale.

Although his job had taught him not to stick his nose into things that didn't concern him, lest others would stick their noses into his business, he got up from his seat without a word to Avery. Guided only by instinct, he went to make sure Hope knew she wasn't alone there.

"Aren't you worried about your employee?" he asked Avery after Hope had exited the place, passing them with her smudgy jeans and tee, leaving the idiot who she had been with to mumble to himself over his empty beer glass. He used "employee" instead of "colleague," hoping to inspire some responsibility in her.

"She's a big girl. I hope that wasn't a date, though she seems to have a thing for douchebags. You wouldn't expect it from her I-initiated-a-food-program exterior."

Jordan gritted his teeth. "Douchebags tend to leach on to good people."

"So, about the model UN," Avery started after a moment's silence, just when he opened with, "What food program?"

"She, and Anne and Connie from Breading Dreams—Oh, you know Connie! I forgot. Anyway, they distribute unsold products from a few shops at the end of the day. Connie's daughter is a social worker, but you know that, too, of course … And Anne is my … Anyway, we have a free-to-all sandwich tray at school every morning. Most of our kids come from good homes, but a few need the help, and since it's free to all, no one knows because everyone can just grab a freebie."

He just looked at her and nodded. It wasn't her face he saw.

They barely managed to get through half their drinks when that Blake guy stood up and walked toward the exit.

"Damn, he's wearing sandals. I *really* hope for her it wasn't a date," Avery sneered.

"I'll be right back," Jordan said, getting to his feet to follow the man.

When he reached the entrance, he saw Hope standing outside, looking at her cell phone, ten minutes after she had left. The guy he had followed cut toward the men's room.

"I think your friend needs help. She's still outside," he said when he returned to the table, knowing he stretched the truth by using the term "friend," but hoping that would move the needle. "Come on; be the big girl you can be and help her out." Another truth stretch.

Reluctantly, Avery got up. "For you, Jordan Delaney," she said, placing her palm on his shoulder as he tucked a twenty bill under his unfinished beer.

~~~~~~~~~~~~~~~~~~

Now the image of Hope and her daughter disappeared from his rearview mirror. Her inability to control her mouth during the ride had amused yet touched him at the same time. It was honest and unguarded, almost vulnerable.

Maybe some of it had rubbed off on him, because he couldn't explain the comment that had escaped his own mouth when he had insensitively asked about her ex. Wanting to know more about her and being unable to fathom her with someone like Eric didn't justify that slip of the tongue. That, along with the image of the little girl bolting toward her reminded him that someone like him couldn't, and shouldn't, come near a woman like her.

Just then, his phone vibrated with a message.

"*You owe me after today! So see yourself committed to the Model UN judge role. I'll email you the details and see you very soon. xoxo.*"

If he was looking for a divorced, single mother to get involved with, Avery was a much simpler option. *If* he was.

~~~~~~~~~~~~~~~~~~~

A few days later, driving again through Riviera View, toward the school that he had attended and where his mother had taught for forty years, Jordan wondered if places had memories. The town's streets and shops, houses and buildings, all had a place in his heart and mind, and he hoped he had a share in theirs. He should check sometime if the wall under Life's A Beach's terrace still carried the graffiti that he and his friends had sprayed there lightyears ago.

With his six-foot-one height, he felt like Gulliver in the halls that were decorated for autumn. Children's paintings of the traditional seasonal symbols—red and orange leaves, rain and grey skies—were hung all around, although the California sun was warm and bright outside in its blue September sky. He could never relate to the need to do or feel things on cue. Although, ironically, that was what he had sometimes advised his clients. *You're visiting a military base? Wear a bomber jacket. It's September? Post a family picture with matching sweaters.*

Despite the two and a half decades that had passed, his legs led him, instinctively knowing every turn on the way to the small hall, as they used to call the smaller assembly room.

Besides Avery, there was one other person he knew who worked here. Hope Hays. He wondered if she was around.

Avery waved at him from the hall's door and stepped outside to greet him, speaking while he walked toward her. "We have a small crowd in there, but that's just the prep for the regional campaign. Have you read the instructions?"

"Skimmed over it."

"Thanks for agreeing, JD," she said when he reached her.

JD? Now she had a nickname for him? He had to fix that and fast.

"You sent my mother after me."

"In love and war, you know?"

He didn't know. What love? What war?

"Four teams of two. Only one team will get to represent us in the regionals. They're fourth, fifth, and sixth grade kids, so don't expect much."

"Trust me; I don't."

"Kids are not your strong suit, huh? I should take note of that."

"Shall we?" He led the way to the door, ignoring her words. This wasn't a topic he was capable of touching these days.

Avery pushed the door open, and the raucous of children talking and yelling to each other hit them like a concrete wall.

"Wait here," she said as they entered.

The small hall looked almost exactly as he remembered it, except the UN and various countries' flags that were hung around. The crowd consisted of five long rows of seated kids and three teachers who attempted to shush them.

A science fair poster hung next to where he stopped to stand while Avery went to speak to the two teachers who were to share the judges' bench with him. The printed instructions on the poster culminated in, "*Signup with Ms. Hays.*" Below it was a handwritten sentence, "*Chemistry rocks! It can melt rocks! Join us.*" It was signed, "*Hope Hays.*" He didn't know about rocks, but his heart clenched at this, and warmth spread in his chest as if the damn thing was melting. Maybe there was something wrong with the chemicals in his brain these days because he had rarely been affected by such trivial, mundane things before.

"Follow me," Avery said, showing up next to him and guiding him to a table covered with the UN flag map.

He shook hands with the two teachers who sat there and introduced himself.

"Chris Kominski," one of them said while shaking his hand. "From D.C. politics to Riviera elementary? I hope you'll survive it." He smiled.

"We'll see." Jordan smiled back, taking his seat.

Eight kids sat at four tables facing the judges. Each table carried a different flag.

"After the break, they'll switch flags and representations," Chris said, leaning sideways toward him to get over the noise that was loud enough to reverberate from the walls.

"Yes, read it in Avery's instruction manual."

"She's a close friend of yours?"

Jordan eyed him, wondering what Avery had been telling people. "No. We were just in high school together."

Twenty minutes into the simulation, it was obvious that one student there was better than the rest, though she received the least applauds from the audience. When someone from the crowd cut into her speech, she looked like she was going to explode, and the effort to contain herself was written all over her face.

"Don't pay attention. Carry on," Chris called toward her just when Jordan opened his mouth to say the same.

Ten minutes later, the girl got up, pushed her chair, and stormed out of the room after someone from one of the rows called in a mocking voice, "Cry baby," while she was delivering her closing speech. Avery scolded them and announced a fifteen-minute break.

The spectators, all not surpassing five feet in height, stormed onto the floor to encourage their favorite contestants and throw insults at the others.

Jordan felt his phone vibrating in his pocket and exited the hall.

"*Can I call?*" The message carried the familiar D.C. area code, though the number was unidentified, and his heart sank.

"*Yes.*" He stood at the window and gazed at the playground. School was a survivors' jungle. Just like in politics, it had alliances, cliques, a pecking order, running over the competition, circling the strong, isolating the weak. He had seen it all. It was sadder to see it in kids.

He picked up at the first ring.

"How are you, Jordan?"

"Fine. You?" he said with no patience for niceties.

"Great. *Really* great now. I had to call from a pre-paid phone, though."

He waited.

"Not yours. Hundred percent. No chance."

He didn't reply. His gaze was glued to the yard outside where a first-grade gym class was being held. Were six-year-olds really that small?

"Jordan?"

"Yeah, I'm here."

"They'll send you the email with the results, too. I'm so relieved. I bet you are, too. Now we can go back to normal without this hovering over us."

"Yeah."

"Okay. Great."

He was silent.

"Are you coming back? Heard Warber is interested in you."

"Not for the time being."

"Okay. If you do, I'll help."

"No need, Sharon, thanks."

"My offer stands."

"Bye." He hung up.

Seconds later, the email arrived.

This was exactly the news he had been waiting for, the one phone call and confirmation that had been gnawing at him for months until a confidential DNA test could be run on the amniotic fluid at a certain week of gestation. But now he had to admit that, while relieved, he also felt a strange void permeating his body, crawling and settling in his insides, his heart, his throat.

A rhythmic sound of metal being rapped repeatedly called his attention. Jordan turned around but didn't see anything. He veered his head to peer further into the corridor. From behind a locker, a flame of curly, reddish-blonde hair caught his eye. The girl who had rushed out of the hall was kicking a metal locker. Her kicks weren't forceful; they were rhythmic and served as an accompanying metronome to her mumbling the same sentence to herself over and over. "We can benefit. Every life. On this earth. If we join forces."

Jordan tore himself from the window, shoving the phone back into the back pocket of his chinos. Stopping next to her, he reached out his hand. "Jordan Delaney, UN Model judge and former student in this school."

The girl stopped her kicking and chanting and, looking into his face, hesitantly reached out, took his large palm, and shook it with her much smaller one without a word.

"Hannah, right? Listen, don't tell anyone I said this, but you're the best one in there. That's why they don't clap for you, okay? Because you're killing it in there." He paused. "But—there's a but here—you need to tell a story and not just lecture them. Make them visualize what your suggestions mean by painting them an image of what could happen if your policy isn't implemented. If you do, they'll be too busy listening to you to call out things from the sidelines like cowards."

The girl narrowed her green eyes as she took his words in. "So, like, tell them that, if other countries don't help out with disposal of plastic waste in smaller island countries that don't have the budget to do it themselves, then baby dolphins could choke and die?"

"Exactly."

"Will they clap?"

Her question squeezed his heart. "I don't know. All you need for this competition is to convince the judges. And all you need for yourself is to trust yourself and keep going, even if they don't clap." He paused, and she slowly nodded. "But I understand why you want them to. I know it's hard. But being applauded doesn't always mean you're winning. It doesn't mean they're friends with those they're applauding, either."

She bunched her lips and drew her mouth to the side, as if she were pondering his words.

"Remember, tell a story. And don't let them see you're upset. Trust me; someone like you will get enough applause when you're older."

The girl bit her upper lip, then slowly nodded again.

"Hannah!" Avery peered from the hall's door. "Oh, there you are. Jordan, hey. Come in; we're reassembling."

He winked and smiled at the girl, then they entered the noisy hall.

When it was her turn to represent her stance, Jordan was proud of his youngest advisee. More kids applauded her than before. He sent her a small smile, unable to openly support her over the other contestants.

But he did when the moment came for him to announce his verdict.

"Not everyone can do what these guys did," he said, waving an arm toward all eight participants. "It takes guts and hard work. It requires nothing, especially no guts, to hide behind someone's back and discredit that. Don't be the ones hiding behind others." He then looked at Hannah. "You should all be proud of yourselves. All teams were good, but Team Three did the best."

The two other judges voted with him, and he watched Hannah and the boy who was her teammate receive the congratulations of their classmates. She beamed when hers and the boy's names were cheered in a chorus.

"Like mother, like son, JD," Avery said from behind him, her hand loitering on his shoulder.

"What do you mean?"

"You both have an eye for the underdogs."

He stood up so her hand fell to her side. "I don't know about that, but that girl, that team, was the best one here. It was unanimous." He looked around. The two teachers who had judged with him had left.

Avery ignored the annoyance in his tone. "Well, I'm done for today, no meetings or classes to substitute in. I'll go get my things and meet you in the parking lot?"

They never made such an arrangement, and he wasn't sure where this was coming from. Perhaps she read the old him right. If he was the man he had been a decade ago, she probably would have had him in her bed by now … though out of her door soon after.

"I can't. Sorry. *I* have a meeting," he lied.

It was too noisy for her to reply, so she just followed him outside, where they were surrounded by a flock of kids that flowed into the hallway.

"Listen, Avery," he opened, intending to make sure she understood he wasn't going anywhere with her. But before he could continue, a loud yell compelled both him and Avery to look ahead.

"I won! Mom! I won!" The girl he had coached flew from within the herd of kids toward a woman who plowed her way toward them, her copper hair tied in a ponytail and her bangs reaching just above her green eyes. Jordan's heart stammered in his chest.

"Oh, there's your project," Avery muttered. "I never reveal the contestants' network to our outside judges for objectivity reasons."

Hope bent to hug her daughter then raised her eyes, and their glances met just as he and Avery reached the two. He should have known. The hair, the eyes, the sticking to a list of dry facts while her real emotions were written all over her face should have clued him into whose child this was.

They were an island as the kids swerved around them on their way outside.

Jordan was pretty sure that this time Hope's blush was mirrored on him because he couldn't ignore the sudden furnace that heated up the blood in his veins.

"Hi," they both said at once.

"Hope, congrats. Hannah ended up doing very well in there. We had a minor issue, right, Hannah?" Avery said.

"She was great. I didn't know …" He faltered, holding Hope's gaze.

"Thanks for the advice," Hannah cut in, drawing his gaze from her mother several inches down toward her.

He smiled. "You're very welcome. You'll do great at the regionals."

"We gotta run," Avery said, pulling at his elbow as if they had something planned.

"Congratulations, sweetie," Hope said, wrapping her arm around her daughter's shoulders. "I'm so proud of you." She then raised her eyes back to his. "Thank you."

"My pleasure. It was well deserved." His gaze lingered on her as she was then dragged away by her excitedly chattering daughter.

"See why I didn't mention whose daughter she was? I didn't want you to be biased," Avery said.

"Why would I be biased?"

"Isn't she your brother's fiancée's best friend or something? Weren't you her knight in a shining car the other day?"

"You don't know me, Avery. If I let personal connections bias me, I wouldn't be able to do my job, and I did it for fifteen years."

"It was nice of you to help her. You should have seen her last week when she lost the student council elections. She was mad at one of the girls who promised to vote for her but then made a deal with another girl. I told her she wasn't even close, and that vote wouldn't have changed much, anyway."

He had only just met the flame-haired girl, but a small dagger shot through his heart, both at the pain caused by her friend's betrayal and at the cold bucket of words that Avery had poured on her right after. "It's the betrayal that stings the most. Not the actual loss. And she didn't have to know she wasn't close."

"Well, Mr. Political Advisor. A soft heart in your position isn't a good thing, am I right?" Avery teased as they reached the main entrance.

"Thanks for inviting me. I think my debt—whatever it was for—is now cleared. Take care, Avery," he said in a tone that he hoped left no doubt as to his intention to never see her again.

Chapter 7

"I told it as a story, and it worked. And they clapped, Mom. Even Brittney. I saw her."

The sheer happiness on her daughter's face was like a glow feeding Hope's heart. "I'm so proud of you for doing this. It's not easy to compete and speak in public. And you won! Don't pay so much attention to the applause. Focus on what you came there to do and say."

"That's what the judge said."

"He did?"

Hannah went on to tell her about their conversation, and Hope swayed between feeling a new warmth toward the man who had supported her daughter when she wasn't there to do it, and a strange pain in knowing that Jordan Delaney had witnessed her daughter's hardships, as well. The warmth she felt cooled off when she remembered he was there because of his association—whatever it was—with Avery.

She didn't tell Hannah that Avery had texted her during class. "*Hannah stormed out in the middle of the simulation. We have to talk.*" Her heart had sunk like the corn syrup had inside the water in the experiment she had been doing with her students at that moment. She couldn't leave, though every instinct in her begged her to run and console her child. She had texted Chris, knowing he was there, but his phone must have been switched off.

She had rushed toward the small hall the minute she could, only to find a glowing Hannah. And it was thanks to the advice of the silver-tongued political advisor who made her wayward heart thump, rendering her able to utter only the two words that she had ended up saying to him.

Picking up Naomi from the second-grade hall, Hope smiled as the two girls chatted excitedly, walking in front of her toward the car.

"Mommy, can Lia come over today?" Naomi turned around to ask. "I want to show her the Barbie Dad bought me and tell her that Hannah is going to the regilands." Naomi ended her sentence triumphantly. Her shiny, blonde hair bounced in a ponytail as she climbed into the car. This girl, who was conceived when Hope and Eric had tried to patch up the fragments of their marriage, looked so much like him, but where he used to augment someone's insecurities, she reminded them of their wins and strengths. Hope was proud of both her girls.

"Sure you can, sweetie. Hannah, do you want to invite someone over? I can make chocolate chip cookies for everyone." Happiness was contagious.

"I'll think about it," Hannah said, her eyes still glowing, her smile wide.

~~~~~~~~~~~~~~~~~~~

"Your future brother-in-law was at our school this week."

"What was he doing there?"

"Avery invited him to judge at our Model UN."

Libby tilted her head, narrowing her eyes in a skeptic grimace. "Really? Jordan?"

"Yes. I was surprised, too. Maybe she has good convincing skills."

"I bet she does," Roni said, sticking her tongue against her inner cheek and accompanying it with the relevant hand gesture.

They all laughed, but an uncalled-for icicle pricked Hope's stomach.

"This is something I'd pay to see," Libby said.

Roni burst into laughter and nearly choked on her drink.

"No! Not this!" Libby called out, snorting with laughter. "Oh God, no! Yuck! No, I meant Jordan judging in the school's Model UN."

Roni coughed and laughed, and while Hope laughed, the thought of Jordan in such a position made her sweat a little, despite the cool night air. But the additional image of Avery with him made the leek quiche that she had just eaten threaten to make its way back up her throat.

"He was actually really sweet about it," she said to push the bile down. "He saw Hannah having a … difficult moment outside and helped her." Hope lowered her voice. They were sitting in her backyard for their weekly meeting and, while the girls were asleep upstairs, she didn't want Hannah to hear her in case she woke up to pee. "She says his advice is what helped her team win. But I think it was also the fact that she felt someone was on her side, that someone … *saw* her."

"Sounds like he's better at this than his teacher of a girlfriend," Roni muttered from her place on the deck chair. "I can't forget what she said to Hannah after the students council elections. What a bitch. And I'll never forget that she once told Lulu to act her age. Bitch, she was acting her age! She was eight!" Roni's temper flared fast on some topics.

"I don't think she's his girlfriend," Libby said.

"What does Luke say?" Roni asked, cooling back down as fast as she had flared up.

"That Jordan has been pretty cagey about things ever since he came back."

"Interesting," Roni muttered. "Maybe he and Avery are like Luke and you?"

Libby shrugged. "I don't know. I don't know how close they used to be. I swear Hope sees more of him than I do."

Hope had told them about the incident at the bar with Blake and the ride Jordan had given her but hadn't gotten into too many details.

"Luke says Jordan never had a serious enough relationship to bring someone home for the holidays or anything," Libby continued. "I think he's a bit of a player. He could be just … having fun with her."

"I bet." Roni made that tongue-hand gesture again.

Though she shouldn't care, Hope listened attentively while trailing the condensation on her glass.

"Speaking of …" Libby continued, turning the ring on her finger from side to side. "We decided to have an engagement party. At Jordan's."

"What? Why?" Hope blurted. It was one thing to run across Avery and Jordan; it was another thing to spend an evening with them in his house … for so many reasons. For one, she didn't care much for Avery and didn't want to socialize with her indirect boss. She had also experienced too many uncomfortable moments with those two together and apart. And there was the unhelpful and unhealthy fact that, despite herself, Jordan made her feel things, physically and … non-physically.

"We want to bring everyone together. Gabe will come with Tammy and the kids from L.A., and our apartment is too small to accommodate everyone. The house in Wayford is bigger, and he offered."

"But weren't you weirded out by the fact that Luke lived there with Lilac?" Roni asked, sipping her white wine.

"We both were, at first. But it's water under the bridge now."

"So, are we invited?" Hope asked, her lips hovering over her glass.

"No," Libby said. Then, giving Hope's thigh a little smack with her napkin, she called, grinning, "Of course you are! You're my sisters from different misters!"

While they enthused over it, Hope wondered what calamity would befall her in front of the eldest Delaney brother this time.

"How's the science fair committee going with Chris?" Roni redirected the conversation while they were devouring the carrot cake that Hope had baked for the evening. "Any chemistry or physics in action there?"

"Kinda. But with him being recently divorced …" Hope placed her cake plate on the grass next to her chair. She looked between her two friends who sat facing her on their deck chairs, wearing soft smiles. "Eric, Blake … I'm gullible at best. I should avoid men altogether."

"You're not. You're just a good person who thinks well of and gives credit to people. It's just that some don't deserve it. Don't deserve you," Libby said, leaning forward in her chair and placing her palm on Hope's knee.

"They're not all made equal. Men, that is," Roni said. "And besides, Chris is divorced almost a year now. Weren't you and Eric divorced that long before he got with Jenna and married her?"

"Thanks for the reminder." Hope chuckled.

"What I meant is that men are usually faster to land on their feet in these situations."

"Do you like him?" Libby asked.

"Yeah. I mean, he's a teacher, too, and he knows what it's like to be divorced and a single parent. We're both nerdy. It's easy for me to talk to him. We have a lot in common."

"Sounds like you should give it a try," Libby replied.

~~~~~~~~~~~~~~~~~~~

She thought of that conversation two days later when Chris and her were left alone to do the final preparations for the science fair. They were at different sides of the small hall, but at some point, when they were nearly done, she found him standing next to her. His plaid-shirted shoulder, which was only two inches higher than hers, brushed against hers when he helped her hang a large poster of the periodic table.

"I was thinking …" he opened, pivoting toward her. "Would you like to go for a cup of coffee or something sometime? We can discuss the fair."

"The fair's tomorrow."

"We can discuss other things, too." Chris smiled. His black hair was close-cropped and receding a bit, but it served as a great contrast to his light blue eyes that weren't hidden behind his rimless glasses tonight.

She returned his smile. "Yeah, we could do that. But after tomorrow, I don't want to hear about this fair again."

"Avery gave you her 'if it ain't broken, don't fix it' over every new idea you came up with?" Chris asked, smiling at her.

Hope raised her eyebrows. "I was also honored with 'don't try to invent the wheel'." She couldn't believe she would have to see Avery at her best friend's engagement party.

"No shop talk, I promise." Chris chuckled. "I have Mason over this week, but next week, he's with Linda."

"Great."

They smiled at each other, *like the dorks we are*, she thought, gazing into his blue eyes.

Had she just agreed to go on a date again? Because, if this didn't go right, she couldn't quit school like she had done with the pottery class.

Chapter 8

The living room looked like it was ready for a *Good Housekeeping* photoshoot, mainly thanks to his brother's ex-girlfriend and the designer that she had hired. If his life was in limbo, at least it had this serene setting—off-white sofas, plush sea-palette cushions and throws, rustic-looking wood furniture, and a second-line ocean view washing in through the large doors that opened to the balcony.

The silence was broken only by the far sound of the waves, the breeze, the seagulls, but in two hours, it would be replaced by music and the cheerful chatter of twenty people.

Jordan picked up the only things that were out of place—the two suitcases waiting to be relieved of their cargo of clothes, books, and other belongings that he had brought back with him from his short trip to Washington D.C.—and carried them to the back

Not wanting his assistant to handle his personal business, he had been forced to spend a few days there to pack up his apartment and return the keys after it had stood empty for weeks. He had never bought a property in the city, as if, deep down, he had always known it wouldn't be a real home to him. Being back there had reminded him how sick he had become of it.

Yet, while there, he had met with a few people, knowing it would be easier to maintain some connections than building bridges from ashes later. His main goal had been to kill any rumor that Dana Brin had tried to spread for her client. Given his track record, reputation, and the fact that Dana wasn't as good at her job as he was, no one really believed her, anyway. Still, he was glad that he had managed to avoid crossing paths with her or Sharon Rush while there. It was enough that everyone knew the congresswoman was pregnant, which had been brought up in almost every meeting he had held, rendering it impossible for him to forget.

Sharon's words over the phone had delivered good news. It had saved them both a plethora of immediate issues and long-lasting problems, the media being the least terrible of them, which said a lot about the pit that they had almost dug for themselves.

Yet, there was this strange void in him.

Having time to think about it while performing the mundane task of packing up his apartment, he had concluded that the emptiness he felt was the kind of disappointment one felt when you let someone else decide between two options that you couldn't choose from, and you only realized which one you preferred when they picked the other one. In some fucked-up way, he had wanted it to be his. A pregnancy that resulted from a momentary lapse of judgment with a woman he respected as a professional but had no feelings for.

The only thing he hadn't figured out yet was *why*.

Was it his age? Because, when he had accidentally impregnated one of his ex-girlfriends at twenty-four, despite having been willing to do whatever it took to care for her and a baby, her decision to terminate the pregnancy just two days after she had peed on a stick had been a relief. But now, knowing that a pregnancy that shouldn't even have been his in the first place, indeed wasn't his, stung. And that was ironic, because *that* hadn't been his first reaction.

When Sharon had told him she was pregnant and didn't know if it was his or her husband's, who she had separated from, his instinctive reaction had been cold calculations of professional implications and damage control strategies—how to keep the media at bay, where to book a confidential paternity test, what to say, to whom, and when. Those tactics had become second-nature, imprinted in him. The fact that there was a child involved, potentially his, had penetrated his mind only after.

He had realized then that he didn't know who he was anymore and, repulsed with himself, used his sister's wedding as an excuse to leave.

And now he was an outsider in his own life.

Spending time with his family helped. So did being in his hometown, in the place that had known him before he had become what he was now. And, in some unpredictable way, so did reaching out to another outsider—a girl who had kicked a locker alone in a hallway, feeling like a public and private failure.

Jordan pushed the two suitcases into the bedroom's walk-in closet then took his clothes off. Stepping into the shower, he thought about that girl's mother. The look on her face that day had caught him off guard.

Every shred of her daughter's hard-earned victory had been reflected on her face. This woman, who had experienced divorce from a man who probably still lived up to his reputation and who raised her daughters almost alone, fought to keep it all beneath the surface. But, at that moment, the maelstroms in her eyes had revealed it all.

He had seen it. The things you notice when you really look. Like the ocean through his window, with its sunken ships of hopes and dreams. Her artless, and sometimes awkward, honesty revealed time and again that whatever corroding powers worked against her, inside and out, she wasn't bitter, ruined, or cynical like the miasma that had penetrated his soul. And this unvarnished, unscathed quality of hers should be left unsullied if it had survived until now. It shouldn't be tainted by people like the horrid man who she had been with at Fred's. It shouldn't be marred by someone like him, either.

There was one thing he could do without much risk—let her know that her words had been taken seriously; that, although he had been amused by her open-bookishness at first, he wasn't laughing at her.

Quite the opposite.

Chapter 9

The beach house, though it was in Wayford, was more in line with the more modest beach houses of Riviera View. The interior was beautiful and the catered buffet looked promising. However, the ocean and the beauty of the sunset over it drew everyone out to the large porch.

Hope clandestinely pulled at the shaper she wore under her blue, V-cleavage dress, wondering if she would be able to eat anything with this thing on. She had taken a bit of extra care getting ready today.

"Mom, your hair looks pretty like that," Hannah had said when she had finished with the curling iron.

"I wish I had your beautiful curls," she had replied, patting her daughter's hair. Hannah liked her curls now, but there was a time when she had gotten back from school and asked why she didn't have straight hair like Brittney's.

"You have my mother's hair, and it's beautiful," Hope had told her.

Roni's and Donnie's reactions when they had picked her up confirmed that she had succeeded in looking her best. The wink Roni had given her had also confirmed that her friend knew that Jordan Delaney was the cause of her digging out her fancier makeup kit.

Yes, she had a date set up with Chris for the following week and shouldn't care about the man who wasn't supposed to interest her due to several reasons. Reasons she enumerated in her head again now—his relationship with Avery, his temporary status here, him being Libby's soon-to-be brother-in-law, and him being unlike her in almost everything. Nevertheless, she wanted to look good when she next encountered him, especially after he had been privy to her not-so-great moments.

But, except for the initial greeting between them, when he had shaken her hand and her breath had shallowed under the depth of his gaze and the level of sexiness and masculinity this man effortlessly exuded, she hadn't had much chance to speak with him. All she needed was a short opportunity to properly thank him for helping Hannah and rid herself of this debt of gratitude.

Though Libby had told her the day before that Avery wouldn't be there—"All I know is Patty said she wasn't expecting her"—Hope was still relieved to see it for herself. It wasn't jealousy, she told herself.

There were enough people to meet and greet— Ava and Zack, who thanked her for attending their wedding; Gabe, Libby's brother, and his wife and kids; Luke's parents; and Libby's aunt, Sarah.

At some point, when she stepped from the porch and back into the living room to pour herself another glass of juice, she found Roni standing by the table that carried an array of freshly squeezed citrus juices.

She stopped next to her, holding a lemonade, and followed Roni's gaze. She was watching Jordan and Gabe, who were standing at one corner of the room, conversing.

"They were friends, not just neighbors, growing up," Roni explained quietly. "But their lives took such different turns. Kinda like Libby and Luke. Gabe had to work after his dad had left them, and Jordan went to Cornell, and then for this high power career … Can't get more different than that."

"They don't seem that different now."

"You can take someone out of Riviera View, but you can't take Riviera View out of someone, I guess," Roni said. "Cornell-Schmornell, he must still be a Riviera View guy under all that." She made a sweeping gesture aimed at Jordan from head to toe. "He's not a bad guy."

"You never said he was bad." She tried not to stare at Jordan, which was hard given that his light-blue, button-down shirt, the dark tie, and matching dark chinos fit him in a way that made her heart beat erratically.

"No, but I did hint that he was a player. We were four years younger than him; anyone who got some action back then seemed like a player to me. But I stand by what I said—he looks like he could shred …" Roni didn't finish her sentence because, just then, her husband appeared and handed her a cell phone.

"The babysitter," Don said as Roni took the phone from him. "Where's the bathroom?" he asked Hope when Roni went to take the call.

"Over there, I think," she mumbled, gesturing with her head toward the hall that opened from one side of the living room.

The mental image that Roni had begun painting made her almost ache. Good thing she had that date planned with Chris. It was time.

Most of the others were still outside, watching the sunset, and the kitchen buzzed with action.

Hope lingered a second more, which was unfortunate, because just at that moment, Jordan looked away and caught her gazing at him from across the room. Gabe was telling him something, and Jordan replied without taking his eyes off her.

She was the one to avert her gaze first, taking advantage of the fact that Anne Drecher and Connie Latimer had just emerged from the kitchen with trays of specially made pastries that they had brought from Breading Dreams.

"Hey, Anne." Hope turned to her enthusiastically. "These smell great! I love the wedding cake you made for Ava. I was at the wedding. Can't wait for Libby's. I'm going out to the porch. Come with me?" That verbal diarrhea made her forget that Anne hadn't been invited as a guest.

"I'm not staying. I just came to deliver these." Anne placed the tray down. Then, maybe seeing the look on Hope's face, she added, "I'm busy. I have to deliver today's saves. The boxes are in my car."

Though Anne was Libby's and Roni's age, and her parents had bought Connie's bakery when the Latimers had been in debt and let Connie stay as a salaried employee, Anne mostly kept to herself and never really meshed with them. That was strange, because Hope liked her and thought she could have easily fit into their little group. Being an outsider, she seemed better able to befriend Anne, and the two of them were involved with donating the bakery's and other shops' daily leftovers to local institutions that needed them.

"Is Avery here?" Anne asked, skimming her gaze around the room.

"No. Were you expecting her to be?"

"Heard her say she's working on snagging Jordan Delaney, so I … Please, don't say anything. I shouldn't have said that."

Avery was Anne's cousin, but there wasn't much love between the two. Hope felt even more connected to Anne over it, though she didn't know the roots of Anne's dislike of Avery.

Regardless, the words *snagging Jordan* remained with her.

She looked toward Jordan again. It was as if he felt her gaze on him, brief as it was, and their eyes crossed paths again.

Just then, those who were out on the balcony came inside and cut their line of sight. Hope took a deep breath and parted with Anne.

After a toast raised by Luke that was followed by the buffet opening, trays of cocktails were brought from the kitchen and placed on the drinks table.

Hope, who was just reaching for a plate, did a double-take upon seeing them. She raised her eyes and caught Libby's gaze.

Libby shrugged, curled her lips down, and raised her eyebrows in a *I had no idea.*

Hope surveyed the cocktails. The glasses contained cherry-red or apple-green spheres that could only be made using reverse spherification. Others had foam fluffing the top of the liquid, and some had colorful droplets, looking like little gems at the bottom, such that were formed by spherification.

When she brought her gaze up a second time, she found a deep, dark amber gaze resting on her, piercing her from across the room. The smile that spread on the face, the deep brackets that hugged the mouth, the tan skin under the light-colored shirt, made her swallow.

Hope cleared her throat, which had suddenly become dry, when Jordan made his way across the room toward her.

"Thanks," he said, stopping next to her.

"What for?"

"Getting me almost drunk all week long."

"What?"

"Making these. I had to practice. Spherification and reverse spherification aren't as easy as you made them sound."

Those eyes, that smirk, that wall of a chest, his fresh-woods smell. And he had just verified that he had attentively listened to her lame lecture to Josh.

She tore her gaze from his. "It looks fantastic. I want to taste it all, but I probably shouldn't."

"You can start with one." He pointed. "Green and red combination—gorgeous."

She felt his gaze skimming her face and automatically reached up to touch her hair. She then took one of the glasses, and Jordan took another.

She raised her eyes, and their gazes landed on each other.

He clinked his glass with hers. "To chemistry."

"To chemistry," she echoed.

She took a longer sip than one would normally take from a cocktail, but she needed to alleviate the desert in her throat at the thought that this man had taken such notice of her words. Eric had always forgotten what she had said a minute after she had said it.

She used the long sip to build the next sentence in her mind so it wouldn't come out as a convoluted speech.

"You like the result?" Jordan said over a huffed chuckle, watching her prolonged sip, putting his own glass down.

She stopped drinking and gazed at him from over the rim of her glass, feeling the shaper clinging to her heated skin. "Yes, it's great. Thank you," she said as soon as she could muster the words, despite his scrutiny. She placed the nearly empty glass on the table and spoke without looking directly at him. "And thanks for the ride home from Fred's, you know, that day. It was … And I'm sorry I … I don't usually …" She was doing it again. "It's … It was very kind and …"

"No problem. My pleasure," he cut her off, giving her a second to collect herself.

"And thanks for helping Hannah at the Model UN—the advice you gave her." She now lifted her eyes to his face. "And more than that, for making her feel she could do it. I appreciate it. It meant a lot to her. She still talks about it." *She talks about you.*

"Again, my pleasure. She's a bright kid. She did well even before I talked to her and deserved better than the treatment she received there."

Her heart missed a painful beat. He hadn't sugarcoated it, but coming from someone who had taken the initiative to help Hannah, it wasn't abrading to hear her daughter's social issues openly stated. Quite the opposite. She felt seen, understood, empathized with.

"Hey, sweetie! Are you enjoying the evening?" Libby turned up next to them and swept Hope into a hug before she could reply to Jordan. "So, how about the surprise drinks that Jordan prepared for us?" Libby gave her a brief yet meaningful look before moving her beaming face to Jordan.

"They're great. I was just telling him that …"

Just then, Patty Delaney called Jordan from the kitchen.

"You know he made these for you, right?" Libby said as soon as he excused himself and left them.

"But, why?"

Libby shrugged. "He likes you?"

She didn't reply, not knowing what exactly to say.

"It's not a bad thing," Libby said.

"It's not. But …" It wasn't a bad thing; it was only confusing and a little frightening that she couldn't remain indifferent to him despite every logic.

"I'll ask Luke to dig deeper about Avery."

"Don't. It's not just her. He's … We're not … And there's Chris," she mumbled, knowing Libby would understand.

She did, given the way she rubbed her arm then.

While eating later, Hope chatted with Libby's aunt as they stood close to the back wall that overlooked the packed living room.

"Just look at those Delaneys," Sarah said with her mouth full. "A great pool of genes right there." She chuckled at her own joke. "And if he wasn't a little intimidating with all this"—she jiggled her hand in front of her the way Roni had done before, the mini-quiche she was holding sprinkling tiny crumbs on the front of her fuchsia pink blouse—"I'd tell you it's time to forget about your ex, get out there, and grab yourself the last Delaney kid left, dear." Sarah's hair fluttered with the incoming ocean breeze, its color-of-the-month mahogany. "Now that I think of it, it's like meeting a real-life version of Alain Delon. It's a bit scary." Everyone knew Sarah had a lifelong crush on the French actor. "I can't believe he grew up next door." She chuckled again, but her words, spoken in true Sarah form, echoed Hope's own thoughts. "Oh, I almost forgot, dear," she continued. "I'll be available to babysit next week. I had to finish the inventory check. You can't be too careful in a pharmacy."

"Thanks. That'd be great," Hope said, looking over at Jordan.

Being the host, he had been busy most of the evening, and she hadn't found another chance to speak to him. At one point, she had overheard his sister half-whispering to him, "Great party! Your diplomatic experience shows. Pity to let it go to waste in this place."

"Who said I'll let it go to waste?" he had replied, squeezing her fondly to his side.

She wished Libby had heard that. Because, yeah, there was also that—he wasn't here for the long run. Poor Avery.

~~~~~~~~~~~~~~~~~

"You wouldn't mind if we stayed longer, right? We're finally together, all of us," Roni whispered to her when Luke's parents, his sister, and her husband left. Connie and David had left with Libby's brother when his kids had fallen asleep. Aunt Sarah had left with them.

"It's okay. Eric's mom knows I might be late."

It was just the rhyming couple, Roni and Donnie; the "L's," as Roni nicknamed Libby and Luke; Jordan; and her on the porch with music playing in the background. And, as Libby sat in Luke's lap on one of the Adirondacks and Don was getting all cozy with Roni, Hope felt her couple-less status acutely, just as much as she felt Jordan's presence.

Because Don was there, the conversation soon revolved around real estate costs and the difference between Wayford and Riviera View.

"If you're considering buying this house, you should try Riviera View first," Don addressed Jordan.

"We don't know if he's staying," Roni said pointedly to her husband, but it was clear she was trying to gauge Jordan's reaction. "And maybe Riviera View brings up too many memories, what with Avery Miles and others." She now smirked at Jordan. Roni wasn't famous for her subtlety.

"If I stay and buy a house, I'll hire you, Veronica. I hear you're one of the best interior designers around," Jordan replied, unfazed, using Roni's full name, which she hated.

"*The* best," Roni said. "Can you afford me?"

"I might have to go for second-best, then," Jordan replied flatly.

That was a battle of equals, Hope thought. Most men were confused around Roni, but *he* wasn't.

Don, always one to try to dominate the conversation, moved to talk about politics, calling Jordan's attention time and again with things like, "*You* know what I'm talking about, Jordan. Am I right?"

Eloquent and fluent, it was easy to tell Jordan ruled that arena—well-versed in confidently communicating his opinion, short and punchy, explaining without mansplaining, contradicting without sounding criticizing. And to imagine he had done all that not just with small-town lawyer Donnie but with D.C. sharks on a daily basis for many years.

At one point, he had removed his tie and opened the two top buttons of his shirt. Sitting across from him, Hope conducted a private biology experiment—could she look at him without her heart rate rising or her palms sweating?

She failed the experiment time and again.

"I saw you gawking," Roni whispered to her when they both went in to put on a jacket as the night became chilly. "Can't blame you. Even *I* could hardly help myself. To think that you tried to flirt with Josh when this specimen of a man was there. Josh is a kid next to him."

"Roni! What if Don hears you?"

"What? I'm married, not blind," Roni said, laughing. "Don doesn't mind. He knows I'm his, heart, body, and soul. Didn't you and Eric joke about these things?"

"*He* did. God forbid if *I* ever said someone was attractive. He'd get all, '*It's very common here in California to see people who keep in shape,*'" she mimicked a man's whiny voice.

"I wonder if that applies in Nevada and for his new wife, too. God, what a douche!" Roni exclaimed, her face contorting in contempt.

Hope didn't reply. While Jenna, Eric's wife, was a civil engineer like him and had begun dating him just six months after her and Eric's divorce had been final, she was okay. Most importantly, she was nice to Naomi and Hannah.

"Are there any more of those special cocktails, Jordan?" Libby asked when they were back.

Hope shot a glance at her friend, her heart rate speeding up yet again. She was wondering about that gesture of his, too, but would never dare to bring it up.

"All gone," Jordan said with a smile. "I was tricked into thinking they'd be easy to make. They're not. Maybe a real bartender, like Josh, could whip those out faster."

On the porch that was lit by strings of fairy lights, the moon, and the backyards of the houses in the front row to the beach, Hope could clearly see his wink in her direction.

She failed another biology experiment just then.

Through a dry mouth, she managed to say, "They looked like they were made by a pro."

A bit later, when the two couples spoke quietly between themselves and Jordan went inside after his cell phone had rung, Hope got up and went to lean against the railing of the porch. *Who would call him at eleven p.m. on a Saturday night?* she wondered while trying to shut herself up internally. It was none of her goddamn business.

Gazing at the waves breaking in the distance, she checked for messages. Nothing. That was good news.

She was dying to pee, but just the thought of pulling down the shaper and then back up again had kept her from going until now. However, there was no way she would survive the ride back if she didn't go.

Approaching Libby, she quietly asked where the restroom was, then went inside, leaving her jacket with Libby.

Jordan's voice was coming from somewhere in the house but she didn't see him.

After using the bathroom, which was a door away from the open door of the bedroom, she snuck a peek in. It was immaculate in comparison to her house, which held evidence of kids in every corner, including her bedroom.

Back on the porch, while the rhyming couple was quietly conversing by the railing and Luke and Libby on an Adirondack, Hope decided to hint that she was ready to leave. She gathered as many glasses as she could carry from the side table and went inside to put them in the kitchen.

Jordan was still nowhere to be seen.

After depositing the glasses in the sink, she washed her hands under the tap. When she pivoted to take the dishtowel that hung by the fridge, Jordan entered the kitchen.

"Hey." He stopped a few inches from her.

"Hi. I think we're leaving soon, so I thought I'd help clear some of the dishes."

"Been avoiding the make-out sessions outside?"

She chuckled nervously. "Kinda." Wiping her hands, she stared at the towel as if it was fascinating, then hung it back.

He pointed at the row of containers on the counter, labeled "*Calcium Lactate Gluconate*" and "*Sodium Alginate*." "What am I going to do with all the leftover powders? Are they powders, by the way, or do they have another name?"

"Powders is correct. You can use them to wow other guests of yours." It was as close as she could come to hinting about Avery.

He traced his glance over her. Brief as it was, he heat up everything in his path up to the roots of her hair. "Everyone I wanted to wow was here today."

She cleared her throat. The silence that followed was deafening.

"Why chemistry?" he suddenly asked, his voice low, raspy.

"Like physics, it's at the basis of everything. And I've always liked watching how elements react to one another. You know, if they'll blend well, repulse each other, or create an explosion. Explosions are fun." She chuckled again. "I've loved it ever since they took us to the science museum in St. Paul in third grade."

His gaze rested on her as he just nodded at her words slowly, as if he was taking them in.

They stood less than a foot apart, and she could see every line and edge of his face and smell a hint of his aftershave and detergent. She ensured her gaze didn't drop lower than his chin because, whenever it did, all she could think of was the small gap between his shirt and his skin.

"Why politics?" she asked. Maybe if she stuck to short sentences …

"Like chemistry, it's in everything. And I wanted to influence the important things from within." A small lopsided scoff clouded and disappeared from his face. "Are you happy with your choice?"

"Yes. You?"

"They say that politics changes people more than people change politics."

She stared at him, sensing, not for the first time, an underlying element in him that made her heart thrum in her ears. It wasn't just her body. She felt as if her heart had been breached.

His ensuing silence and penetrating gaze compelled her to speak again, to revert to things she understood. "By the way, I use reverse spherification in baking, too. It exploits a chemical reaction between the calcium ions and the alginate, which is what you have here." She pointed at the counter, happy to break eye contact. "Did you know it's a polysaccharide found in the cell walls of brown algae? When you add calcium, its ions will cause the alginate molecules to cross-link with each other and form a gel. It's … very useful and better than gelatin"

"That simple?" He had a little smirk on and a spark in his eyes that held hers unflinchingly.

She shrugged and swallowed. "Yes, if you mix it right, then you can use it for all sorts of things in the kitchen … I just explained it."

"Not in English," he said, his smirk widening.

Their gazes were glued to each other like alginate molecules. The amber color in his darkened.

She was sweltering. "I could try to simplify it. If you compare the reactivity of …" She faltered. Somehow, Jordan was closer, and her sight blurred. She could feel his breath on her as her own breath shallowed. "Sodium and … calcium—"

Her heart rate spiked out of control when his breath intermixed with hers.

"The gelation process—"

His lips closed on hers, shutting her up mid-sentence.

God, his taste. She opened her mouth to his almost immediately, her body succumbing to her yearning to taste him, a yearning she had tried to defy. In damn vain.

And that was all he needed to back her up against the pantry door that was right there, pinning her between it and his strong body, slipping his fingers into her hair so he could meld her mouth further to his and deepen the kiss.

His tongue in her mouth, and the feel of his body against hers, sent clenches that were almost painful down her body, evaporating every logic, igniting and setting her on fire.

Her arms rose, as if by themselves, her palms landing on and trekking his hard biceps and wide shoulders over his shirt until she linked them around his neck. Sandwiched between Jordan's hard body and the surface behind her, Hope's head lulled back, and she heard a little moan escape her throat.

She devoured him shamelessly, her body humming, as if an electric wire ran through her.

Jordan slid his hands down her neck and shoulders, over the sides of her breasts, and down to her waist, gripping and pressing her harder against him. She felt him lingering on the thick waistband of the shaper that was felt through the fabric of her dress as he smoothed one hand across her waist. He then traced his hand down over her hips, along the shaper, as if searching where it ended, while raking his other hand under the hem of her dress, hiking it up her bare leg, his touch making her knees gel, until his fingers met the shaper at her mid-thigh.

Jordan tore his mouth from hers and pulled his head back a little. With less than an inch between their heaving mouths, he smirked and rasped, "Is that a protective armor?" His eyes were hazy, but a flame burned behind the dark honey.

"No," she managed to croak.

He then slid his mouth along her jaw to her ear. "I didn't think so," he whispered, causing her eyes to flutter shut from the sheer force of the arousal that his raspy voice sent through every nerve ending in her body.

Jordan kissed the hollow below her ear then down the column of her neck and clavicle, his hand under her dress trailing in the opposite direction— up—until it cupped her shaper-covered ass, pressing her against him. He trekked his other hand over the underside of her breasts, his large palm splaying along her ribcage, while he trailed his lips over the cleavage of her dress where the pushup bra kept her breasts where they used to be two pregnancies ago.

Hope raked her hands up his neck then weaved them into his hair, pressing his mouth further to her. She bit her bottom lip, stifling the moan that hovered there.

If it wasn't for the shaper, she could have felt that hardness in his pants much more acutely. And, as if he realized she was aiming for more friction, Jordan wedged his leg between hers, and Hope realized she was grinding unashamedly against him and that he was helping her by pinning her ass that was cupped in his palm further into him.

When a little whimper escaped her lips, Jordan crashed his mouth back on hers, and she was filled again with his taste and the maddening feel of his tongue in her mouth. She could come right there, in a fully lit kitchen, trapped between him and that door.

But the sound of shattering glass, followed by laughter and voices approaching caused them to break their kiss, tear their lips from each other, and push themselves off the door.

Breathless, Hope ran a quick hand over her hair then over her mouth. And right before Roni and Don entered the kitchen, laughing and carrying more glasses, she managed to ensure her dress was where it should be after Jordan had hiked it up.

"Sorry, Jordan, one of your fancy glasses slipped and broke," Don said. "Libby and Luke are sweeping it from the porch."

"No problem," Jordan said, running a hand through his hair. His tone and look were as if nothing had just happened.

Maybe *he* was used to snapping right back to normal in such situations, but Hope couldn't. She used the opportunity to slip out of the kitchen and back out to the porch to collect her things, hoping no one would notice her. She was still breathless, and her body throbbed with need.

"Wow, it's later than I thought, but we had to wait until Don was ready to drive," Roni announced, returning to the porch and shoving her cell phone into her purse. "I've had way too much to be driving."

They both hugged Libby and Luke and congratulated them again before they escorted them to the front door where Don and Jordan were already waiting.

In the mix of voices and goodbyes, Jordan managed to bend toward her and whisper, "Sorry about ..." He gestured with his head toward the kitchen. "I shouldn't have ..."

She brought her eyes up to his. Did he regret kissing her? She had never been kissed like that before. Eric had been a decent kisser, especially at the beginning, but he had been *nothing* like that. She couldn't even remember the man-wannabes whom she had kissed before him.

He held her gaze until Roni stepped between them, but didn't say another word.

Chapter 10

Fuuuuuuck. He'd had no intention of doing that.

Yes, the cocktails were for her. He had wanted to see her smile, make her feel confident in herself near him, but he had never intended to take it further. He had *wanted* to, but he had every intention to withstand the desire, the need. He could blame those fucking cocktails for getting to a point where he just couldn't resist kissing that unstoppable mouth of hers with that freckle at the edge of her upper lip that drove him mad when she spoke about something she loved. And once he had started, he couldn't stop. He had a pretty good inkling of how it would have ended if they hadn't been interrupted.

Jesus, he wanted her. And no, he couldn't blame alcohol.

And it wasn't even her looks that had done him in. Cute as she was, he had never gone for cute. It was that she was the woman with the most heart in her eyes. Those eyes betrayed everything she felt, and she might have even known it, though she couldn't do much about it. And in those large greens that were half screened by the copper bangs that kept falling into her face, he had seen that she had wanted him to kiss her.

And he had longed to do it. So he had. But he shouldn't have.

That was why he had apologized. Because someone like him shouldn't be involved with someone like her. She had too much on the line for him to risk. A man whose first instinct had been to treat a pregnancy as a public relations problem and had never celebrated a two-year anniversary with anyone shouldn't fall for a single mother who probably had enough shit to deal with as it was.

He was just unable to force himself to stop thinking about her. Not even two days later.

Driving to Fred's to meet with Luke, Jordan smiled to himself when he thought of that rubber thingy she'd had on. Was it rubber? It had felt like rubber, but it couldn't be, right? He had peeled off thick pantyhose before, a corset even, but never that … thing.

Hidden under that sexy blue dress of hers, it was probably aimed at stifling her curves. She looked her age and her life experience reflected on her, and he loved it. She wasn't like the million and one fresh-out-of-college assistants and assistants to assistants who swarmed into D.C.'s halls of power every year. In recent years, he had felt that they were getting younger, but it was just that he was getting older.

He wasn't interested in their clean slates and lost patience with their I'm-still-learning-to-be-me place in life. While figuring yourself out was a lifelong journey, he wanted someone who at least had decent mileage on that path, someone who knew what it was like to stumble and fall, pick yourself up, dust yourself off, and keep going.

Hope Hays ticked all those boxes and so many more. But he wouldn't tick most of hers. And that was the problem.

Parking his mother's barely-used car, which she had let him borrow for as long as he was in California, Jordan went inside to find his brother already seated alongside the long bar. He looked around, but no clay-splattered redhead was there.

A beer and short chitchat later, Luke watched him closely.

"You look more lost now than you were when you first arrived. What's going on?"

Jordan breathed out a puff of air in place of an answer. Was he becoming readable, too?

"Class president, homecoming king, head of your class in Cornell, top of your game in D.C.; what more do you want, Jordan?"

He turned his head to look at his younger brother. "Everything else."

"What does that mean?"

"I don't know yet, but you probably do."

A big grin spread on Luke's face, the one he now often wore, especially when Libby was near or when she was talked of.

"Ambition, money, competition, winning, being wooed from job to job, offered more weight in decision making, fancier car, better pay, closer to the zenith of power—it's not enough anymore," Jordan said. "Not even knowing that the projects I pick have a good aim."

"So, what's stopping you from going after everything else?"

Jordan threw his head back and sipped the last of his bottle then plunked it down on the wooden surface. "I don't score as high on other scales. I'm pretty shit at it."

Luke nodded. "Dad will wonder what he did wrong raising us. As far as he can see, there's nothing more to want."

Jordan scoffed. "Yeah. Did you notice that, between him and Mom, you and I took after Dad then did a one-eighty?"

"I don't think we've ever been like him. But are you doing a one-eighty, or a three-sixty with a stop here on the way?" Luke asked, his lips hovering over his beer bottle.

"I don't know if there's something here to keep me." He hadn't expected it to hurt, but saying it out loud did.

"Libby thinks you're interested in Hope."

"She does, does she?" Jordan grinned, though his heart hammered quicker.

"Is she wrong? I mean, the cocktails and all. What the fuck, man?"

"Yeah, I figured that would draw attention, but I had to do it."

"Don't do those things if you don't have any intention of sticking with it."

"I was just trying to ... you know, because of ..."

He couldn't bring himself to tell Luke the truth about what had happened later. And it sounded like Hope hadn't told Libby, either, or Luke would have mentioned it.

"This isn't D.C. Don't play those games here."

"I wasn't playing a game. That was the last thing I wanted. I just wanted to close that loop from Ava's wedding; make her smile over that, instead of …" He gritted his teeth. It sounded bad enough even without the additional info of what he had done after. He shouldn't have done *any* of it.

Regret serrated his flesh in every direction.

"Make her smile? Didn't you help her kid or something in school?"

"Is there anything those two aren't talking about?"

"You tell me. Is there anything else we need to know?"

"*We*? No, there's nothing else to know." He hated lying, though he was good at it. Anything he told Luke would go straight to Libby. No. That was something he had to deal with alone.

"Good. Because you can't escape something like this if shit gets too real, you know. So don't start anything you can't commit to."

It wasn't commitment, or wanting to escape, or shit getting real that he was afraid of. It was what that woman made him feel and knowing how fucked up he was.

"You're preaching to the choir, Luke. I know. Trust me; I know." He had never meant to start anything. Not with her. She didn't deserve it. And he didn't deserve her.

All that was left to do now was damage control … if only he could find a way to do it without succumbing to touching her again.

Chapter 11

"Are you sure there's no other way? Like, maybe wait until you or Luke are back, or your mom?"

"The ceiling is leaking. It's urgent, Hope. Please."

"Okay, okay."

Great. Luke was at the San Francisco airport for one of his forty-eight-hour shifts, Libby was away in San Luis for a conference, and Deidre from the bookstore below their apartment had called to say that her ceiling was dripping water that obviously came from some burst pipe in their home. Connie and David were away with Libby's aunt, Sarah, at a doctor's appointment out of town, and Roni didn't have a key. That left *her* to hand over her set to Jordan Delaney.

Oh no.

After the engagement party, she had spent the rest of the weekend with her daughters, wondering if there was any outward change in her. After all, it had been the first kiss that she'd had in over two years, and the first man she had kissed who wasn't their father in the last million years. It must have reflected on her. Or maybe not because, on the way back home from the party, Roni and Don hadn't seemed to notice how she had been an open flame in the back seat of their car. All they had spoken about was the catering and the beach house.

Hope hadn't told anyone about the kiss. It had been so tantalizing, yet his apology right after so much like a bucket of cold water—a bucket she had needed because it had snapped her back into rational thinking—that she didn't know what to make of it. She had been dying to tell Libby, but Libby was practically related to him, and when she had tried to hint something to Roni, she couldn't go through with it.

What would she say? *I wanted him to kiss me, and he did, he* so *did, and I wanted so much more, still do. It was just like you said, Roni. He could be what I need, but I can't just have sex with someone, can't just have sex with* him *because the way he looks at me makes me feel like I'm me again, not just someone's mom, ex, teacher, friend, daughter, sister. Me. Hope. And it's scary. Because I forgot who she was, but I see her in his eyes. And the difference between us is insurmountable, so nothing can come out of it, so it's better that I don't see or hear from him again.*

No, none of it made sense. She couldn't say that. So, she didn't say anything.

Good thing her date with Chris had gone well earlier this week. Maybe, just maybe, just a hypothesis—all this confusion over Jordan was caused by the fact that he had been the first man she had touched in ages. She should treat it like an experiment, where Jordan and Chris were the variables, and her response to them, her feelings, would be the observed result.

When Chris had offered they meet at Life's A Beach for their date, she had offered an out-of-town place. "We don't want people to start gossiping," she had said. In truth, she had wanted to avoid running into Josh, who owned the place with his father.

In his car afterward, she had leaned in so he would get the hint and kiss her, mostly because she wanted another kiss to obliterate the taunting memories of Jordan's mouth, and hands, and body. Memories that had her send her hand into her panties the night it had happened and at least twice since. After nearly a thousand days without that type of physical contact with a male body, *his* male body had worked like narcotics on hers, even if she left her heart out of the equation.

But Chris hadn't kissed her.

"It was a really nice evening," he had said *twice*.

Later, she had realized that it had been his first date since his divorce. At least it hadn't been as traumatic as hers had been with Blake.

Now, exactly a week after he had pinned her between his body and a door, Jordan was on his way to her house. She had thirty minutes at best.

She would meet him at the front door so he wouldn't have to come in, and it'd be quick.

Rushing to her bedroom, she changed from the faded blue sweatpants and stained Tweetie pullover to a pair of jeans and a T-shirt. She brushed her hair with her fingers and was just about to apply some concealer to the circles under her eyes when the doorbell rang. *Sonofabitch.* How was he here so fast? She hadn't had a chance to clear the mess from the living room, at least the part of it that could be seen from the front door. And she looked horrible.

"I'll get it," she called loudly. But, while rushing barefoot from her bedroom to the living room, she heard a deep, bass voice, somewhat raspy, over Naomi's squeaky one.

She halted mid-jog upon reaching the entryway. Sending a smile in the general direction of the tall form at the doorway without looking directly at him, she addressed the four-foot munchkin first. "Naomi, what did we say about opening the front door? How did you even manage the key?"

"It was easy-peasy," Naomi said triumphantly.

"We'll talk about this later."

Feeling his gaze on her, Hope shifted hers to finally look at him. *Jesus Christ.* From the height of his six-plus-feet, Jordan was smiling at her, light brown eyes, dimples, and all.

"Hi." She plastered a smile on.

"Hi," he echoed, locking his eyes on hers.

She was about to open her mouth to say that she would get him the key when a tiny voice next to her said, "Don't stand outside; you'll catch a cold."

"Thank you," he stressed with a chuckle, his attention back on Naomi.

The house looked about as messy as she did, Hope thought when Jordan strutted his well-built frame into her living room. She noticed his gaze swooping it all in—the hill of unfolded laundry on the couch, Hannah's sneakers thrown near the coffee table, Naomi's Barbies and LOL Surprise dolls scattered all over and around it, Hannah's homework and her students' exams waiting to be graded spread on the dining room table. At least the walls had been recently painted and the accent ocean-blue one Roni claimed was out of fashion looked great with the white curtains that let the sun in, warming the space up though exposing its state.

"I'll go get you the key," she finally said.

"What's your name?" Naomi asked.

Hope left him at the mercy of Naomi and went into the kitchen, hearing him tell her his name and explain that he was Luke's brother and Libby's friend.

She huffed a silent breath as soon as her back was turned to him. It was the first time she had seen him in a T-shirt and a pair of jeans, and by God, it didn't make matters easier. All the muscles she had felt under the fabric of his shirt with her eager palms were now exposed and were in every way as mouthwatering as she had imagined they would look. And just where the sleeve of his blue tee ended, over his left bicep, was a tattoo. A wave rising and curling in black and grey ink.

To battle her unwarranted attraction to him, especially in light of what had happened, she had told herself that he was just a slick-talking Ivy League and Ivy life champion who was circling way out of her orbit, crashed against her accidentally, caused a little earthquake, and regretted it immediately. Somehow, though, a tattoo made him seem so … down to earth.

Silly as it was, it had now become an intervening variable in her experiment.

She took the key out of the top drawer, internally smacking herself for not taking it with her before she had gone to change, which would have saved her from letting him in.

Entering the living room, she stopped in her tracks at the sight.

Jordan was standing by the dining table, and Hope had to suck in her lips and bite them from the inside so she wouldn't laugh. With all his height and width, and with Naomi looking up at him intently, barely reaching his hip, he was trying to jam a straw into a juice box, but the thing kept bending, and he was cursing under his breath.

He looked up from his task. "We have Siri and Alexa, but these things are still around?"

"You're doing it wrong," she said, hardly able to contain the laughter that bubbled inside her. Approaching him and reaching for the box, she took it from him and easily jammed the straw in. "There," she said, smiling first at him then at Naomi.

"Thanks," Naomi said, taking her drink and rushing back to her dolls on the other side of the living room.

"It was nice meeting you, Naomi," Jordan called after her. "Sorry I couldn't help with the straw."

"That's okay," Naomi replied in a comforting tone. She then waved at him with the Barbie that she had lifted from the carpet.

"Seems I'm forgiven," Jordan said as they both turned to look at each other.

"Naomi goes easy on people," she said, wondering if they were talking about Naomi or something else.

Avoiding looking directly into his face now that she stood closer to him, she stared at his chest and neck. It was either that, which wasn't easy, given how well that shirt wrapped him, or looking at his lips and remembering what they felt like on her skin.

"Great craftsmanship, by the way," Jordan said. "It went right in."

"Experience." Her eyes met his for a brief second as she smiled. "The key," she said, handing it over.

"Thanks."

They just stood there for one drawn-out moment, eyes locked together, before he spoke again. "You did this?" He pointed at the orange- and red-glazed, shallow bowl in the middle of the round dining table, which she used for her keys, used batteries, spare change, misplaced scrunchies, and lost dice of old board games.

"Yes."

"It's pretty."

"Thanks. Sorry about the mess." She chuckled nervously as that bowl was surrounded by open textbooks and stacks of papers.

"It's a family home," he said.

She sneaked a peek at his face, feeling his eyes boring a hole into hers.

Eric, who had never lifted a finger in his parents' home, and had them pay for a cleaner when he had attended college, had wondered at first why things hadn't magically found their place. "It's a family home," she used to say. "Not a museum."

"Did you leave that class?" Jordan suddenly asked.

"I'll take it again sometime." She broke eye contact. The memory of Blake and what had followed

114

made her apprehensive, and she really wanted Jordan gone.

"No one should be deterred from doing something they like and are good at because of others' shitty personalities."

He looked like he was going to say more, but just then, Hannah came strolling into the living room. It was Saturday morning, and Hope was less stringent on the weekends, letting the girls stay in their pajamas until lunchtime if they wanted. Growing up, she had hated having to be up and ready, her bed made, even on Sundays, so she was lenient in her own home. Now she kind of wished she had made them change, because both girls were in their long unicorn nighties, their hair unbrushed.

"Hello there," Jordan said, "the best United Nations representative west of New York that I've had the honor of meeting."

Hannah smiled coyly. "Thanks," she said, her eyes sparkling.

"When's your regionals?" he asked.

"Mom, when is it?" Hannah looked at her.

"There's time. It's in San Francisco, right before Halloween," Hope replied.

"Will you judge there?" Hannah asked, her head bent back so she could look up at Jordan.

He smiled. "No. They didn't invite me."

"And if Miss Miles invites you?"

"I don't think she can or will," he said, his gaze briefly crossing paths with Hope's.

"Can I invite you?" Hannah asked.

Hope snapped her head to look at him just when he looked at her.

"I'm sure Jordan is very busy," she said.

"I'll have to check," Jordan said, his smile on Hannah.

"Okay." Hannah hesitated then added, "Do you want to see my room?"

"If your mother agrees," he replied, looking at Hope.

"Jordan has to go and check a burst pipe in Libby's house," Hope explained. "We should let him get to it."

"Just for a minute," Hannah said. "I'll just show him my new globe."

"It'll just be a minute," Jordan echoed, looking at Hope with a smile and a half-wink.

As soon as he followed Hannah into the hall leading to the bedrooms, Hope quickly stacked the papers on the dining table and shoved Hannah's shoes under the coffee table. She halted to look at the laundry waiting on the couch but decided there was nothing she could do with it at this point. Remembering that the bedrooms weren't in a much better shape, she darted toward them, at least to close the door to hers so he wouldn't see the bed that was rumpled mostly on one side. After Eric had moved out, having the bed just for herself used to be a silver lining, but after a while, she missed having a warm body there that was taller than five feet.

"I did, but I knew how to talk my way out of it," she heard Jordan say. "It's okay if you don't know exactly how. It's better to say what you want instead of bottling it and then …" He must have done some pantomime instead of ending the sentence because she could hear Hannah giggle.

Hope pressed her fingers to her lips. She didn't want them to know she was eavesdropping.

"Yeah. Brittney, she could make even … even Gandhi explode," Hannah exclaimed.

Hope took a deep breath. Her daughter was telling him things that she herself had to work hard to get out of her.

She tiptoed closer, glad that she was barefoot, just as Jordan's voice was heard again.

"I know the type," he said. "They're everywhere. But—and remember this because it's an important but—you have to do it with style, okay? Don't yell, don't insult, just say why something isn't fair or isn't working. Try not to cry right then—it's okay to cry afterward—and don't ever, under any circumstance, use bad words. Those give you away immediately. You can say them in your heart, but don't tell your mom I said that."

"Mommy, what are you doing?" Naomi's voice startled her from behind.

"Hi, sweetie," she said in an *everything's normal over here* voice. "I was just putting some things away. You two left so much stuff in the living room."

To ensure no one thought she was lying, she entered Hannah's room as if she had been on her way there.

Jordan was sitting on the edge of Hannah's bed while she was on her rolling student chair across from him, holding her globe.

Surrounded by all the pinks and lilacs, the stuffed animals and cuddly dolls, Jordan looked gigantic and rugged with that stubble on his jaw.

They both looked at her.

117

"Sorry, I was putting stuff away," she said, wishing she wasn't empty-handed. "I think we've kept Jordan here long enough, and that leaky ceiling at Books And More isn't going to repair itself." She said this looking at her daughter.

Jordan got up, further dwarfing everything around him. "Yes, I'd better go and see how much plumbers charge here on the weekend." He smiled at her, and she wished he didn't. It only served to make her heart race faster in her throat.

"Do you like my Barbie?" Naomi, who strolled into the room behind Hope, said, holding her half-naked Barbie in front of Jordan. Hope had asked Eric to buy the newer model that at least vaguely resembled normal-proportioned women, but he had bought the classic one.

"It's very nice."

"My daddy got it for me. Hannah got a globe. That's what she wanted." Naomi's expression indicated her sister didn't know what a good present was.

Jordan smiled and patted the blonde head. "Those are great gifts." He looked at both girls. "Thanks for showing me your presents. And, Hannah, thanks for the drawing." He picked up an A4 paper that was on the bed. It had a quirky colorful globe painted on it with markers.

"You're welcome," Hannah said.

Hope bit the inside of her bottom lip. The happy expression on her daughter's face pinched her heart.

"Bye, girls," he said.

"Bye, Jordan," the two replied together.

Hope led the way through the hall, toward the living room, feeling his gaze on her back the entire way.

"I'm sorry they kept you," she said when they reached the living room.

"That's okay. I was … glad." His gaze was soft. Though she hadn't seen much of him, she knew she'd never seen *that* look in his eyes. "Heard an appropriate reference to Gandhi," he added with a smirk.

She couldn't help but smile back. "She reads a lot."

"Naomi's a natural rockstar. And Hannah will do great. Model UN is definitely her thing."

"It ticks many boxes for her." She smiled warmly at him. While it might have been easy to spot Naomi, it wasn't as easy with Hannah, and he had succeeded. The drawing he was holding was one proof of that.

They stopped by the front door.

"Listen, Hope," he started as she was about to open it. "I'm sorry about—"

"That's okay," she interjected. She didn't want another apology for that kiss. Not when standing here with him reminded her of how he had cornered her between that body of his and another door and how they had touched, and touched, and touched.

He nodded once. "I'd like to explain if possible. I … It's not that I … I'd love to …" It was the first time she had seen him faltering and searching for words.

"I'm seeing someone," she blurted. One date. No kiss. It didn't really count, but it came right out. She didn't want him to think that that moment in his kitchen had meant anything to her when it hadn't meant much to him. She wasn't sure if he wanted to ask her out or what, but even if he did, doing it only because he happened to be here wasn't good enough. It had been a week since he had kissed her, the best kiss she had ever had, and touched her in a way that still had her burning and yearning. However, he hadn't shown any interest in her since.

This wasn't the type of man who would beat around the bush. If he wanted something, he would take it, like he had in his kitchen … which he had apologized for twice already. So, if he hadn't done anything, it meant he didn't really want to.

He nodded slowly. "You're seeing … I hope it's not …" The look in his eyes told her exactly who he was referring to.

"It's someone from school. He's a teacher. We have a lot in common." She was sickened by her own blatant overcompensation and managed to shut up right before adding, *And he's leading our Model UN program.*

Jordan pressed his lips together. "That's great." His expression was sincere, but his eyes were like bronze. "I'd better go check that leak. Bye, Hope."

She closed the door behind him and leaned against it. Even if he wanted her, as tempting as it was, she shouldn't, couldn't, and wouldn't. She needed a Chris, not a Jordan. And not just for herself; she had other people to think about. People who could get attached.

If only she could think of him again as the insensitive jerk that she had thought he was at the wedding.

Chapter 12

Seeing her like that—no makeup, barefoot, everything around her so *her*—this *realness* of hers again made him want her even more.

But meeting her daughters proved yet again how delicate this thing was and he wasn't the gentle type. Luke's warning, which had felt redundant at the time, came in handy now. He almost congratulated himself for not pressing the *send* button on his phone a million times like he had almost done during that week. Finding her number hadn't been difficult, and he had typed and deleted so many versions of texts until he had ended up not sending a single one. Unusual failure for a man who wrote public speeches for others.

His silence was even worse. Yet another proof that he was shit at what really mattered.

Then he stood in front of her and had to recruit every shred of willpower left in him not to kiss her by that front door. He had begun explaining, but she had reality-checked him. Good.

After calling in a plumber, who had taken half a day to find and fix the leak, Jordan went downstairs to help Deidre clean up the bookstore.

He pushed the heavy counter, which she had already emptied, exposing the original color of the floor.

"It must be very dull here for you after D.C.," Deidre said, mopping the area before he pushed the counter back into place.

"It's not dull. It's different. In a good way, actually."

"I guess there are enough politicians in California if you want to work out here."

"Oh, there are," he scoffed.

They put everything back in place on the counter, working quietly as he handed her stacks of books, and she put them in the right order. He then cleaned the remnants of ceiling plaster that had fallen onto the floor while Deidre wiped the bookshelves. Luckily, the water hadn't damaged most of the books on them.

"It's funny that you and your brother both came back at the same time. Him, I remember well. He used to come here a lot with Liberty when they were kids, and it's wonderful they live up here together. Well, except this," Deidre said, pointing toward the wet circle in the ceiling. "But that's not their fault. These buildings are old. You, your mother had to drag you to buy books for school. How did you end up in Cornell?"

"I read newspapers instead of books." He chuckled. "I had a lot of catching up to do later. Though I wanted to be a policeman, not a politician."

"At least they both start with the same syllables." She chuckled.

When they were done, Jordan stalled next to the car. His fingers clutching the driver's side handle, he tried to convince himself that going back to Hope to return the keys was a bad idea. The logical thing would be to keep them until Libby and Luke were back in case the leak continued, but his mind kept sifting through excuses to go back to her. He found none. If he went to give it back, it would only be because he wanted to see her again.

He couldn't, and shouldn't, and wouldn't … for many reasons. The recent one was the fact that she was seeing someone. A teacher.

For the first time, Jordan regretted not becoming one as his mother had once offered.

Chapter 13

"Linda says that Mason needs to spend time with the both of us, knowing that we're going to separate homes after. It will make him feel more secure seeing that we can be together and apart, and he can be safe in both situations. It might lessen the bedwetting. And you know what? I agree with her. How did you and Eric handle it?"

Hope played with her spoon, and it clinked against the saucer. "You're very unlike Eric—in a good way. While he still lived here, we just … To be honest, he was okay with whatever I decided. I offered shared custody because I wanted the girls to have us both, but then he …" She was too ashamed to say it. "He gave it up because he decided to move to Nevada, to his girlfriend, now his wife."

Chris smiled, but he seemed a bit disappointed, as if he was expecting her to shine some sort of light on a solution to his predicament and she had failed to supply it.

Hope looked away and scanned the coffee shop. It wasn't as homely as The Mean Bean, but Mocha & Chino was on the 101, and it was better than being at one of the Riviera View cafés, bumping into colleagues or parents who would gossip about the English and Chemistry teachers dating. It was the kind of place that the Silicon Valley crew would hold their business meetings or come to work on their laptops when they weren't up to driving all way to the Bay area, or felt too cooped-up at home and wanted to be surrounded by this addicting smell of special brews and the soft music that played in the background.

"Linda offered we continue with the bi-monthly joint meetings with the therapist, and I agreed. At least until Mason turns six. Right?"

Hope pressed her lips together, creasing her chin in a *I dunno* way. It was better than the *Can't you talk of something other than your ex?* expression that she stifled. "You two know what's best. It's never exactly the same for everyone."

"No, of course not," Chris replied.

It was their third date, and the second that Chris had spent talking almost solely about his ex. She hadn't minded at first, but it was a one-way street. He didn't ask her about her issues, except when he needed her to corroborate something for him. During summer school, they used to talk about books, share movies and series recommendations, come up with funny ways to improve Show & Tell, but now it was no more.

They had kissed after the previous date at a restaurant. Chris had said that she had been his first kiss since Linda. She had smiled sympathetically and hadn't revealed that he hadn't been her first since her divorce, or the best.

"Do you want another coffee or …?" she asked. It was afternoon, and they had only been here thirty minutes, but she was getting restless.

"No, I'm fine. Thanks," Chris replied.

She sneaked another peek at the room. A man was sitting alone near the windows, his gaze fixed on his phone. At the sight of him, a hot coil ignited under her ribcage, diffusing heat all over her, from her toes to the roots of her hair. *Oh shit.*

Jordan Delaney.

Why was he there? He hadn't been there a few minutes before, and she hadn't noticed him come in. Was she doomed to see him at every café or bar?

She must have been staring, because he raised his eyes, as if he felt someone was watching him, and their gazes collided. He seemed startled, too.

They looked at each other for a moment. He then shifted his eyes to Chris, and a slow smile curled his lips. He nodded once then returned to his phone.

Thrown off balance, Hope shifted on her seat and resumed playing with the spoon's handle, half-listening to Chris, who was telling her about the new mealtime routine that he and Linda were trying to get Mason on, so his schedule would be the same at both homes.

Distractedly, she shook her head in a quick motion, as if she could churn up her thoughts and feelings like the flakes in a snow globe. Because here she was, with Chris, but her reaction to Jordan indicated that her experiment was evincing a disaster.

Chris wasn't someone she was ashamed to be seen with. True, his too-large Hard Rock Café Los Angeles T-shirt made him look far less enticing than

Jordan with his white button-down shirt that was cuffed at his elbows and sat so well on his broad shoulders. But, so what? Chris was a nice, normal, regular guy, and his shirts weren't bespoke like Jordan's probably were.

She tried to forget that tattoo on his bicep, the one that told her that Jordan had facets that she hadn't known, like some lost key to an underlying essence she had sensed in him. She tried to forget that Libby liked him and that she appreciated Libby's opinions on people. Or that he had been kind to her daughter and sweet to both her children. Chris dealt with kids every day and had one of his own.

When nothing else worked, she reminded herself of Avery's words from a few days before, when they had sat next to each other in the teachers' lounge. *"Congrats again on Hannah winning. I knew bringing Jordan would be a good thing. I can't wait for him to meet my son."*

"What did you and Eric do in such cases?" she caught the tail of Chris's question.

"Let's get out of here," she said. "We can drive to the market in Cambria. Wouldn't it be fun?" She hoped she didn't sound like when she was trying to convince her daughters to tidy up their rooms.

"We can go, but I have to be back by seven."

"We will."

Chris excused himself and went to the bathroom. He was the only buffer between her and Jordan, who sat a few tables away with no one between them now. She watched him as Chris's movement caught his attention, and he followed him with his eyes for a moment before looking at her. He smiled again.

To her alarm, he got up. But instead of approaching her, he went to pay at the counter, leaving a bill in the tip jar. Then he detoured toward her.

"Hey."

"Hey." Her throat constricted.

"I swear I'm not stalking you," he said with a smirk. "I was supposed to meet with a realtor here, but he just texted me that he couldn't make it." He angled his right wrist, exhibiting his phone, as if to drive his point home.

"Oh." She didn't think he was following her. She just attributed her bumping into him to sheer luck, or lack of.

"That's my co-judge at the UN Model," he said, angling his head in the direction Chris had gone to.

"Yes." She hoped he didn't notice the catch in her voice. It was just that facing him … She recalled Aunt Sarah's sweeping gesture at the engagement party—the whole package that was Jordan Delaney.

"Enjoy your afternoon, Hope," he said, giving her a small, tight-lipped smile.

"Thanks. You, too," she said when he turned to leave.

"The market?" Chris asked, remaining standing when he reached the table.

"Yes." She hurried to get up. "The market." Maybe it was time she and Chris took this relationship up a notch. She was obviously ready for more.

Chapter 14

That man was perfect for her. He could tell. Even before he realized where he knew him from. He had only spoken to him once, and briefly, but he looked like husband material.

He vowed not to ask Luke or Libby about Hope and now regretted he had cut the line with Avery. She would know what this guy's story was. But that would come with a price—Avery.

It was none of his business, anyway. Yet, he was relieved to see that this man was nothing like the asshole he had seen her with at Fred's.

Men in general, and men in his position in specific, had radars that told them what breed other men belonged to. His radar told him that this guy was the good kind. The type who would stick around, who wouldn't make mistakes that could potentially end up in him impregnating a woman over a one-night stand, or get his hands dirty with other people's affairs, tax evasions, lies, and fucked-up lives. He had the look of someone who would marry his high school sweetheart.

Jordan watched himself in the sun visor's mirror. That crease between his eyebrows. The man that reflected there was callous, jaded, and whatever other synonyms there were to describe why he wasn't like that man she was with.

Feeling that someone had been watching him and raising his glance to find those green eyes, half-curtained by copper bangs, had been like being hit in the gut unexpectedly with a kids' foam-covered baseball bat—slaying you softly.

He should have just walked away as soon as he had gotten the text that his meeting was canceled, but no, he'd had to stop and talk to her, drawn to be near her again. To what end?

She had acted so different. No rambling long sentences that made her self-conscious, just short, monosyllabic replies. Three, he counted. Three syllables were all he had gotten until she had wished him a good day.

What a fucked-up thing to pay attention to.

And that goddamn warmth in his veins …

If he needed something to fill the empty spaces in his soul and the hollow in his chest, then he could find a good cause to spend his time on instead of thinking about *her*.

In fact, that was exactly what he should be doing.

"*I won't be looking for a property after all*," he now texted the apologizing realtor back. "*I'll be in touch if anything changes. Thanks*." They were supposed to meet because the beach house owner wanted him to move out sooner than expected. The house had been sold, and the new proprietors wanted to start the renovations, willing to cover the costs of the lease breach.

It was a sign. He had missed it the first time, but it was clear to him now. It was time to snap himself out of this stupor, out of this place, to course-correct and go back to his natural habitat, to what he was good at, great at, what he fitted to do, what fitted him, and away from the danger of losing his heart to a woman who, come to think of it, he hardly knew.

Chapter 15

Hope looked at her two friends. They were sitting on the turquoise beach blanket that she had spread on the sand, the ocean breeze playing with their hair. Naomi, Hannah, and Roni's kids ran back and forth, bringing water in their colorful buckets and filling the hole they dug in the cold sand.

She had initiated this early autumn picnic at the beach because the days were still warm enough, if you didn't go in the water. The sun wasn't as blazing, but with their freckled skin, she made sure both she and the girls wore long sleeves and hats.

"Maybe he could come later," Libby suggested with a shrug.

"No, he said they'd be all day," Hope replied.

"Doesn't it bother you that he lives on the same street as his ex and spends so much time with her?" Roni asked pointedly, as always, removing a strand of black hair that flapped her face.

"Veronica," Libby muttered. They only ever used Roni's full name in anger or joke. "Of course it bothers her, or we wouldn't be talking about it."

"No, it's okay. We can talk about it," Hope said. "None of it bothers me *that* much. It's okay for the stage we're at, but … going forward … I guess then it would …" She didn't finish the sentence. Instead, she stretched and handed Naomi her yellow plastic shovel. "The girls know him as a teacher, not as my boyfriend. It's too early. We haven't given ourselves that title yet, and we haven't even slept together." She lowered her voice at the last part, although the kids were two feet away and way too busy to pay any attention to the three of them.

"Yeah, what's up with that? You've been seeing each other for some time," Roni said before biting into an apple.

"Nothing's up—"

"Yeah, I bet," Roni cut in.

Hope nudged Roni with her elbow. "Don's dad jokes are contagious?"

The three of them laughed.

"Shit, I should be more careful," Roni said, laughing. "I don't want those to rub off on me."

Hope pushed back her straw hat. "We only get together once a week. I think we're both okay with taking it slow. I mean, we meet almost every day at school, and with his ex and all the issues they have with Mason, it's just too complicated. And, to be honest, I'm not *feeling* it … yet." She sighed. "But he's a great guy, so …"

"So it's worth trying," Libby said, handing Hope a cold soda can.

"Yeah," she expelled. It was true, but the more time they spent together, the more alone she felt. She began wondering if he was ever going to get over

Linda. They had been together since high school. While her own divorce had been painful, she had initiated it. And it wasn't Eric she struggled to get over; it was the failure.

"D'you guys have a wedding date in mind yet?" Roni turned to Libby.

"We're thinking May. We're more focused on finding a house, to be honest."

"I saw Jordan the other day," Hope said, jumping on the opportunity to gauge some info without directly asking. "He said he was meeting with a realtor." She felt bad for lying to her friends by omission. She hadn't told them about that kiss or about the fact that Jordan Delaney occupied more space in her thoughts than he should, and that all her efforts to bash him from there had been futile so far. And as *they* hadn't mentioned him since she had begun seeing Chris, she hadn't brought him up, either. Now that she had, her palms turned clammy.

"Yeah, he has to move out of the beach house soon. He's spending more time in D.C. these days, anyway, coming and going. I don't know what's up with that. I think he'll go back there eventually."

It made sense. Yet, Hope's stomach clenched with a sudden twinge.

"Poor Avery," Roni scoffed.

"I don't think they're a thing," Libby said. "I poked around, but he knows how to divert the conversation."

"He's a politician, after all," Roni commented. "Words are their weapon."

"But he's one of the good guys," Libby said.

"Mom, I decided what I want to be for Halloween." Hannah appeared next to Hope, sand sprinkling from her clothes and over her mother. "I want to be a jellyfish."

"Sweetie, what about that unicorn costume we saw on Amazon?" The girls were big on unicorns.

"Mom, people underestimate the jellyfish. I want to be a jellyfish."

"You'll be whatever you want to be, sweetie," she said before Hannah ran to join the other kids.

"Lulu changes her mind daily, too. Don't worry about it," Roni said, already guessing Hope's concern that, once again, Hannah would find herself as a social outcast.

"It's one of the year's highlights for them. I want her to enjoy it. Last year, she got tired from carrying her ice cream stand costume and trying to keep up with everyone," Hope said, watching her girls filtering wet sand from their fists, creating shapes on top of their sandcastle.

"Let her choose, even if she makes a mistake," Libby said.

"Yeah, that's what I'm doing, at least with the little mistakes. I wish someone had warned me from some of the big ones I made. But you live and learn."

"Or not," Roni said with a wink.

If only she could tell her friends …

"Hannah," Hope called. "Next week at the fair, they'll be selling Halloween accessories. Let's see what they have there. Knowing you, you'll find many things you'll love."

"Deal," Hannah said then returned to her sandcastle.

"Luke and I won't be here for the fair. We're going to New York," Libby said.

"Will you two finally join the Mile High club?" Roni grinned.

"Once an air marshal, always an air marshal," both Libby and Hope quoted, laughing.

Chapter 16

Jordan stretched his legs on the hotel's king-sized bed and put the phone next to him, on the sheet. He had to think before replying to the text that he had just received from an unknown sender.

"Rush is praising you around every corner. She's tired of Dana Brin and wants you back on her staff, or overcompensating for something? She's due in a few months if I'm not mistaken."

Even the fourth-grade Model UN contestants of Riviera View's school would be able to read the plain threat that was poorly concealed behind the words.

Jordan got up and went to the tiny kitchenette to pour himself another coffee, although it was nine p.m. This hotel suite was his home when he was in the city and fully paid for by his new employer.

He had developed an allergy to D.C. but hoped that the renewed exposure would immune him rather than poison him further. This text wasn't helpful.

His new project, which he had carefully selected, enabled him to spend half his time in California if he chose, in case he needed breathing space, an escape route, an outlet, or heartbreak.

Sitting down on the bed's edge, he picked his phone up. "*No need for recommendations*," he texted Dana, knowing she would understand that they should shut up about him.

Though they hadn't met, she and Sharon knew he was back in the city. He didn't need Sharon's regret and overcompensation in putting in a good word for him. What the fuck was she thinking? And Dana should know better than that if she knew how to do her job.

Jordan suspected the text had been sent by the disgruntled staff member whose failure he had been hired to fix. The fact that he didn't have anything to do with that guy's situation or that he hadn't dipped his hands in those cheap tactics to screw others over didn't save him from being on the receiving end.

Usually, he would disarm those things without much effort. But the grain of truth in this one was gunpowder he had to handle with care.

Sipping his coffee and looking around at the large, luxurious, empty, soul-less room, he decided not to respond. In his experience, this was sometimes the best way to handle these things. It didn't hurt that he was due to return to California to sign off his brother's lease and pack up the beach house.

Still in limbo, he was half-here, half-there. Having nothing here and nothing there.

Chapter 17

She needed to talk to someone. It was rare that Hope felt the lack of an immediate family in Riviera View, but this was one of those times. Though, if she talked to them, her mother and older sister would just tell her to come home, as if this could solve anything. If she called Libby, she knew Libby would leave everything and listen to her, but she didn't want to dump her issues on her friend who had finally found happiness and was away on a romantic weekend.

She was being silly because she had pushed Eric to spend more time with the girls, so why were tears stinging the back of her eyes?

Hope made her way up Ocean Avenue and away from where the town fair's happy crowd brimmed the sidewalks. Sarah's pharmacy was closed, but Breading Dreams was open.

Going in, she was disappointed not to see Connie Latimer, the closest thing she had to a mother in Riviera View.

"She's at the fair with David. Didn't you see her there?" Anne asked from behind the counter.

"No. There are so many people out there. More than I've seen in years."

"I know. It's great. Many out-of-towners came today. We're getting a lot of business. And we need it." Anne's almond-shaped eyes were restless, their dark brown a sharp contrast to her fair complexion.

"Are you okay?"

"Yes, I'm fine. Thanks. It's just ... I'll be fine."

Hope creased her chin, pressing her lips together. She wished she could talk to Anne more. They both seemed to need it. The crowd in the bakery left no room for that, though.

"Do you want unicorn cupcakes for Naomi? I know they're her favorite, and we're running out fast today," Anne said.

The mention of her daughter made the tears prick the back of Hope's eyes again. "No, thanks."

"Oh, I'm sorry," Anne said. "They're at Eric's?" Anne's face contorted, probably without her even noticing. She hated Eric. And for a good reason. It was Roni who had told Hope after her divorce that, in high school, Eric had started the nickname "Plain Jane" for Jane Anne Drecher. The first name her mother, a Jane Austen fan, had given her had been forsaken, and the middle name, which was also after an Austen character, had remained. And so had the hate. But Anne was discerning enough to never mention it until Hope had entered the bakery one day and apologized to her, feeling terrible for having seen her a million times without knowing. *It's not your fault. If anything, you improved him. But he still didn't deserve you,*" Anne had said.

"They're with him, yes," Hope said now. "But we had plans for the parade. He called out of the blue on Wednesday and offered to take them to Disneyworld. In Florida! I can't compete with *that*, and I couldn't stand in their way of having that much fun with their dad. So, his parents took them, and they flew there …"

"I'm sorry, Hope." Anne, tall and thin, reached over the counter and placed a comforting hand on Hope's forearm.

"It's okay. Thanks. I should go home. I'm happy they're having fun. I guess it's just the short notice and our plans that—"

Just then, the bell over the door rang, and a procession of tourists and locals entered.

Hope was about to leave when she noticed Anne's face turn paler than usual, and her slender fingers, which had never seemed fit for the hard work of a bakery, clutched Hope's forearm.

"Anne?" Hope asked.

Anne didn't reply.

Hope shifted her head and saw the dark-blonde-haired man with prominent, grey-blue eyes that Anne was staring at.

Her grip on Hope's arm loosened as she pulled her hand back.

The man approached the counter. "Hi, Jane."

"Finn," Anne said.

"I'll see you later," Hope mumbled, walking slowly toward the door, wondering what she had just witnessed.

As she made her way back down Ocean Avenue, Hope noticed the crowd had thinned. Chairs had been folded or stacked, waiting to be picked up, the plastic jersey barriers removed, and the road had opened for vehicles. The beach promenade in the distance still swarmed with people.

She had come to the fair because she had promised her students that she would see them there—that was before she knew the girls would be with Eric—and Roni had made her promise, too. But Roni had her hands full with her three kids. So, after strolling along the booths and buying a few knickknacks that she knew Hannah and Naomi would love, Hope had had enough.

Chris had told her in advance that he had agreed to meet Linda and Mason there. She had seen glimpses of them. They looked like a family. They *were* a family. In fact, things between her and Chris had slowed down so much that they had wordlessly agreed on a timeout. They met at school almost daily, but they hadn't met or spoken outside of it.

Hope continued down the street. She was surrounded by people yet felt like an island.

As she neared Books And More, she looked up at the three red deck chairs on Libby's balcony. She missed her.

Her phone buzzed in her pocket, and she took it out, thinking how funny it would be if it were Libby. Stopping to stand near the beautifully decorated window of the bookstore, she opened her phone.

The bright smiles of her daughters lit up her screen. Her ex-mother-in-law had sent pictures of just the girls, the girls with their two grandparents, both and each individually with Eric, and the last picture had the girls, Eric, and Jenna standing with Cinderella's castle in the background.

A family. Eric, Jenna, and the girls looked like a family. She was happy for her daughters, but she missed them so much and felt so alone that it hurt physically. The tears she had held back began streaming freely, though she reproached herself for them. She didn't miss Eric, far from it. She didn't even miss the family that they had once been. She missed the family she and her daughters were.

Hope inhaled deeply, struggling to stop those unwanted tears. Her daughters were happy and that was all that mattered.

She wiped her palms over the salty paths that had reached her chin. Finding a single tissue in her jeans pocket, she dabbed at her eyes and nose, knowing her makeup was ruined, anyway. Walking toward the nearest bin to throw the soaked tissue, she fumbled inside the pretty paper bag that held her daughters' presents, remembering that one of the booths had used wrapping tissues. These would do at her state. Then, walking back from the bin that was near the curb and blearily looking inside the bag, she bumped right into a hard mass.

Two large palms gripped her arms and stopped her from stumbling back.

"Hope!" a voice called just as she mumbled, "I'm sorry."

"Are you okay?" he asked just when she recognized him and said, "Jordan!"

"You first," he said, still gripping her biceps. A soft smile spread on his face, which was a few inches from hers.

"I'm sorry. I was just trying to …" She faltered, breaking their brief eye contact, aware that her face was wet and tear-stained.

"What happened?"

She sent her hands to wipe her eyes and face again, and he released her arms.

"It's nothing. I'm sorry. I'm okay."

"You just apologized three times in a row, and you've been crying. That's not okay in my book."

She chuckled despite herself, wiping her nose in a quick motion. She really needed a tissue. "No, I'm fine. I swear." His eyes … Even through the mist in hers, she could clearly see the warm bourbon in his, and the expression on his face tangled her heart.

"Do you want to come up and wash your face? I have the key. *Your* key. I was just up, leaving the Wayford house lease and a few documents for Luke. I forgot about the fair and was waiting upstairs until I could move the car."

"No, that's fine. I should go home. It's a ten-fifteen-minute walk."

"I know. I'll drive you."

"It's okay."

"Are Naomi and Hannah here, too?" He looked around.

This crashed reality back down on her and brought fresh tears to her eyes, which he found the moment he shifted his gaze back in her direction.

"No," she croaked. "They're with Eric."

"Is that why you're crying?"

She couldn't speak just then. She just nodded and pressed her forefingers to the corners of her eyes, trying to absorb the tears that shouldn't even be there before they could fall.

"Hope," he said, placing his hands on her biceps again and lowering his head so he could catch her gaze. "Let me drive you. Please."

"Okay," she relented. Damn him and damn her fickleness.

"Come on. My car's here."

She felt his hand on the small of her back as he guided her toward the car. It was warm, and strong, and comforting.

They climbed inside, and her tears dried again. When he didn't notice, she drew her sleeve quickly across her nose, feeling like the last and least student in her class. How embarrassing.

Just then, he suddenly leaned toward her. She froze for a moment until she realized he was reaching for the glove compartment. With his back stretched like that under the dark grey fitted Henley, so close to her, his nape nearly in her face, she inhaled his smell. Even in her state, his proximity affected her.

He straightened into his seat and handed her a small pack of Kleenex with a smile.

"Thanks." She huffed a chuckle.

When he reached his hand to close the compartment, she noticed something colorful and familiar in there.

"Is that …?" She sent her hand toward it, and their palms touched.

"Yes," he said.

She dug out Hannah's drawing, protected in a clear sheet cover.

"I liked it." He shrugged, straightening into the driver's seat. "And I don't have a fridge anymore, so …"

She swallowed and nodded, then placed the drawing back in its place. She looked at him, unable to remove her eyes from his. Her heart thumped. Was she in love with him? She suddenly realized her experiment had been finished some time ago, though she hadn't had the guts to admit what the results said. He was the single variable that directly impacted her feelings.

"We'd better …" He tore his eyes from her and buckled up.

She did, too.

After he backed out of the spot, making her conscious of his arm on the back of her seat, he spoke again. "Can I buy you coffee? Or … do you wanna go down to the beach? I have a feeling going to an empty house right now won't do you good. Am I right?"

She hesitated then slowly nodded. Deep down, she knew he could have asked her to mount a rocket at that moment and she would have probably relented. "The beach."

They were silent until he parked the car above the stretch of beach not far from Life's A Beach. It was on the other end of the promenade, away from the fair's path. She wondered if he, too, remembered how they had met when she had tried to hit on Josh.

They went down to the beach in silence. The sun was mild and the breeze cool.

"We used to come here a lot, growing up," he said when they reached the part of the beach where the sand was damp.

"Yes, Libby told me they did, too."

"Yeah, I guess almost everyone who grew up here did. The kids today still do."

They were silent again, just strolling closer to the water. The tide was out and the water edge far. When they reached it and stopped out of the waves' reach, he asked, "So, what happened?"

She took a deep breath. "The girls were supposed to be here, but Eric's parents took them to meet him and his wife in Florida. They're at Disneyworld. We were excited about the fair—we go every year—but I couldn't say no when he told them. And he bought the tickets already, so …" The words were half-choked in her throat.

Jordan looked at her then sent his hand to rub over her arm. It was probably supposed to be a comforting gesture, but the touch, his hand on her skin, sent ripples down her body. This man's touch wasn't something that she could be indifferent to.

"I'm encouraging him to see the girls more, but … this last-minute thing and leaving me no choice … I'm glad they're having fun; I just … I don't know. It's silly."

"It's not. Not at all. He doesn't see them much?"

"At first, he was very involved, but then he moved and thought that me having to report and check with him on everyday things was equal to being involved." She had no idea why she was spilling all these truths on him, except that he listened, even with his eyes that were intent on her. "And I probably shouldn't have come at all, but I promised Roni and the kids … my students … They were excited to see me."

"I bet." He smiled at her.

A little sunshine rayed her insides.

"And you're alone because …? What about …? You're seeing that teacher … Chris, right?"

"He's here. But he's with his son and wife. Ex-wife. And they …" How come they were both faltering with words?

Jordan nodded, and she could see he got it. He gazed at the ocean.

She wanted to add that she wasn't really seeing Chris these days but didn't. She didn't tell him that she had seen Avery and her son at the fair, too.

"It's so relaxing here." Jordan expelled a breath.

"Yes, it is." She loved the sound of the constant white noise of the ocean and the tiny salty droplets that the breeze carried. She thought of the wave tattoo that was hiding on Jordan's left bicep, under his shirt.

"Can I ask you something?" A muscle twitched in his jaw.

She hesitated. "Sure."

He turned to look at her. "How did someone like Eric Hays get *you* to marry him?"

She scoffed. From his tone, she knew the question wasn't an insult to her. "I thought he was the one; the perfect combination of a cool, blond surfer from California who was also smart enough to study civil engineering and dream of building bridges and cities. He was charming and said all the right things."

"What would those be?" He huffed a little chuckle.

She scoffed again. "That my eyes were green like seaweed, my hair reminded him of the sun. It was poetry in comparison to the *wanna hook up?* we only ever got from the guys in my hometown."

Jordan laughed, and his laughter was deep and husky, making her heart flail and her lips curl into a wide smile. It was strange that, despite the way her body reacted to him, she didn't feel uncomfortable with him now. Maybe because she had felt out of place all day and he was a sort of a familiar, comforting presence.

"So, how did you find out?" he asked, and they both fleetingly glanced at each other before returning to gaze at the crash of the waves. It was clear he meant to say, "*that Eric was a douchebag.*"

"It was gradual. You know that saying about boiling the water with the frog in it? I was the frog. First, it was the university we went to that wasn't good enough; he kept saying how it was a compromise for him, that he could have done much better. Then it was the town I came from, and what my parents did, and what their house looked like, and who my sister married. Then the projects he got were never good enough for him. He offered we'd come here, and I was in love enough, and hopeful enough, to think … But after we moved here and things looked up, *I* wasn't enough. Nothing I did …" She faltered.

"*He* made you feel you weren't enough? *You?*" He looked at her, and that muscle twitched in his stubbled jaw again, as if he was biting back a curse.

"I let him. You didn't know me then." She watched him, feeling her color rising, because she couldn't believe she had just admitted something like that, something she had only ever told her best friends.

"I didn't, but I know *his* type."

The intensity of his gaze was such that she forced herself to avert hers and fix it on the rolling waves of the ocean, unable to face him at that moment and feeling his gaze scorching her profile.

"And he remarried?" he asked.

"To an engineer he met at work. Not the type of wedding where the girls were bridesmaids and all that. A Las Vegas one. But we'd met Jenna—that's his wife—and she was okay. I know what people say about him, and I know what he can be like, but he's not like that with them—the girls. He's good with them ... when he sees them." She was silent then, still feeling his eyes on her profile, as if he knew she had more to say. "They met when we were still married, but he didn't cheat on me. I initiated the divorce, and they got together only after."

She turned to look at him as he ran his hand under his mouth, as if he was choosing his words.

"And you stayed here?" he asked, returning her gaze.

The breeze that swept her hair back swept his onto his forehead. She yearned to reach out and rake it back with her fingers. He was so close, and she was flooded with vivid memories of what that mouth felt like on hers, on her skin, what those hands felt like on her body, what his hardness and that rock-hard thigh felt like between her legs.

She shook her head in a single, quick motion to bash it all. "I love this town, I love my job, made good friends here, and the girls were born here. It's their home. I like visiting Minnesota, but I always feel relieved to come back here again. It's home."

"It is."

"For you, too?"

"Yes." His gaze drifted from her to the view. "But I'm leaving again tomorrow."

Though she knew it, and though there was nothing real between them, Hope felt as if her insides had become void. The breeze felt cold on her skin, although, up until now, all she had felt was heat.

He turned his head, and they watched each other again.

"And now you're dating Chris. Also born and raised here."

"Well, I don't know if … We haven't really … I think it's over."

"Oh. I'm sorry." He averted his gaze back to the sea and chewed on his lip.

"It's getting chilly," she said, rubbing her palms over her arms. She wasn't sure if the cold was outside or inside of her.

"Do you want to get something warm to drink?" he asked, pivoting his torso toward Life's A Beach.

She hesitated, torn. She wanted to be with him some more but knew she probably shouldn't.

"You don't still … because of Josh?" he asked, cocking his head and looking at her with a grin. But it was such that it made her feel like that thing with Josh had been a shared experience and not something she had done and he had witnessed.

She didn't reply, just pressed her lips together in a tight smile and rolled her eyes up.

"Come on; you'll have to go in sooner or later. Living in Riviera View, you know that."

When she rocked undecidedly on her feet, Jordan smiled and grabbed her hand, pulling her to go and evaporating what was left of her resistance. "He might not even be there," he added.

When she walked beside him, he let go of her hand, and they crossed the sand and went up to the place.

The bar was right next to the entrance, and Josh was definitely there, taking out clean glasses from a large, plastic tray and placing them on a shelf under the bar.

"Come on." Jordan put his palm between her shoulder blades for the brief moment she hesitated at the door. "Like ripping off a Band-Aid."

He approached the bar with her in tow. "Hey, Josh. What's up, man?"

"Hey, Delaney, good seeing you. How are the bride and groom?" He then noticed Hope and nodded at her in recognition.

"My sister? Great. We're having another wedding soon. Luke and Libby."

"Congratulations."

Hope looked at them. Josh was probably fifteen years younger than Jordan, but it wasn't just the age gap that made him look like a boy next to him.

"Thanks. But listen, if we do the bar with you, we'll want the cocktails festive. You know, with foam and spheres and all that. I did it for their engagement party, based on advice I got at my sister's wedding, and it was a hit."

"Sounds good," Josh said, looking between them.

"Great. I'll see you around. Can you bring us two coffees, please?" Jordan turned to look at her. "How do you take yours?"

"Black, please."

"One black, one double espresso. Thanks, man." He reached his arm out, and the two shook hands.

"He's a good guy," Jordan said as they made their way toward a window table.

"And you're good at diplomacy," she said.

The place was rather empty, as most of the town was at the fair, and the music in the background was 90's rock.

They sat down. It was now or never, and so she just let the words roll out of her lips. "What about you? Are you seeing Avery?"

"No." If he was surprised by her question, it didn't show.

"Are short replies recommended in politics?"

He chuckled. "Sometimes. But no, I'm not seeing her. Never have. We were in high school together, but we didn't go out then, either. Ran into her at Ava's wedding. She offered a coffee, so we had coffee and that was that."

"And the Model UN."

"Yes. That was what she wanted to have coffee about," he said, and she could tell he knew that Avery didn't offer a meeting just to discuss it. "And I'm glad I did *that*." He held her gaze, and she could hardly hear the music anymore.

"Me, too," she said honestly, feeling her earlobes burning. She was pretty sure he could see her flushed skin. "So, you grew up here, huh?" she added, bunching her shoulders and clasping her palms between her knees, though she wasn't cold.

"Yep."

He didn't have to have verbal diarrhea like her, but he could at least give her more than that.

She pressed on. "Left your mark on the town and its inhabitants then went to make it big in D.C.?"

"Left graffiti on the wall beneath this porch is pretty much all I did."

She laughed. "I'm sure you had more impact than that. It's not there anymore. What did it say?"

"The graffiti?"

She nodded.

He shifted his eyes sideways with a little lopsided grin of embarrassment. Then, bringing his gaze back to her, he said, "Swallow the world and shit it whole."

"Ouch." She laughed. "Sounds like childbirth."

His burst of laughter caught her off guard. It was raspy and made her unclasp her palms, turn them, and claw the insides of her thighs.

"I'm sorry," she said, chuckling and becoming even hotter in the face.

"No," he said through the laughter. "That's perfect. We were kids; didn't know what the fuck we were talking about."

"And did you?"

"What?"

"Swallow the world?"

"No." He shook his head, still chuckling.

But she had a feeling he had gotten pretty close. This man, who looked so good in the simple Henley that clung to his shoulders and delineated his athletic arms, had spent most of his adult life in suits with people the rest of the nation and the world only ever saw on TV.

They were still worlds apart, and she should remember that, though it was becoming harder by the second.

"What about you? What was your last name before Hays, by the way?"

"Peterson. Minnesota, you know." She smiled and shrugged. He was interested in her "before," and she liked that. "I left no graffiti behind."

"You love science. Chemistry. Did you ever want to become a scientist or—"

"Or have I always dreamed of being a school teacher?" she guessed the rest.

His gaze pinned hers. "My mother was a teacher. It's a tougher job than most. And crucial to get right."

She hadn't expected his reply. He kept surprising her, shattering patterns she had grown used to.

"I didn't always want to become a teacher. I love the experimental part, but not so much the math and processes that lab research requires. I took up a job as a teaching assistant in college and fell in love with it. It turned out well because, when we moved here, it was easy to find a teaching job, and it works well when you have kids. I get to do experiments in class or at home. I don't have the patience and resilience that being an academic requires."

"I don't know about academia, but you seem plenty resilient to me."

She had to force herself to break eye contact, force herself to remember he was good with words. A pro, in fact. She should remember that.

He was going back to Washington, and she belonged in this small town. Worlds apart. She should remember that, too.

Chapter 18

She was resilient; she just didn't know it. Or didn't realize the extent of it.

"I wasn't always," she said. "Like I told you—"

"I didn't know you then. Yeah, you said." He smiled. "But I have a feeling I'd think the same even if I did." He scanned her face—those eyes that were still a little red from the tears she had shed, the windswept hair, the creases of life that showed on her face. Jordan tried to downplay the fact that his heart was pounding erratically in his chest for fear that what she made him feel would reflect on him and scare her off. It was the most comfortable that she had been with him, and he wanted more of it. More of her.

Just being next to her amplified everything. Usually, the opposite happened to him—the closer he got, the less he felt; the more he came to know, the less he found to like. But not with her.

She made herself seem—maybe even thought of herself as—a simple, small-town school teacher. But she was so much more. To him. He found himself looking up to her, admiring her, wanting that elusive, unscathed quality in her, that genuineness, that

157

agenda-less goodness, to rub off on him. He wanted to be more like her.

He wanted *her*.

But, for that, she would have to get closer to him, to know more about him, and he was pretty sure that the opposite would happen to her—the closer she would get, the less she would like him; the more she knew, the less she would think of him.

Maybe not if she had known him years ago, when he had been different, more like her. But it was true what he had told her in his kitchen—politics changed people more than people changed politics.

He hoped to reach a point where he could look her in the eyes, tell her everything, and add with confidence, "You didn't know me then," certain that he had succeeded in leaving the stench in the past. But he wasn't there yet. So, he kept his mouth shut.

Chapter 19

When he pulled over by her house, she remained seated.

They both turned to look at each other in the orange glow of dusk.

"Thank you," she said, when what she actually wanted to ask was, "*Do you want to come in?*" and what she really wanted was to continue being warmed by that gaze of his that was a mix of soft and scalding, caressing and penetrating. She wanted to know more about him and liked that she could admit things about herself.

Maybe they could be friends, a little voice in her whispered. But it was drowned by the roar of laughter of the rest of her. Because what her body desired was to feel this mouth of his everywhere on her. Everywhere. Just the thought made her pulsate. And that gap between his shirt and skin would be her undoing.

But her logic said that, while he denied it, she thought he was *exactly* the type to swallow the world whole, and she was the type that would anchor someone like him behind. She had been led to feel like she had done that before. She wouldn't let it happen again. So, she unbuckled, instead.

"Thanks for today," she repeated.

"It was my pleasure," Jordan said. "Not to find you crying, but … the rest. Are you okay now?"

Damn him. Why did he have to make it so hard?

She smiled. "Yeah. Thanks." After another beat, she bit her lip, stopping the words that now threatened to come out, then opened the door. "Have a good trip back to D.C."

"Thanks, Hope." His eyes grew darker brown.

She wasn't sure what she could see there, but it was like standing close to a volcano—feeling the heat and sensing an approaching eruption. She noticed the flexing muscle in his jaw.

When he drove away, she went in, thoroughly regretting that she wasn't more brazen, but comforting herself that her logic was impeccable.

Chapter 20

If he continued to watch the rearview mirror a second longer, instead of bringing his eyes back to the road, he would have smashed right into the SUV that reversed into the street from one of the houses.

Jordan raised his palm and mouthed, "*I'm sorry*," to the man who glared at him from the driver's window.

He drove on, making his way out of Riviera View and toward Wayford.

The twilight sky turned purple that deepened with every mile that came between him and the town, and the woman, he had left behind.

He couldn't stop thinking about her. Ironically, his flight tomorrow, at noon, never seemed so enticing. Back in D.C., he could put all this energy into work and hope for the best.

Hope.

Even the word unsettled him now.

Feeling an urge to talk to someone, Jordan shifted his gaze to where his phone was supposed to be, in the holder between the two front seats. It wasn't there. He patted the warm seat next to him, which brought involuntary thoughts of the backside that had been sitting on it. Fuck, he had been celibate for too long if thoughts like that came to his head.

Noticing a flash of light from beneath the passenger seat, he sent his hand, but it was too far under the seat.

Reaching the only safe spot before the exit to the highway that connected the towns, he stopped at the side of the road, unbuckled, and stretched toward the floor. His phone was the first thing he grabbed, but there was something else there. He picked it up and looked at it. It was the small paper bag with the gifts that Hope had bought for her daughters.

Jordan ran a hand over his mouth and chin. Then, deciding, he shifted the car into gear, turned the left blinkers on, and did a semi-legal U-turn.

He could easily tell why his heart was pounding when he slammed the car door behind him and made his way to her front door. The light on her stoop was on, and he went toward it, holding the little pink gift bag.

Jordan hesitated for a moment then knocked. The lights in the house were on, and he could hear the music that played inside—"Hungry Heart" by Bruce Springsteen. How befitting. He knocked again, louder, when the door opened, revealing the face that was still burned into his retinas.

She had a surprised look on her face.

"Hey," he said, lifting the bag in front of him. "Thought you'd need this."

"Oh! I do. Thanks. Sorry."

"What for?"

"Um … The bother, I guess."

"It's no bother," he said just when she said, "Would you like to come in?"

He could see that her breathing pattern changed by the way her lips remained parted and did his best not to stare at them. Instead, he raised his eyes, and their gazes locked. *What was she doing?* What was *he* doing?

"Sure."

She moved aside, and he stepped forward without them taking their eyes off the other.

Two steps, and he was inside, hearing her close the door behind him.

Turning around, he found her leaning back against the closed door, staring at him. Her throat moved as she swallowed, and her forest-green eyes looked huge. Velvet flowed in his veins at the sight. What he saw in them prepared him for what she did next, but he remained still, as if a movement from him would frighten her away.

Pushing herself off the door and taking a step forward, Hope rose to her toes and placed her hands on his shoulders.

He remained still for a moment when she kissed his lips, but then he did what he had been aching to do almost since the first time he had met her. He melded his mouth to hers, letting her taste permeate every part of him, grabbed her hips, lifted her, and pinned her with his body to the door.

Chapter 21

Finding Jordan on her doorstep, Hope wondered if someone had heard her wishes, her regrets, her fears. From the moment she had left his car, she had thought of what Libby had told her not long ago, when they had talked about her and Luke. *"It's the what-ifs that sting the most. I'd rather regret doing than regret not doing."*

Changing into her comfort clothes—the stained Tweetie sweatshirt and loose, dark lounge pants—she had walked around the empty house, putting things in place and wishing her daughters were there, or at least one of her friends. To banish the silence, she had turned the music on.

The beat of the song made her miss the first knock, but when she had heard the second one, her heart rate mimicked the fast rhythm of the music without her even realizing why.

From the moment she saw Jordan standing there, she knew she wasn't going to regret *not* doing this time. Like a guided missile, she locked her eyes on his lips and didn't even feel herself moving until her mouth was on his.

164

The soft kiss she placed on his lips was answered by a deeper one as Jordan wrapped his arms around her faster than mercury could spread. He lifted her, and she was clamped between his hard body and the door, the back of her head nestled in his large palm, his fingers threading in her hair and fiercely welding her mouth to his.

Their breaths were rugged. She drank in his taste and smell, and everything inside her head vaporized, leaving a thrumming heart and a hungry body that now, with clothes that enabled her to feel every inch of his hard body, was pulsating with desire.

Acting on their own need to feel as much of him as they could reach in this posture, her hands raked into his hair then slid to his neck, shoulders, the plains of his chest, then crossed to his back.

Eagerly, she tugged at the dark grey Henley that had taunted her all afternoon, lifted it, and took it off him. Now she could graze her hands over every ridge of his exposed, warm skin—the muscled expanse of his wide chest, the corded arms.

God, he was five years older than her but so taut. Everything was in its place, and everything so well shaped. His muscles weren't bulges; they were well defined, and her lower belly clenched just from the feel of them under her palms. She thought of what hid under her clothes, and knowing there was no way she was going to give up now on feeling and seeing all of him, she knew it also meant he would have to feel and see all of *her*.

Two plus years without sex, and longer than that with a critical male gaze for a companion, had left her self-aware, even now, even through the haze of this man's panty-melting touch.

"The bedroom. To your right," she whispered into his ear. The living room was washed with too much light.

"Door, bedroom, table, we'll get there," he rasped against her neck. Supporting her by pressing his weight into her, his hands were free to roam all over her. If this was how it felt over her clothes, she couldn't wait to feel him under them.

She kissed his neck and shoulder, and before her eyes flickered shut again, she caught a glimpse of his tattoo that was completely exposed now. The surge and ripple in black and grey mimicked what he was doing to her body with his mouth and hands before he even took her clothes off. She moaned against his mouth that was back on hers.

Though she wanted him to pummel into her right there at the door, when Jordan attempted to remove her sweatshirt, raking it up to her armpits with one hand and eagerly caressing the skin he exposed with the other, she broke their kiss and rasped again, almost begging now, "The bedroom."

With his arms wrapped around her, his hands splayed on the heated skin of her back, Jordan moved away from the door. He could easily carry her, even if her legs weren't wrapped around him, but she clasped him tighter, craving to maintain contact with the hardness in his jeans.

As soon as they entered the bedroom, he threw them both unceremoniously onto her bed.

She hadn't realized how much she had missed this—a strong, male body on top of hers, the weight pressing into her. Everything in her soared, soared, soared. She kissed him hungrily, feverishly, hardly letting him pull himself back a little just so he could take her sweatshirt off.

While he raked it up, exposing her untucked skin, she reached to the bedside lamp that she had switched on when she had changed before. It yielded enough light for her to see the hard angles of his jaw, his lips, the fire in his eyes, the muscled shoulders and arms. Just the sight of his pecs and abs could make her come. She was sorry not to see more of it when she found the switch and turned the light off.

She lifted her arms and let him take her shirt off. Then she felt one of his hands leave her body. A click was heard, and the light was back on, seeming stronger than before because of the momentary darkness that she had bathed them in.

She watched his face as he glanced down at her, his gaze sliding then rising, sweeping, eyes meeting, before he bent to kiss her neck and shoulders, sliding off the straps of her bra and kissing his way to her breasts that were cupped in his palms over her bra.

She lifted her hand again and switched the light off.

Jordan grabbed her wrist when it was halfway back, pinned it above her head, then turned the light back on, stilling above her and looking into her face in the softly lit room.

"I prefer the light off," she expelled into his face.

"And I prefer to see you," he rasped, his eyes flaring, searing hers. "I want to see this," he half-whispered, skimming his gaze over her face, caressing her with his eyes from her hair to her lips, drawing his thumb over the same path, parting her lower lip, and sliding down her chin. "And this." He traced his gaze further down, sliding his palm with it to her breasts and further south to her belly. Then, bringing his eyes back to hers, as if he was making a point, he slanted his head and kissed the flesh she was sure just flabbed above her bra without taking his eyes off hers.

She ached for him.

The touch of his lips and tongue on her skin made her eyes flutter shut.

She thought of the stretch marks, half-hidden beneath the waistband of her pants.

And, as if he read her mind, Jordan hooked his fingers into it and dragged it down to her hips.

She swallowed and opened her eyes.

He was watching her. "I want to see it all. All of you." He exhaled the words, and the way his lips curled around them made her raise her head and meet his mouth in a deep, slow kiss that became frenzied as she gave in, and in, and in.

He flipped them over until she was on top of him so he could take off her bra and bring her breasts into his hot mouth.

"God," she heard herself moan loudly as he cupped, sucked, and licked.

As soon as she had any planning capacity, she brought her impatient fingers to undo his jeans and slipped her hand into his briefs, where she was welcomed with an even bigger surprise than she had imagined through the denim.

She forgot about everything when she heard him groan at her touch. She forgot herself, too, until Jordan was on top of her again and she was dragging his jeans off him. The dim light in the room proved how good he looked fully naked. *Damn him.* She kissed—no, she *licked*—and caressed all those beautiful ridges, a voice in the back of her head taunting her for reveling in him, in this beauty, so damn much that she throbbed with need.

She had nothing on except the pants that were already down to her hips and simple cotton panties that she was pretty sure were soaked by now.

Jordan kissed his way down her body again, lingering at her breasts, kneading with one hand and bringing them into his mouth with the other. His tongue and lips induced moans and whimpers from her before he continued down to her belly, where he drew the waistband of her pants farther down, probably exposing more stretch marks. He didn't seem to care or notice as he licked the skin over the edge of her panties.

When he grazed his mouth over the thin fabric, she shivered with desire, but a sudden apprehension made her reach down, grab his shoulders, and try to drag him back up.

"I don't think I'm ready for …" she gasped urgently, fighting her own need to feel his tongue there yet pulling him up.

Jordan stopped and looked at her, surprised. He pushed himself up until his face was at level with hers. "I'm sorry. Is it something I did?"

A sudden prickle wrenched her heart at the expression on his face.

I've given birth twice, and my ex-husband wouldn't go near there since after the first.

"No. It's not you. It's me," she said out loud. "I'm ..." *And I haven't slept with anyone in ages, and maybe as a way to wall the option off ...* "I haven't ... I'm not ... styled." *God*, she wanted to die. *Did she really just admit to this sexy as hell man that she wasn't ... coiffed?*

"Styled?" A smirk she could see he was trying to suppress flitted across Jordan's face, and a cloud sailed away from over his eyes. He looked relieved. "You mean ...?"

She shrugged with one shoulder in an embarrassed admission. If the bed collapsed right then and trapped her shut in the linen box, Hope wouldn't have minded. "I'm not ready for ... And it's not that I ..." She faltered, mortified, losing control over her mouth even in bed.

Jordan moved his eyes between hers, then bent and kissed her, caressing the side of her face with one hand while slipping the other into her panties. She knew he would be soaking in her. If only he could find his way down there. Oh. He could and just *did*.

She exhaled against his mouth at the torture of his touch.

"You seem plenty ready to me," he graveled, looking at her.

God, she *was*. She was. She just didn't want him to *see* it all.

"And as for the rest, like I said, I want to see you—all of you."

She could come just from this—the low timbre of his voice, the flame in his eyes, his hand in her panties, and the feel of his hardness pushing against her.

Without lingering further, Jordan kissed her again then glided down her body, and with one pull, he took her pants and panties off, stretching his arm far until they were off her and discarded to the floor.

He touched her, smoothing, soaking, kissing her inner thighs, and before any coherent thought could return to her head, she felt his mouth on her, full-on, lips and tongue sucking, licking, sinking, his wide shoulders nudging her legs farther apart.

She gasped and moaned, fisting the bed's covers, her head floating with an excess of oxygen.

He continued until she pulled at his hair, fumblingly. "Please," she exhaled, bucking against him. "Please." She needed him inside her *now*.

Jordan stormed up and stopped when his gaze was at level with hers, leaning on his forearms, looking at her. She could read in his eyes that he knew exactly what she wanted him to do. She could smell herself on him.

With a glint in his eyes, he pinched the tip of his tongue with his forefinger and thumb, as if removing something. He then smirked at her. "You were saying?" he teased before capturing her lips in a deep kiss, his tongue doing to her mouth what he had just done down below, what she craved he would do now everywhere.

When he broke their kiss, he smoothed his thumbs over her cheekbones. "Now it's my turn to interrupt." He smirked. "Do you have a condom? I don't carry any, and I wasn't planning on …"

"They're three years old."

"I doubt they'd—"

171

"IUD. I have … for hormonal purposes …" *This*. This info exchange was why she wasn't looking forward to being with someone new. Jordan made it easy, though, comfortable, unawkward.

"Good. But what about the rest? You know I could just continue—"

"Can I trust you?" she cut in, knowing he would understand. She had no idea how many partners he'd had and when, but until now, he hadn't given her a reason not to trust him.

"Yes."

She reached between them and smoothed her palm over him, up and down, inducing a groan from deep in his throat. She watched his eyes inflame as she brought him to her entrance.

Jordan hooked her thigh high over his waist and used it as a lever to sink deep into her in a rough thrust.

God. She exhaled. That was exactly what she needed. He was stretching her, filling her.

He threaded his fingers with hers, pinned their joint hands over her head, and caught her mouth in a deep kiss. He thrust deeper and harder, making her gasp and moan against his mouth, building a helix of fire in her.

Eyes locked on hers, he reached between them with his free hand and touched her, adding to the friction inside her, until she broke into a million shiny pieces under him, against him, reaching high, high above.

She tried to muffle the sounds that emanated from her, but Jordan growled without taking his eyes off her, "No, I want to see you and hear you. Let me hear you come."

That launched her higher, and as if from a distance, she heard him groan as she dragged him up there with her, their gazes clinging to each other as much as their bodies were.

~~~~~~~~~~~~~~~~~~~

Detonation, explosion, combustion. It was all that and more. She was pretty sure that, although the windows were shut, the sounds that Jordan emitted out of her were heard in the street. Whether in speech or otherwise, she just couldn't be quiet with this man.

Lying wasted next to him, Hope didn't care, at least for the time being, that the light was on and that he could see all the stretch marks, freckles, untucked tummy, breasts, and all.

He didn't seem to mind any of it, either. Because, as soon as he caught his breath, Jordan rolled on his side and trailed his gaze all over her.

She would have blushed if there was any breath left in her.

He then leaned his forehead against her temple and let his hand trail the same path his eyes had taken over her body. Her skin was still sensitive, and she shuddered.

"Is this what you didn't want me to see?" he whispered, his mouth hovering at the side of hers.

She nodded but barely.

"You're beautiful, Hope. Just as you are. Please don't ever think any differently." He then scooped her up in his arms and pulled her to lie on top of him as he rolled to lie on his back.

She breathed in the skin of his neck and closed her eyes, feeling the thump of his heart under her palm. While she didn't regret doing what she had done, Hope knew that things had developed way beyond Roni's advice. She knew for a certainty that it wasn't only her body that he had just made his. It was her heart, too.

Maybe she could hold on to him a little longer, until the morning, until he would go back to a life that was thousands of physical and metaphorical miles from her.

Chapter 22

The taste of her still in his mouth, the scent of her body ingrained in him , her body wrapped in his arms, Jordan wondered how he was going to board that flight to D.C. the next day when his heart was no longer his own.

The flight. It was a reality check that added to the long line of other realities that he had to face with this green-eyed surprise.

He pressed Hope closer against him and breathed in her auburn hair that was tousled across his chest. Reality would have to wait a little longer. He needed savoring this moment.

"Chemistry-ly speaking, what just happened here?" he asked, smiling at the prospect of a lecture that might follow this question.

Hope tilted her head up and saw his smile.

"You're asking for real?"

"For real." He kissed the freckled bridge of her nose.

"Dopamine, oxytocin, serotonin, to name a few hormones. We're flooded. They're like opiates to the receptors in our brains, and just like opiates, they'll soon subside."

"Romantic." He smirked at her. "And then what happens, at least according to science?"

"It varies."

"Can we raise the levels again?"

"We can. Some studies show that …" She didn't finish the sentence and blushed.

"That what?"

"That, like opiates, they're addictive." Her cheeks glowed, and her smile was that awkward one he had seen before, as she hurried to rest her head back on his chest.

He loved that smile. This woman was full of surprises. If he had to be honest with himself, he hadn't expected the wild version of her that he had just experienced—he was pretty sure that his back was thoroughly scratched. Then again, he shouldn't have been surprised, given how often she had lost control of the feelings that reflected in her eyes and the words that dropped from her mouth. Her body reacted to his like a loose cannon and drove him to the brink.

But what caught him off guard the most was the explosion of feeling he had experienced, along with the physical. It surpassed anything he had ever felt before. And she was right. It was addictive.

He veered his head and caught her mouth in a kiss. "Can science explain why I don't want to go?" he half-whispered against her lips. Were unintended, premature truths dropping out of his mouth uncontrollably now, too?

Hope raised herself again and leaned her cheek on her elbow. A mess of emotions collided in the green forest of her eyes. She was slaying him with those.

He reached and swept back the bangs that had fallen into her eyes.

"Didn't you just take on a new project and pack up the house?"

"I did, but I can do some of the work from here. And I need the space to be away from there."

"Why?"

He gritted his teeth. Could she handle even part of the truth?

"It could be rewarding. Not just financially, I mean in many other ways. But it can also take over you, over your soul. There are so many covert and conflicting interests. Words can mean one thing one day and another the next until you don't know what's and who's real anymore. Until you doubt yourself. It's like poison—you think you get used to it, but it's killing you slowly from the inside."

"And still you go back."

"That's why I need the space—to keep myself real."

She scrutinized him, but her gaze was soft. Could he tell her more? The whole truth?

As if she had sensed his inner thoughts, Hope's next question unsettled him.

"How was it working for Sharon Rush?"

"She's a very capable lawmaker."

"Did you like working with her?"

"It's not so much a matter of liking. A lot of times, it's a matter of agreed common agendas." He traced his thumb over her eyebrows, over the gentle creases that were showing on her forehead. She was so beautiful. Natural. He loved her freckles and the laugh lines.

"Didn't she withdraw her sponsorship from several social welfare bills? Including ones that would help single parents?"

He looked at her. Was she testing him?

"You follow her career? Most people have no clue."

She blushed. "I read about her after …"

"After you heard I worked with her?" He couldn't help but smile.

"Yes."

"It's a give-and-take game there. You give your support to something to get the support you need for something else. I was tasked with getting her the votes she needed to pass a bill against pollutive industries."

"And that bill passed."

"You read about that, too?" He played with the strands of hair that fell over her naked shoulder.

"Yes. So, she believes in social welfare but also in cleantech, and it's a matter of choosing what's more important?"

"In a way."

"Did you advise her on—"

"Not to vote for this? No. That was her decision, based on alliances she had to form on other topics."

"I saw on the news that she's pregnant. Maybe she'll work harder to support working mothers now."

He watched her. And there it was, plain as day. If Hope knew what Sharon had said on the matter, she wouldn't despise just her, she would despise *him*, although he didn't stand behind it. Just as he feared—knowing him more, she would like him less. How could he tell her about the rest? It was a catch-22.

"So, why did you leave that job?"

"I was only contracted for that one project. I prefer not to be a regular staff member, exactly for the reasons you mentioned."

"And you took time off once that finished, and now you're going back for the new project?"

"I wasn't planning on taking it on, but this new project is flexible. I don't have to be there all the time. There's a lot of prep and infrastructure work that I can do from anywhere." He felt like he was in a job interview, one where he wanted to kiss the interviewer and roll her under him again.

"So, you'll be around."

"Disappointed?" He smirked, but inside, his heart pounded hard against his ribcage. He wondered if she could feel it since her palm was right there on his chest.

"No." She chuckled.

"So, what happened with Chris?" he asked after a beat passed.

She broke eye contact, lowering her gaze to his chest, bringing her fingertips to kill him with light caresses. "It didn't really go anywhere. We haven't seen much of each other outside of school … We haven't even …" The familiar red heat rose to her cheeks.

He wasn't a jealous man usually, and he had no right to be in this case, but fuck him if he didn't feel a grip twisting his stomach at the thought of this man touching her. Any man.

"You haven't even what?"

"Slept together." Her eyes flitted back to his.

He caressed her cheek, and she pressed it against his palm, closing her eyes. His heart melted beyond recognition, congealing back in the shape of her.

"You probably have many exes," she suddenly blurted, opening her eyes and watching him.

"I don't know if many." He threaded his fingers into her hair.

"More than my two or three."

"Is it the quantity that counts? Because I've never loved anyone enough to want to have children with them, and you did."

"Never?"

Not until now.

Fuck. Where did that come from? He couldn't tell her *that*. The thought kicked him in the gut like a motherfucker. This wasn't anywhere near his belated disappointment when Sharon's accidental pregnancy wasn't his. Because it hadn't been about Sharon at all. He didn't want *her*. He didn't love her. And he knew beyond certainty that this was the name of what he felt for Hope—love. He fell in love with this woman who wouldn't even like him if she knew what he was hiding, though he was inching closer to the core of what he would tell her if he wasn't afraid of losing her immediately after she had taken a chance on him.

His silence must have goaded her to speak, because she added in her usual fumbling way, which he loved more than any polished blather, "I did love Eric when we had Hannah. But Naomi … things weren't good. I think he would have preferred … I don't even want to say it. Once Naomi was born, he

180

loved her, obviously, and we kept going for a few more years, but ..." Her eyes blazed with the inconvenient truth that she had just shared.

And that was it. What she had just told him tied his tongue. He couldn't now tell her that his past was sprinkled with one abortion and one almost pregnancy. It didn't matter that he would have supported both. What mattered was how his fucked-up instincts had him initially react regarding the latter.

Not until now.

His unspoken words seared him.

Instead of replying, and knowing, knowing, knowing he had no future with her until he could tell her the truth, and maybe no future *because* of the truth, Jordan tightened his arm around her, and with the hand that was threaded in her hair, he pulled her down for a kiss that deepened with every second.

At least he would have tonight.

He hoisted her to lie on top of him, each stroking the other's body, their gazes connected. "You're amazing, Hope. So amazing it's scary."

She bent to kiss him, and he grabbed her thighs so she straddled him. He slowly rose to sit up with her on top of him, holding her, as their kiss became fevered.

"I want to look at you," he said, leaning back against the pillow, raising his hands to caress her face, her neck, sliding to her breasts as she positioned herself and sank down along his hardness. He brought his hands up to cup her face, fingers drowning in her hair as they moved in synch, slowly, savoringly.

He loved that she didn't seem self-conscious of the light anymore. At least not until she grabbed his shoulders and pulled him to sit back up and hold her as they kissed all the way to the end.

~~~~~~~~~~~~~~~~~~~~~

"This song was playing when you left with Roni and Don after the engagement party," he said much later, when they stood half-dressed in her kitchen, making grilled cheese sandwiches. The music she had turned on before he had arrived was still playing in the background.

Hope finished buttering the bread and inserting the cheese and the tomatoes that he had sliced. In her loose pants and that Tweetie sweatshirt that he found endearing because it was so her, she was efficient, like a sandwich production line. He could imagine her doing that for Hannah and Naomi.

"It's from that TV show, *Big Little Lies*. It's part of the playlist, I guess. Libby downloaded Spotify for me, and I love how it just guesses what I like." She put the ready sandwiches on the griddle.

"It's called "Cold Heart." Michael Kiwanuka sings it."

"And you remembered it played then?" she asked, looking up from the griddle.

"I remember everything about that evening."

She bit her lower lip for a second. "Yeah, me, too."

He would tell her, just not tonight. He would tell her that he remembered that song out of all the others because it had played just as he had seen her out of his apartment after kissing her, and the lyrics punched him in the gut—she was the hope for his

182

cold, bleeding heart, yet he feared that neither one of them could get over knowing him as he was.

After a lingering moment, Hope averted her gaze. "So, when's your flight tomorrow?" She flipped the sandwiches over.

It felt like some sort of a deflection mechanism from too much emotion when reality hovered above. And it worked.

"I have to be there at noon." He took the plates that she had given him and went to put them on the dining table. Absentmindedly, he ran a finger over a box of crayons that had been left there. "When are Hannah and Naomi coming back?"

"Tomorrow evening." Hope emerged from the kitchen and placed a platter with the ready sandwiches on the table.

"Tell them I said hi? No one has to know what I wore when I said it."

They grinned at each other, and he saw her gaze tracing over his bare chest and down to the jeans that he hadn't bothered to button. Then, when she brought her eyes back to his, they were a strange combination of hazy and sparkling.

Jordan grabbed her wrist and pulled her to him, wrapping his arms around her and crashing his mouth on hers. The sigh that escaped her throat made him rasp her name against her lips.

Whatever else he had to tell her would have to wait. He needed to muster the courage to face the risk.

Tweetie landed on the grilled cheese sandwiches three seconds later, and Jordan hoped to God the table was sturdy enough to last through it all.

Chapter 23

At no point during the previous day had Hope suspected, even for a moment, that she would wake up the next day naked, in her rumpled bed, with a naked Jordan next to her, his heavy arm splayed across her waist.

A sweet languor flowed in her veins, and it took her a few seconds to realize that the buzz she was hearing wasn't coming from inside her but from her phone on the nightstand.

She reached out for it. A video call from Hannah.

She sat up abruptly, flinging Jordan's arm in the process. He stirred and squinted at her.

Another glance at the phone verified that it was just seven a.m. on a Sunday, but it was three hours later than that in Florida.

"Hey," he rasped, caressing her nape.

"Hey. It's the girls. In a video call. I have to take it. Sorry." She reached to the floor, but neither his shirt nor hers were there. "Would you mind if ...?" she asked, looking at him.

It took him a second to understand. "I've already seen it all, you know," he said with a teasing smile.

"I know." She amusedly gave an eye roll. The phone ceased buzzing.

Jordan smiled and threw a deliciously muscular arm over his eyes. The sheet that covered them was so low on his pelvis that it would have had the same effect if it hadn't been there at all. She was sorry to leave the bed.

Getting up, she reached the closet and grabbed a T-shirt, managing to put it on just when the phone began vibrating in her palm again. Grabbing a pair of panties from the drawer, Hope rushed to the living room, placed the phone on the dining table, hovering over it so only her face would be seen. She put on her panties while sliding the green key to accept the call and pushing away the memories of what she and Jordan had done on that table just a few hours before.

"Hey, sweetie," she said as soon as Hannah's face appeared on the screen. They seemed to be in the hotel room. "How are you two doing?"

"Mom, we want to stay more, and Dad said we could, but Nana said we have to go to school tomorrow and that you'd never agree. Will you, Mom? Please."

The flow of words was disrupted only by Naomi shoving her little face into the frame and joining Hannah with an urgent and dramatic, "Please, Mom, it's the most fun I've ever had in my entire life."

Hope chuckled at their sweetness, though, inside, she thought of the words she would exchange with Eric and his mother later. Convenient for them to make her the bad guy.

She picked the phone up from the table. "I'm so happy you guys are having that much fun, but you do

185

have to be back for school tomorrow. I'll tell you what, next time, we'll plan it properly, and then you can stay longer."

Their disappointed expressions clenched her heart.

"I'll see you tonight, and we'll talk to your dad and plan another such fun vacation soon, okay?"

Naomi was too disappointed to remain calm. She left the phone, and Hope could hear her whine in the background, to which a chorus of adult voices responded.

"Your hair is funny, Mom," Hannah said. She seemed to be over the disappointment really fast.

Hope ran a hand over her ruffled hair. "There. Is that better?" She smiled at Hannah. "I saw your pictures yesterday. They were lovely. I miss you and want to hear all about it."

"We have to pack up now. I have to go. Dad got me a T-shirt that says, '*Unicorns are Real. Just Look at Me.*' I'm gonna wear it for the flight. And we got other presents, too. Bye, Mom."

"Bye, sweetie. Tell Dad and Nana I'll be in touch." They blew kisses at each other before ending the call.

The house was so quiet that Hope could hear the faucet running in the bathroom adjoined to her bedroom. Her yoga pants were on the floor, not far from the table. She put them on and went to start the coffee maker, taking chewing gum from one of the drawers until Jordan would be out and she could brush her teeth.

Given that he had a four-hour drive to San Francisco airport and that he had to stop in Wayford to pick up his luggage, she knew he might not even have time for coffee.

"Good morning," he said from the kitchen entrance.

She pivoted to look at him, her breath shallowing at the sight of him all dressed, knowing what was beneath. "Good morning."

"Everything okay with Hannah and Naomi?"

"Yes. Just having too much fun." She smiled. She loved that he used their names and not something like "your kids" or "your daughters." "They wanted to stay more, but I told them next time. I'm the bad guy now."

Jordan pressed his lips into a thin line. She wondered if he was holding back words. "Never," he then said. "You couldn't be bad if you tried."

She swallowed. His gaze was warm, but there was something in the way he said it that made her feel there was another layer of meaning to his words. Maybe he preferred people who could be a little bad.

"I hope you have time for coffee," she said, turning toward the gurgling machine and throwing her gum into the sink. "Or I could prepare it in a takeaway cup. I have all sorts …" She trailed off when he reached her and slipped his arms around her waist, drawing her to him, pressing her back against his chest.

He kissed the crown of her head. "You never asked why I kissed you that time or why I didn't get in touch after," he said, his lips on her hair.

"You never asked why *I* kissed you last night, either," she said.

"True." He huffed a chuckle.

"I wanted to." She pivoted in his arms and looked up into his face. Their eyes connected.

Jordan dipped his head and kissed her, soft and gentle. He smelled of sex, and toothpaste, and remnants of aftershave, and she inhaled his neck over the edge of his Henley when she leaned her cheek against his chest.

"I wish I could stay. If Luke was on shift, I could stall some more." As an air marshal, Luke could help him through a rapid security check.

She nodded against his chest.

"I know this wasn't the plan yesterday when you ran into me, but I'm happy this happened," he added, and she could hear his voice reverberating in his chest. "Can I call you when I'm there and see you when I'm back here, and we could …" His voice faded.

She pulled herself back a bit. "Yes."

"You still haven't asked why I didn't—"

"You didn't know what to do with it, and neither did I."

He huffed a dry chuckle. "Something like that, just more complicated. Can we talk about it when I'm back? Because, Hope, I want to uncomplicate it."

"We can." She smiled. "I'll make coffee." Reaching for a regular mug and a plastic travel one with The Mean Bean logo on it, Hope tried to stifle the happy dance her heart was doing. There was a lot to analyze.

Jordan leaned against the counter as she handed him the travel mug.

"I'll return it when I'm back," he said, raising it in cheers.

She raised hers, too, and they both sipped. Hope felt almost like she had when she had tried the cocktails—needing to continue sipping because she didn't know what to say and worried that, if her mouth was free, it would reveal too much of her heart. Her feelings for him had first snuck in then raided her heart.

She hadn't meant or wanted to fall in love with him, but she had. So. Fucking. Much. And it was too late to fight, ignore, deny, or defy. While the promises they had just made were enough for now, she was risking more than she had planned. More than she had thought possible.

She then saw him to the door, where they stopped and kissed again. It was slow, and deep, and searing. But they let go, and then she opened the door, glad the neighborhood was still asleep and not witnessing former town local, Jordan Delaney, coming out of a Riviera View's school teacher's house at this ungodly hour on a Sunday.

Jordan turned to look at her once from the lane and once again before he drove away. Hope closed the front door and leaned against it, her heart bursting in her chest as she rushed to the bedroom and flung herself onto the disarray of sheets that still smelled of Jordan and her.

~~~~~~~~~~~~~~~~~

"This suite is too tidy. I could use some mess on the dining table."

Hope looked at the text and smiled to herself, remembering the pile of papers, uneaten sandwiches, and the sweatshirt that had been shoved together to the far end of her dining table the night before while she was getting the third orgasm of the night.

She sat in her bed, the bedding changed, her left hand caressing Naomi's hair, while the right held the phone. Hannah was sound asleep to her right. Both had been exhausted and so happy, spreading their gifts as she had helped them unpack. They wanted to sleep in her bed that night, and she had agreed.

"What about the bed? Because mine is crowded," she texted back. She wasn't good at flirting, and it took her longer than it probably should have to respond.

"This one's too cold. Everyone's back? Did they like the gifts from the fair?"

She bit her bottom lip and shook her head in disbelief. He remembered the little details. She wasn't used to being noticed like that.

"Loved them!" she texted back. The girls had been thrilled at the things she had gotten for them, and she had smiled at how big the pink paper bag looked in their excited little hands versus how small it had looked in Jordan's.

Hannah stirred and opened her eyes for a moment. "Night, Mom," she mumbled.

"Night, sweetie." Hope caressed the curls back from her daughter's forehead.

"Glad you arrived okay. You're probably beat," she texted, trying to imagine Jordan in his hotel room.

"I am. Hardly slept last night. ;) Talk tomorrow?"

Hope chuckled silently. "*Good night. xoxo.*" Had she really just sent him a "*xoxo*?" Hope covered her face with her palms. She felt like an old teenager.

A cocktail emoji appeared in reply, followed by, "*To Hope.*"

When she closed the chat that melted her heart, knees, lower belly, and everything in between, Hope's eyes fell on the chat she'd had before. Eric's text made her ground her teeth.

"*I might want the kids on Halloween. I'll notify if I do.*"

She hadn't responded yet, knowing that it required more than the intuitive reply of, "*Fuck off. You don't get to notify; you get to ask nicely. And don't talk to them about it until after you decide 'if you want' them and I decide if you get them,*" that she had rammed on the keyboard then deleted. She would phrase it better in the morning. Maybe change the "*fuck off*" to something milder.

~~~~~~~~~~~~~~~~~

"Definitely didn't grow my virginity back." Hope felt her face all flushed, probably exhibiting outwardly the way she sweated nervously under her clothes.

She looked at her shocked yet bemused friends. Roni wasn't perched back on her chair, like she usually was, but leaned forward, her elbows on the table, her blue eyes sparkling with mischief. The expression on her face was the dictionary definition of *I'm all ears*. Libby's mouth was half agape in a surprised smile, her hazel eyes wide, and her general expression was that of *I want to know more, but I also don't.*

"We leave you for one weekend and that's what you do?" Libby asked, laughing, gripping Hope's hand from the moment the words, "*I slept with Jordan*," had fallen from Hope's mouth a moment before.

Sitting on the terrace at Life's A Beach, they had each shared about their weekend, and when it was her turn, she had told them about the fair, how she had bumped into Jordan, how they had gone to the beach then the café, culminating the story with the four words that had them gasping in surprise.

"The moment she agreed to meet here, I knew there had to be something big that made her get over that stupid Josh thing," Roni addressed Libby. Then, turning to Hope, she said, "I want details. How was it? Where? How? How many times? And ... was it indeed something big?"

"Wipe that saliva," Libby said, laughing and looking at Roni. She was pointing at the corners of her own mouth.

Both Roni and Hope laughed.

"I *am* salivating," Roni called. "And I wanna know."

"Shh ... please!" Hope said, looking around at the other tables.

"Okay, let's start simple. Who kissed whom first?" Roni asked.

"I invited him in and kissed him first." She didn't reveal that he had kissed her before. They would be pissed with her for concealing it for this long. She would tell them, just not now.

"Now for the rest of my questions, please," Roni nudged with a grin.

Hope sighed theatrically. It was actually liberating to share. "Three times ... that I can remember," she said sheepishly, though she couldn't wipe the smile off her face. "I had mini ones, too, I swear. And it was bed, bed, dining table. And yeah, *it* was very impressive."

"Oh God. I don't want to know all this about Jordan," Libby said, burying her face in her palms.

"I do," Roni said, jokingly elbowing Libby. "He's not *my* future brother-in-law, and I've been married forever, so I need details. Though, I don't think I could ever eat on Hope's dining table again."

"Then don't eat anywhere in my apartment," Libby said, chuckling.

"You see? You don't want the details," Hope said.

"So, detonation?" Roni asked.

"Oh, yes. But so much more."

"What's *more*?"

"He was just ... amazing. He saw me, heard me. And I don't mean *that*, Roni," she added a rebuking aside to Roni, whose expression said *I bet*. "I mean before we even got to it. I felt seen and listened to, you know? Like he really cares."

"He really does," Libby said, seriously now. "And he's proven it time and again."

"Yeah, sounds like it," Roni agreed. "And you deserve it, babe, especially after losing in the ex-husband lottery."

Hope had preempted her revelation about Jordan by telling them about how Eric had behaved throughout that Florida weekend saga and his text about Halloween.

"Without getting into too many details, he was everything that Eric wasn't and did everything that Eric didn't," Hope said, playing with the margarita straw.

"If I guess, will you confirm?" Roni asked with a sassy smile.

Hope chuckled. "Libby, you'd better cover your ears."

"I'll survive ... hopefully," Libby said.

"He went down on you when Mr. Douche wouldn't," Roni said, stating it as a fact, her tone venomous when she used Eric's nickname. "And he didn't make remarks about your post-preg body, didn't compare you to anyone, and actually enjoyed seeing you enjoying yourself and made sure you were. Oh, and he didn't do that annoying thing that douches do—give your head a little shove down so you'd get the hint."

"Check, check, check, check, and ... check," Hope replied, making both women chuckle along with her.

"I need another drink," Roni said with a sigh and waved at a waitress.

"So, are you guys together now?" Libby asked.

"I know he's Luke's brother and that you like him—hell, I like him, too, with how he treated Hope—but I don't know if he's a long-term relationship material, so don't get ideas into her head," Roni said, sending a protective hand to grip Hope's shoulder. "He's supposed to be her rebound sex, an explosive send-off back into the dating world.

And it sounds like he delivered. She could enjoy him a little more probably, but she needs to find someone who's actually here, who's more like her. Those that make your heart race like crazy are dangerous."

"Guys, I appreciate the concern. It's not that simple because there are ... feelings," Hope said, and it was her turn to sigh. "We did say we'd talk and see each other the next time he arrives. And he texted when he reached D.C. last night and this afternoon. But with him there and me here and used to such different things ... We'll see how it goes."

"Sweetie, I know you," Libby said. "And though you haven't said much about him until today, I can tell that you're deeper in than 'we'll see,' regardless of what Roni says. *We'll see* was Chris. Am I right?"

"You're not *wrong*," Hope admitted without looking directly at her friends.

"Oh no." Roni sighed again. "You two are going to kill me with all this anticipation and angst. First you, now you," she said, pointing at Libby then at Hope. "What would I do without you, though?" she added with a scoff. "Die of my suburban boredom, that's what."

The waitress had just arrived with their second round. Libby raised her glass. "Here's to smooth sails with minimum angst."

They clinked their glasses.

"Speaking of," Libby said, "what about Avery? Did you talk about that?"

"He wasn't seeing her."

"Is it only me, or do you two also think better of him for that?" Roni remarked.

"I mostly know her from your stories, but yeah," Libby said.

"To be honest, I was relieved. I work with her," Hope said. "I saw her at the fair. I saw Anne, too, by the way. I was at Breading Dreams, thought I'd see your mom there," Hope addressed Libby. "Anne seemed strange, especially when this guy entered. I forgot his name. Would you guys mind if I invited her to one of our evenings?"

"Good luck with that," Libby said. "I invited her several times, but she blew me off. I think she's uncomfortable around me because of the bakery, though it should have been the other way around. And, speaking of, her parents pretty much announced they're retiring and Anne is taking over. She offered my mom become a partner."

"Did Connie agree?"

"You know her. Said she didn't want that burden in the last years before her retirement. Besides, I think Anne's a little afraid of our Roni here."

"Me?" Roni stopped mid-sipping her cocktail.

Libby scoffed, bumping her shoulder fondly against Roni's. "We love you, but Anne is so quiet and private; you're probably too much for her with no fault of your own."

"Invite her. I like her. Though I still can't get used to calling her Anne and not Jane. I'll be on my best behavior. Promise," Roni said then resumed sipping her pink drink.

"That guy at the bakery called her Jane."

Libby and Roni exchanged glances.

"What is it?" Hope asked.

Roni shrugged. "It was a million years ago." Then, looking at Libby she added, "Can you imagine how awkward that wedding was?"

"What?" Hope repeated.

"Nothing. Stupid town gossip," Libby replied. "Not worth repeating." She gave Roni a pointed look.

~~~~~~~~~~~~~~~~~

"How was your evening?" Sarah asked as soon as Hope came in through the front door.

"Great. Libby says hi. How were they?" Hope gestured with her head toward the bedrooms, leaving her keys in the red-orange ceramic bowl on the dining table.

"Great. Hannah read until I turned the lights off, and Naomi was out right after her bubble bath. She wanted to put cucumber slices on her eyes and light candles, but I told her a bubble bath was enough spa for one evening."

"We all need to be a little more like Naomi," Hope replied, chuckling.

"Yeah, that girl got it right. You look great, by the way. Donna told me you came in this afternoon, but I don't think you did anything to your hair. I can tell when it's the hair." Sarah smoothed a hand over her flavor of the month hair color—sandy brown. "Facial maybe?"

"Yes, a facial," Hope said with an amused smile. Donna's Fresh Hair was one of three hair salons in town, and she knew pretty much everyone. Although Sarah was the kind of woman you could tell anything to, there was no way she was going to discuss with her the Brazilian wax work that she'd had done.

"It suits you. Well, I'd better be going. Day after tomorrow, *I* have a night out with *my* friends. Deidre—you know her from Books And More—and Maggie who backs me up at the pharmacy. I forgot to tell Luke how well Deidre spoke of his brother. She probably told him herself, but I bet she didn't tell him that she thought Jordan would be stuck up, like their dad, because of all his friends in high places, but that he was so down to earth and kind, helpful, generous, and funny when she met him. He helped her clean for hours, and brought her lunch, and she began wondering if Joe Delaney was even the real father of these three." Sarah was divulging all this in a half-mumble, almost to herself, while she collected her purse, sweater, book, and shoved her feet into her tennis shoes. "She was only kidding. Don't tell Luke she said that. Of course they're his. They got their height from him and that head of hair. Mind you, it's hard to find men at Joe's age with such a head of hair. I should know."

It was the most trivial, offhanded chatter, but it made Hope's blood gush with sudden warmth. Every new thing she discovered and learned about Jordan shed a new, bright, beautiful light on him, warm light that seeped into her and glowed around the ashes of her heart. She couldn't believe she hadn't liked him or thought him a prick when they had first met. *I didn't know him then*, she thought as she walked Sarah to the door and thanked her for babysitting.

~~~~~~~~~~~~~~~~~

"*Heard from Luke you had a girls' night out,*" the text from Jordan pinged as she was getting ready for bed. The bed he had been in just the previous morning.

"*Almost every Monday. Our way of starting the week.*"

"*Afraid to ask what you talked about.*"

"*Be afraid. Be very afraid. They know.*" She added scared, screaming, and laughing emojis.

"*So does Luke.*"

She huffed a breath and, for a moment, covered her face with her hands. Was this really happening? It felt like they had just made it official.

"*Rearranged my schedule so I can come back in three weeks,*" he texted again, sending her heart into somersaults.

She couldn't wait. Her palms tingled, her stomach clenched.

"*I'll be here.*" She wanted to say something smart and flirty but had no idea how.

"*I'm counting on it,*" he replied. A heartbeat later, another text arrived. "*Because I have that travel mug to return.*"

"*Yeah, I need it back. I grade papers with it. In my kitchen, on my dining table, and even in my bedroom,*" she wrote then sent before she could regret it. She could regret it after, which she instantly did.

"*I can think of a few other places,*" came Jordan's reply. "*Ever graded papers on your door? Wall? You have to hold them tight against it and grade real hard.*"

Oh, sweet Jesus. She felt those words between her legs.

"*Interesting approach*," she texted.

"Mommy, water," she heard Naomi's voice from the next room.

"*Gotta go. Water round.*"

"*Goodnight, Hope. Don't freak out, but I miss you.*"

She bit her bottom lip. He was doing to her heart what he was doing to every other part of her.

"*Not freaking.*" That wasn't entirely true. "*And me, too.*" Hundred percent true.

But, was this too fast? She had been divorced for over two years, had had one world-class crappy first date, then a few weeks with someone she liked, which had culminated into nothing, and now this. This man who made her body sing.

She filled a glass with water and drank it standing over the sink, drinking it like she had just gotten back from a bonfire. Only the bonfire was in her heart. She filled it again and went to Naomi's room.

Chapter 24

Like on a rollercoaster, he soared now, knowing the steeper and more painful the fall could be. He tried but failed to slow this thing down—the racing of his heart, the thoughts of a future, the truths that he had just texted her—because there was one other thing he had to admit to her before he could tell Hope that he had fallen for her. Ugly words would have to be said before he could say the three beautiful words that he had never said, at least not with a full heart.

For now, in the sterile, bland hotel room, Jordan imagined her in her Tweetie sweatshirt, in her house that reflected her in every corner, even in the neat stacks of laundry that awaited on the couch to be taken to the various rooms. He imagined her bringing a glass of water to Naomi, patting her head, then going alone to an empty bedroom and an empty bed, a bed he would be happy to keep warm for her.

Three more weeks. He could be there with her in three weeks and, finally, tell her everything and hope to God that knowing him more wouldn't cause this hope of his, this Hope of his, to vanish.

~~~~~~~~~~~~~~~~~~~~~

"Will they connect, repel each other, or explode?" he asked with a chuckle, sitting on his hotel bed a week later.

The sound of her laughter at his question pumped a surge of blood to his heart and between his legs.

"They'll connect. That's the whole idea of the experiment." Hope's half-whisper caused another stir in Jordan's boxers. She had told him that she had to whisper because her daughters had a hard time falling asleep. "Are you really interested in all this?" she asked.

"Yes. Why is it hard to believe?"

"It's so … trivial."

"Not more than what I do here daily. You'd fall asleep if I told you about the sections, and subsections, and sub-subsections I have to go over, and learn, and find holes in, and negotiate day in and day out. All the one-track mind people I have to talk to. Hearing you makes me feel like I'm there. It's much more interesting. And I love it when you talk chemistry to me."

She huffed a breathy chuckle.

Fuck.

"Oh, I saw you in a fancy event the other day on the news."

"What fancy event?" He couldn't remember going to a fancy event.

"A press conference/fundraiser something."

"Oh, that. I only attend those things if it involves meetings between the person I'm working for and others concerning the project I'm on."

He had gone to that event straight from the office, feeling like he stunk inside his suit after long hours of work. He had briefly seen Sharon and Dana Brin there. They had exchanged quick hellos, and he had left as soon as his current advisee had finished a round of short meetings.

"Fancier than our teacher get-togethers," Hope said with another chuckle.

He suddenly pictured Chris, and Hope in a dress much like the one she had worn the night he had her up against the door in his kitchen.

"I saw you and Congresswoman Rush there. They say TV cameras add ten pounds, but she looked great, even with that big pregnancy bump."

Jordan dug his nails into his fist. There he was, jealous over nothing, his guilt drilling apprehensions into him that Hope might be jealous, too … over nothing. The need to come clean to her about it burned in his bones, but he couldn't do this over the phone.

"There were many people there, but I left as soon as we finished a few meetings."

"Anyway, it must be really late for you, and I'd better go, too. That experiment won't prepare itself for class tomorrow."

"Hope, can I take you to a fancy event or restaurant when I'm back?"

She huffed a little chuckle.

"Say yes."

"Yes," she said over another chuckle.

Two more weeks, he thought when they hung up. Two more weeks. And his contract was due to end in a few months. He wouldn't take a new one after that … if all went well.

~~~~~~~~~~~~~~~~~~~

He should have known.

Ten days into his return, the rumors about him and Rush began breathing their way through the office buildings, cafés, and members-only clubs of the capital. He should have been the last one to be surprised by something like that. It was always when people thought that they were clear of danger that things came back to bite them in the ass and every threat materialized. Many times, part of his job was to prevent it.

"We heard. Been getting calls from concerned friends," Dana Brin said the moment she picked up his call. Her tone put air quotes around the word *friends*.

"Thought you would." Jordan ran a hand over his jaw, scanning the news sites, looking for initial indications of the story reaching them. He found none and rejected the thought of gauging it through his media connections. Any interest could only fuel the rumor mill.

"Lost your killer instincts in your small town, Delaney? Remind me what it's called again. Something Riviera? Riviera Ridge? Riviera Valley? Something right out of a Hallmark movie, if I remember correctly. There's no room for our kind in those places. See what happens to someone like you there? You forget how to play the game, then you come back with all your guards down and there's hell to pay. You can't do this job part-time, Jordan."

"Brin, I'll say this only once—we stick to the facts. Only the facts. Don't initiate contact. Don't comment if they contact you. Don't give them ammunition. Right now, this thing runs on nothing, but if we react …"

"How did it start circling, anyway? Who did you piss off?"

He expelled a breath. She was grating on his nerves. "You know Dobbe? He's a legislative assistant to Senator Warber. I was hired to fix his screw-ups. Missed a hole the size of Texas in the offer they submitted to the strategic planning committee. Made Warber look like a rookie."

"I know him. A turdy little shit."

"Yep."

"Don't you have something on *him*?"

"I'm not going down that road."

"I forgot. You have class," she mocked. "I hope they're not gonna dig up any more dirt. We're so close to getting what she wants in the transportation committee."

"More dirt? Why? Were there other … incidents?"

"Not of that nature." She chuckled dryly. "You were the only one. What can I say? You're hard to resist." Another chuckle. "How did it happen, anyway? One drink too many? Working one hour too late into the night like we did?"

Jordan gritted his teeth. It was exactly how it had happened, minus the drink. Working late, a hotel in another state, he had been about to leave for his room when Sharon had suddenly started kissing him. Quick and meaningless. Ten minutes. The same it had been ten years prior with Dana Brin.

Wordlessly, they had agreed to never mention it again … until Sharon had realized she was pregnant and the dates had been inconclusive. He had advised her to not disclose that she had been separated from her husband and contemplating divorce, but say that Phil had been in the family home in Colorado for his work, which was true. A few calls had verified that the hotel staff and cameras had no record of him coming out of her suite late at night. Then he had found a clinic that would conduct a confidential paternity test. Waiting out those weeks, he had realized he hated what had become of him and left the city. Sharon, too, had breathed in relief to see him gone.

Now those few minutes were back to haunt them.

"Forget all that bullshit, Dana. *The Whisperers* might soon get the hang of it. Everyone knows they're more tabloid than TMZ, but if the big guns decide to follow, it'll be a wildfire." He took a deep breath and paced to the window, stopping to gaze at the evening sky. "In less than two weeks, I'm flying back to California and will work from there for some time. There are people there I want to come clean to. My family, my …" He bit the inside of his upper lip. He didn't know how to term Hope. "I'm done hiding this shit from the people closest to me. It only stinks worse when it's hidden."

"Just make sure they don't leak it. I know you don't have a motive to get it out there, so just—"

"You don't know the type, Dana. They're not … us." Motives, agendas. If he hadn't been sick enough to his stomach, this would have made him so.

Though there was nothing he would like more than to separate himself from this, the new development proved that it wouldn't be easy, that it might not even be possible. That he was still *us* with everything this place stood for. Would there ever come a day when he would be *us* with something else? Someone else?

"Seriously, Jordan, it's unlike you. You usually smell a disgruntled assface like Dobbe from a mile away. What happened to you?"

"Can you keep a secret, Brin?" His eyes were glued again to the window. It was closed, and his outline reflected in it, but his gaze was far, hanging on to the lights that sparkled outside.

"Yes." The excited catch in her voice reminded him of the eagerness people here had to possess secrets that could be used as a weapon later.

"I'm in love." It was so fucking liberating to say it. He wished the first time he had said that would have been to the woman he loved, or at least to someone who could understand, like Luke, or Ava, or Libby. But it was so good to say it, anyway.

There was a moment's silence, and then an explosion of laughter.

"Laugh away, Brin. After I finish with Warber, I'm out of here."

"Who's the lucky woman who was able to tame you into this?"

"The opposite of everything and everyone you know. A hope for something real."

"Damn, Jordan, you're becoming poetic. I can't believe I'm saying this, but if this is how she makes you feel, then go get her."

"That's more complicated."

"Why? You're a catch."

He scoffed. "She wouldn't think so."

"You'll find the way. You always do."

"Thanks for the vote of confidence. Now we have work to do."

After hanging up, Jordan called Luke. He would tell him, consult with him. But Luke didn't pick up.

"*Shift. Crazy. Can't talk. Urgent or tomorrow good?*" his brother texted.

"*Tomorrow's fine,*" he texted back.

He went to bed later, his last text being, "*Thinking of your smile,*" which he sent to the woman whose smile could warm him in this cold even from three thousand miles away.

Chapter 25

Hope put her phone down on the nightstand and switched the lamp off, remembering how Jordan had kept turning it on that night. She huffed a deep breath.

She missed him, and not just with her body. Her soul missed him—his presence, his dry humor, the sun of his real and metaphorical gaze on her that illuminated parts of her that had long ago been dimmed.

Less than two weeks. The nearer it got, the less she could wait. And the less she could control her feelings from running wild, her body from going into overdrive.

~~~~~~~~~~~~~~~~~~

"A little bird told me you were driving around town with Jordan the day of the fair," Avery said the moment they stepped out of the room that was used for staff meetings a few days after.

Hope snapped her head toward her in surprise. *Damn those gossips. Took them time, though.*

"I guess that saves me talking to you and Chris Kominski about the expected conduct from staff members who have an outside relationship." Avery smiled. It was obvious she fed off rumors and was trying to get her intel verified.

"If you're mentioning these names, there's something I've been meaning to ask." Hope watched the taller woman tense at her words and thought that Roni would have been proud of her for not taking bullshit from her anymore.

"Yes?" Avery prodded.

"Will there be school funding for the Model UN team's overnight stay?" She knew Chris had been waiting on that info. They were colleagues again. It felt right.

"There won't be. I'll update Chris. Unless you see him first?"

"You go ahead," Hope replied, enjoying this a bit more than she should. She wasn't as good as Jordan thought she was.

They continued in silence toward the schoolyard.

Just as the bell rang and multiple doors opened, setting free flocks of excited children, Avery grabbed her elbow and spoke loudly so she could hear her over the commotion. "I was happy to hear about you and Chris, to be honest. He's a good choice, if you ask me. He won't shout at waitresses and embarrass you in public. And he's here and not smooth-talking anyone on the other side of the country."

Hope shot her a glance that she hoped was as cold as she had intended it to be. "Thanks for the advice. And no, I didn't ask you."

"Just a friendly one."

"Mommy," a little, high-pitched voice called, and then Naomi threw her arms around Hope's waist. Hannah had reached the age where she was a bit uncomfortable to show her association to a teacher, but Naomi still relished it. "Can you buy me a *Frozen* castle like Aisha's?"

"Take care, Hope," Avery said, heading outside and leaving Hope to answer Naomi's inquiries.

She knew Avery's words on this shouldn't be taken any more seriously than what she had said about Hannah's or Hope's work, or any of her colleagues, or the ideas she'd had for the science fair. But, like always with Avery, she knew how to hit the sensitive spots, the ones that hid where the armor was punctured, anyway, usually around the heart, and get her venom into a wound.

~~~~~~~~~~~~~~~~~~~

Autumn was present in the crisp night air. Hope entered the girls' rooms to ensure they hadn't thrown off the covers. Hannah was sound asleep, but Naomi stirred when she drew the blanket over her shoulders.

"Goodnight, sweetie," she whispered, patting the blonde hair.

Back in her room, she sat on the bed. The TV was on, but she was only half-listening while going over the new class materials she was working on. She wasn't in a habit of watching the news at night, or following the ramblings of political commentators on the various channels. If anything, she preferred the lighter-tone shows that had the hosts banter a little while delivering news, gossip, or interviewing people. She had started playing those in the background to glean more into Jordan's work and life in D.C. The more she saw, the more she felt her life paled in comparison. All those big names, power suits, and matters of importance to the nation—there was glamour to it.

She dozed off over the last slides of her presentation when the tail-end of a sentence from the show's blonde anchor penetrated her consciousness. "*It certainly seems like this is the new political scandal, hot off the press, Dan.*"

Hope's heart skipped a beat, and she snapped her gaze to the TV.

"*It sure does, Val. I hope our viewers won't forget they've heard it first here, at The Whisperers. A pregnant congresswoman, a husband away in another state, and a political advisor whose job is to be near and aid? They were seen frequenting the same event only last week.*" The co-anchor's words sealed it.

And just when Hope was trying to swallow the lump in her throat that was really her heart, feeling it beating everywhere, the female anchor named the name.

"*It's strange, though, Dan. Though Mrs. Rush had only been a house representative for two years, Mr. Delaney has been around for over a decade, and if we've ever heard him mentioned, it was always in a purely professional context.*"

"*An impeccable reputation, Val. But there are always skeletons in one's closet. I hope we can bring his response to this soon.*"

"You know as well as I do that there's never a year going by without at least one scandal, Dan. We've had sex scandals, financial irregularities, bribes, tax evasions, extra-marital affairs. The list goes on and on. And political advisors are the ones helping prevent it or clean up the mess. You know the saying about laying with dogs and getting up with fleas."

"Or where there's smoke, there's fire, Val, which is a great reminder that our weather forecast is up next. Forest fires in—"

Hope turned the TV off and stared at the darkened screen. Her ears rang as if she was in an empty soundproof room, but that emptiness rang from within her.

The words spoken in the usual gleeful nightly news style echoed the newest, latest, and final testament to the fact that her instincts regarding men were truly and utterly fucked.

With hands as numb as her heart and mind, she lifted her phone that vibrated on the nightstand.

A missed call from Libby, followed by a text she read through the preview pane. *"Hey sweetie, can I come over?"*

She switched the phone off.

What had Jordan said that night? In *that* world, words were cheap, promises weren't meant to be kept, nothing was done without a return, and that it had poisoned his blood. Now the love that she had allowed to transfuse into hers was turning into poison. Nothing else could explain the relentless grip that settled in her insides.

Chapter 26

"The big ones have it, too, but they're holding off because it's all circumstantial. So stick to the facts, Sharon."

"What facts? That I slept with you?"

"I don't want to split hairs here, but we haven't *slept* together. We're talking ten minutes, tops."

"Thanks for the reminder."

"Stick to the facts. Phil worked from your home in Colorado. Your staff hired me to work on a limited project. You and your husband are expecting your third child. You're pregnant with his child. None of this is a lie. They have nothing to prove otherwise, except rumors. A simple fact check would have killed most of it, but unluckily for us, they're going through a dry spell and this is moistier than tax irregularities."

"I know how to do this, Jordan. It's just that it was never supposed to get to this."

"No, it wasn't. None of it should have happened." He tried to keep the accusation from his tone, for her sake. "Now we deal with this. And trust me; I have as much to lose as you do."

"Really? You have no wife, no kids, just your career to fix, and fix it you will. You'll land on your feet before the week is out."

Her words stung. But not in the way she intended them to.

"Issue a statement and refrain from talking to reporters. And no interviews. It will die out faster that way," he said. A cold pain throbbed in his chest.

"What are *you* going to do?"

"Fly home to try to fix the damage there."

"Good luck."

It wasn't the first call he had wanted to make. The first call he had wanted to do before she had caught him on the phone was to the airline to get the first flight out, then to Hope to tell her that he was coming to explain it all. From there, his list continued with Luke, Ava, his parents. He didn't care about anyone in D.C. enough to add them to his list of concerns. After he had completed his list, he could add one other thing—punch the living shit out of the useless fucker whose damages he had been hired to fix. Maybe he would add that, anyway. He would probably need that outlet even more if he failed to save the only good things in his life.

Or maybe he should punch the mirror because the fucker that reflected in it was the one to blame most of all.

~~~~~~~~~~~~~~~~~~

"Luke, I'll explain everything when I get there. Caught a flight first thing tomorrow." Jordan moved the phone to his other hand then caught it between his ear and shoulder to free both hands to pack his bag. "Hope's not picking up or answering texts. Can Liberty go over there and tell her I'm coming tomorrow to explain?"

"She tried calling. She'll know what's best to do."

"Can you make sure Mom and Dad don't freak out until I get to them?"

"Will do. Just one thing, between us: is it yours?"

"Not mine. You know better than to believe that." He straightened up and breathed in.

"All you told me the other day was that you slept with someone you shouldn't have when she was separated."

When he had finally spoken to Luke a few days before, he couldn't go through with telling him everything at once. The words had refused to come out, so he had ended up telling him the bare minimum, encouraged to add more the next time by Luke's mild reaction. But the next time turned out to be too late.

"Right. And I would have mentioned if there was something bigger than that." Jordan threw the shirt he was holding on the bed then ran a hand over his forehead. "She wasn't sure at first because of the dates, but we checked and it's not."

If it felt this bad saying it to Luke, how bad would it hurt saying this to Hope?

"We got your back, bro." Luke's words were exactly what he needed to hear.

"Thanks. Sorry I'm dumping this on you. I'll tell you everything when I see you. But first, I have to—"

"I know. I was this close to losing everything, too."

"See you soon." He hung up and went back to packing.

If it wasn't for the noise this made in the news, there was nothing in it that should be anyone's business but his own. His family, the people in town, his friends—it wasn't like they had ever known who he had hooked up with or dated. That wasn't the issue. And, although he shouldn't have succumbed to a woman who had still been legally married, it wasn't about that, either. This could have been a storm in a teacup except for two things. One, that what followed had taught him something about himself. Something ugly. And two, that he had fallen irreversibly in love with a woman whose rare silence meant that she was already seeing him in all his ugliness.

~~~~~~~~~~~~~~~~~

After a sleepless night, half of which spent jogging in cold, empty streets so he wouldn't go crazy, Jordan drove to the airport.

Though it was five a.m. in California, his mother called.

"We don't believe everything we hear on the news, but you know how these towns are. Your father is well known in Wayford and Riviera View, so he's worried it'll impact his business."

"They'll enjoy the gossip, but no one is stupid or prude enough to stop working with him, even if this thing were true."

"I know, sweetie. I'll talk to him. I'm more worried about how you're taking it. I'll make you your favorite casserole."

"Thanks. Don't worry about me. I'll be fine. It'll soon blow over. It always does." It was true. He knew it wouldn't even impact his career. But he couldn't care less about all that. The only thing he cared about was Hope.

"My famous big brother," Ava said the moment he picked up an hour later while waiting for the flight. She wasn't mocking. Her voice was tinged with warmth and empathy. "Making headlines to bring the limelight into this corner?" That was pure Ava. Her next sentence even more so. "Seriously, though, Jord, how can we help?"

He pressed his eyes closed for a second, thanking whoever was up there in the sky for his mother and siblings.

"Thanks, sis. Nothing you could do right now." *Except maybe rapping on a specific door in Riviera View and pleading my case for me, because I'm going to fail.*

"Whatever, whenever you need. Can I tell you what I think happened?"

"Do I wanna hear it from my baby sister?"

"Your *married* little sister. And yes, you want to, because I know you too well, although you're a million years older than me. You had a fling with this woman, whom you don't love, when she was on the cusp of divorce. The baby isn't yours. And I think you're in love with someone else. And the reason I know is; one, I know you, and if this was yours, you'd tell us a lot sooner. Two, I know you wouldn't believe it of me, but I read a lot of romance novels—I mean, a lot!—and I could fill in the blanks just from the initial reports and knowing one of the two people involved. And three, you coming here all freaked out is not because of Mom, Dad, Luke, or me. You'd leave it for a phone call if it was just us." She chuckled. "Just tell me if I'm right."

He took a deep breath. "You're right."

"I knew it!" she said victoriously. "You know I don't mean it like that. I just really don't think it's a big deal, and if she wasn't a congresswoman, no one would give a damn. And as for the rest, it'll be all right. I love you, big brother, 'kay?"

"'Kay." He smiled, though the back of his throat pricked unfamiliarly with emotion. "Thanks, Ava. I love you, too."

When he was seated and waiting for takeoff, right before switching his phone off, it chirped. Heart hammering, he looked at the screen. No hope.

"I fired Dobbe altogether. Please know that this is by no means something that I'd accept on my staff, and I know it came from him. His name came up from several people I trust. I offer you my sincere apologies and am willing to issue a statement to that effect. We need you on our team."

"Thanks, Senator. I appreciate it. I'll finish what you hired me to do, because I don't back out of my commitments."

"That's why I offered you a full-time spot on my staff."

"You know I don't take those."

"I know. And for the record, I don't believe that rumor to be true."

"I handed the latest revisions to your assistant. I'll check in with him later." He changed the subject, feeling like a liar still.

"Again, if there's anything I can do—"

"Thank you."

Jordan loosened his tie and gazed outside as the aircraft bolted on the runway.

The more distance the plane closed between him and Hope, the more he lost hope.

Chapter 27

She had switched her phone off because she knew, if she hadn't, she would drown in this murk. And she couldn't. She had kids to prepare for school, breakfast to make, a presentation to deliver, a meeting to attend, and a heart to protect.

Besides, she didn't know what to think or say.

Two missed calls from Libby, one from Roni, and three from Jordan awaited when she turned it back on.

And his texts. *"Hope, I tried calling. Don't believe everything you hear. I'll explain."* Another said, *"Please pick up."* The third had three words in it, *"I'm coming over."*

She made breakfast with a tide of ache gripping her heart.

The reports had gotten worse overnight. Pictures of Jordan with the congresswoman were posted on websites that covered political gossip. In one picture, he was leaning to whisper something into her ear during a press conference. In another, he stood next to her, along with others. Just seeing him, his face, his now-familiar features, knotted her stomach.

Nothing was incriminating in any of these, but the way they were reported made it sound like they'd had sex on camera.

Hope didn't want the girls to see this, so she kept the TV off and used her phone. Her mouth tasted like acid as she scrolled through.

"Mom, I can't find my new socks, the ones with the cats," Hannah called from her room.

"They're here. I'll get them for you," she called back, already skimming through the clean laundry basket on the couch with one hand. She held the phone with the other, her attention divided. She found one sock then the other, then froze on her stand. She reached and plugged her earphone deeper in.

"As for our new story, Val, we hear that Mr. Delaney spent two and a half months in his hometown in California. You know that The Whisperers *will look into that."*

Were they ever on a break on that show? For some reason, that was the first thought that crossed Hope's mind when she could think again. The second was, *Oh shit*. She couldn't, and wouldn't, be dragged into this if things escalated. She had a pretty good idea now what these shows and sites were capable of.

"Mom, did you find them?"

"Yes, sweetie."

She pulled the earbud out and walked toward Hannah's room.

Whether any part of the rumors was true or not, she couldn't tell. What she did know was that she couldn't reconcile the man she had gotten to know with what was said of him.

She refused to believe the worst-case scenario which these websites painted—that he had an affair with a married woman, an affair that was still going on, that he fathered her unborn child then abandoned her to hide in Wayford then returned to D.C. for her.

She chose to believe the best-case scenario, the one Libby had texted her when her phone had been off—that he had had a fling with a separated woman, that it was over long ago, and her baby wasn't his. Not a major sin. She wasn't a prude to think a forty-one-year-old, red-blooded, virile, capable—*God, how capable*—man who looked like Jordan was practicing priesthood before he had met her.

But whichever it was, it brought things to a head—she couldn't cope with his life. The distance, the media, being a public figure, the fame or notoriety resulting from public scrutiny, the danger in brushing shoulders with the powerful when, at any given moment, someone who didn't like his agenda or the candidate he was working for could turn his life upside down. Her life, if she were with him. She had kids. She had an ex who would thrive on this. She couldn't afford it.

Everything she had known or guessed from the first day they had met manifested itself now. The difference between them was too wide, too steep to overcome.

Yet, she had gotten a taste, and now loss and longing for what could have been crushed her. But she couldn't afford that, either. There was one way left. Facts. Logic. She would use science to shield her heart.

~~~~~~~~~~~~~~~~~

"Late this morning? That's unlike you. I guess the news kept you up at night, too," Avery, the ever-sensitive Avery, said the moment Hope rushed through the wide entrance into the main hall, with Hannah and Naomi in tow, each holding one of her hands.

"Hurry up, girls. Run to your homerooms, and I'll consider not writing you down for tardiness today," Avery added to Hannah and Naomi, who weren't waiting for her encouragement, anyway.

"You know who I mean," Avery continued when the girls were farther down the hall.

There was no point in denying it. Instead, Hope began walking toward her class.

"I was so saddened for his family last night," Avery said, hurrying to walk next to her.

"He's not dead," Hope muttered.

"Yes, but everyone will be talking. I thought it was bizarre that he stayed as long as he did. Now I know why. But, I guess he couldn't stay away from her for too long. Who can blame him? She's carrying his child after all." She suddenly halted and put her hand on Hope's arm, making her stop her stride, too. "I hope you weren't too hung up on him, sweetie. He's bad news." She chuckled at her own pun then changed her expression to one of sympathy.

Hope wet her lips. "I'm a facts freak. Love science. Don't believe everything I see or hear until I have data. Speaking of, my daughters arrive earlier than most students and staff ninety-nine percent of the time, so writing them down for tardiness today won't make a difference. Now, I'm late for class, and you can write *that* down." She turned on her heels and walked away, the pound of her footsteps resounding in the empty halls, her heart echoing it in her chest.

She didn't want to give Avery the satisfaction of the curses that rolled on her tongue, one spilling out as she muttered it quietly under her breath after there was some distance between them. "Bitch."

"*Don't ever, under any circumstance, use bad words. Those give you away immediately. You can say them in your heart, but don't tell your mom I said that.*" Jordan's advice to Hannah beat against her heart as she rushed to class. She remembered it all—his words, his kindness, the globe drawing he saved, everything. For the first time since last night, tears prickled the back of her eyes. She breathed in, forced them back, then opened the science class door.

~~~~~~~~~~~~~~~~~

The vortex in the coffee that she was stirring was hypnotizing. Her thoughts spiraled along with it.

"Did you catch the news this morning?"

She hadn't noticed Chris until he was standing right next to her.

"There's a new scandal in Washington, and Jordan Delaney is involved. I thought you'd like to know," he added when she didn't answer his question. "You said his brother is marrying your friend." He pressed his lips together.

This was how genuine sympathy looked like, so unlike Avery's.

"Yeah, I saw it last night."

"Oh. I caught it only this morning. I don't usually ... Pity. He seemed like such a nice guy when he was here. Do you think it's true?"

"I honestly don't know." She stopped stirring and picked up the mug.

"Listen, I know things between us sort of ... dissolved. I blame myself. It's Mason and ... But I was thinking ..."

"Chris, I have to get to a meeting. Don't worry about it. I think you and Linda need time to process everything. I gotta go. Good luck."

Holding on to her coffee like it was a lifeline, she hurried away from there. She couldn't deal with this right now.

~~~~~~~~~~~~~~~~~

Libby and Roni had used their group chat to write that they didn't believe the news.

"*It's only the gossipy sites. If what they wrote was true, then half of America slept with the other half, and I swear I haven't slept with anyone but Don.*" That was Roni, injecting her sarcastic humor into the worst situations and always succeeding in making her smile. Even now.

The one from Libby said that Roni was right, asked again if she could come over, and culminated with, "*How can I help?*"

She read those when school was over and she treated the girls to tacos at the pink car, as Naomi and Hannah referred to the food truck on the Promenade. When they were busy eating and comparing notes about Elena of Avalor, their TV hero, she phrased a reply for Libby and Roni.

"*Girls, sorry I haven't replied. I don't feel like talking, and I was at work all day and with the girls now. So, let's sum it up like that: I don't know what's true or not, I'll listen to him when he calls or comes, but either way, it's not right for me. I shouldn't have let it develop further this fast. I have responsibilities. And though it's unpleasant, I'm fine. It's not like we've been together, really. I slept with him once. We haven't even had a chance to start something, so it's better this way. The rest will resolve itself.*"

A second later, the chat said that Roni was typing. A moment later, her text appeared. "*Honey, if everything was that simple, as you bravely try to pretend, we wouldn't get this long lecture. I appreciate the effort, though.*"

"*I hate to admit it, but Roni has a point. We're here for you. Can we get together tonight? We could come over. We were there for your divorce; this couldn't be worse.*"

It couldn't, but it was. Because, back then, the pain was different. It was over her kids, the breaking of their home, the sting of failure, the fear of a new and unfamiliar life. It wasn't about Eric, because she hadn't loved him anymore for some time at that point. And now … now her heart was breaking in a new and different way. Because she loved. It broke for her, for the man she fell in love with, and for the hope she had allowed to sprout and flourish.

Just when she was about to reply that she would get back to them, a message came in from Jordan.

"*Landed in SF. Driving to RV. Pls talk to me when I get there.*"

Her heart, her goddamn heart, went out to him. She thought of how he must feel to see his life smeared like that in online and TV tabloids, knowing his family could get hurt. His career, his reputation. And knowing him enough by now, she knew he was hurting about her, too.

"*I will*," she typed.

"*Thank you*," was all he typed back. And, for some reason, this … this simple answer broke her heart for him even more.

Chapter 28

When it shitstorms, it pours. When you have to get somewhere fast, everything goes wrong.

He had never cursed the aviation industry in its entirety as he had when the pilot announced that they were going to land in Colorado to switch aircraft due to a minor technical issue.

Jordan's mind raced, and he could already picture the tabloids inventing that he had landed in Colorado to confront the scorned husband of the woman whose child he had fathered.

He finally landed in San Francisco in the afternoon and, from there, he had a four-hour drive, if Silicon Valley afternoon traffic wasn't worse than usual.

All this time, he checked his phone time and again, updated his mother and Ava that he landed, spoke to Luke briefly only to hear that Libby was trying to get Hope, and read the only two words that injected some hope into the perimeters of his heart. "*I will.*"

Waiting for the rental car, he skimmed through the sites. The credible ones hadn't gotten into it yet, but more tabloids were gleefully covering it. His heart, that felt like a stone in his chest, a rock only chemistry could melt, sank to his stomach when he saw *The Whisperers* promise to look into the months that he had spent in California. He knew how Hope would take it if she saw it.

That was one of the things he feared—that he would implicate her. Maybe it was wrong of him to even go to her now. He wanted her, but here was the proof that he had been right at first to avoid her. Now it was too late. Now he would explain so she would know the truth. He owed her that. But, if she asked him to leave her alone, he owed her that, too.

Him and her—he shouldn't have let it happen, for her sake.

Speeding on the 101, Jordan tried to form the right words, sentences, speech in his head. Nevertheless, he had gotten to know Hope enough to expect that planning might not work, that she would surprise him with some curveball that he wouldn't know what to do with.

~~~~~~~~~~~~~~~~~~

And a curveball it was.

It started raining as he reached Riviera View, and he wondered if that was a sign.

Just when the stone in his chest pounded until it hurt, as he pulled up next to her house and walked up the wet lane to the front door—the door that he had stood at with a living, thrumming heart just two weeks ago, the one he had kissed her against—it was thrown open.

Through it rushed out a painfully beautiful redhead who made the stone stop its throb for a moment. Her arm was wrapped around Hannah, who was holding a bloody kitchen towel against her mouth. In her other hand, Hope held an open umbrella. Behind them, a Hello Kitty umbrella with legs ran, a little voice beneath it calling, "Hannah, I'm sorry, I'm sorry. I didn't know you'd try to eat it. Mommy, I swear I didn't."

Jordan halted, and Hope, who until then had her eyes on the two girls, raised her gaze and noticed him.

"What's the matter?" he called, taking a step forward. The rain wasn't more than a steady drizzle.

"Oh, my God, I can't do this right now, Jordan," Hope said.

"Hope, Hannah, what happened? Can I take you to the hospital or—"

"We're going to the dentist. She broke a tooth on a marble. A marble that someone wrapped in a candy wrapper," Hope said, turning her head toward Naomi.

Hannah looked at him and attempted to smile. "Hi, Jordan," he thought she said.

"Jordan, tell Mommy I didn't mean to." Naomi ran to him, shifting her umbrella back and grabbing his leg.

He looked below at the little face, automatically caressing her head.

"To the car, *right now!*" Hope exclaimed.

"I don't want to go," Naomi wailed. "You're mad at me."

"I'm angry with what you did, and you need to help me now, Naomi. This isn't the time. We'll talk about it later."

"Hope, let me drive you."

"No, that's okay. My car's over there. Thanks. They said they'll wait … at the dentist's." She pointed at a blue Prius that was parked on the other side of the street. "I leave it outside … The garage door, it's broken, and I didn't get around to it. Sorry, I have to go," she added in true Hope form.

"I'll see you to the car."

He then looked at Hannah. "Hey, Hannah, you're a champ, you know that? You're taking this much better than I would have, and I'm twice your size."

Hannah smiled a crooked smile, only a half of which was visible due to the towel she was pressing to the right side of her mouth.

Hope stared at him for a moment.

He shifted his gaze to hers, and they just looked at each other. He couldn't take the emerald gaze. It was so beautiful, and clear, and messy with the turmoil behind it.

Jordan careened his gaze to the little blonde fireball that still leaned her little palm against his leg, as if it was a column she was leaning against while waiting for the scene to unfold.

"Come on, Naomi; I'll walk you to the car with your mom," he said, holding out his hand for her.

Naomi put her hand in his, where it disappeared inside his palm, and he turned to walk down the lane. Hope and Hannah followed. He could feel Hope's gaze drilling into his back.

"If your hair gets wet, you'll catch a cold. Do you want my umbrella?" Naomi said when he stopped at the curb before crossing the street.

He looked down at her tiny, round face and smiled. "Thank you, but we're almost there."

They crossed to the car, and he folded their umbrellas as Hope helped the girls in.

"You'll be fine, Hannah. Keep that tooth," he said. "Bye, Naomi. Be good and help your mom."

"Bye, Jordan," they both said; Naomi cheerfully and Hannah in a muffled voice.

He straightened up next to the driver's side after reaching in to place the umbrellas on the floor of the empty passenger side. Hope stopped next to him. The whole thing had taken three minutes from the moment they had come out of the house.

"Thanks," she said. The rain droplets fell on her hair and face. They were scattered and looked like tears. He yearned to wipe them for her, to wrap her in his arms and etch her on him.

"Sure. I'll wait," he said instead.

"I don't know, Jordan. It might take time."

"Okay."

She gave her head a little shake, as if to banish something out of there, then opened the door and climbed inside.

He closed it after her and waved at the girls as she started the engine and drove away. He just stood there and watched until the blue car disappeared from view.

Only then he crossed the street and went toward the grey rental.

But before going in, he continued walking toward the house but not to the front door. To the garage door that was to its left. He looked at it. The hinge on the left side was broken. He gave the door a push and it moved. It was open.

Going back to his car, he drove to the town's center, to Harden's hardware store.

Chapter 29

She could tell herself it was just great sex, an infatuation, and that the rest of it would figure itself out all she wanted. It had been a falsehood before she had seen him standing there in the rain, and it was a blatant lie after. Even with everything she had to attend to at that moment, at the sight of Jordan, her heart had jostled with a mix of pain and happiness, distress and relief. And then the girls' reactions to him and his to them—she could see how good this could have been, and how harmful if she let them be drawn into this whirlwind.

"Ms. Hays, ibuprofen if she experiences pain, and no food or drink except water for two hours, but the tooth is fine for now. We've put bonding to keep it in place. I want to see her again and assess in a week." The dentist handed her a prescription.

"Hannah, this is for you"—the dentist handed Hannah a pink toothbrush—"for being so brave and calm, and my best patient."

"Thank you. Can I get a sticker, too?" Hannah asked.

"Sure, you can. The nurse outside will give you as many as you'd like."

"Can I get one, too?" Naomi asked.

"Of course."

"She made my tooth break," Hannah tattled.

"I didn't mean to."

"Thanks, Dr. Perez. Come on, girls. We'll talk about this at home."

Hope led them to the car after a short stop at the nurse's desk for stickers for both.

During the car ride back, relieved that Hannah was fine, she gave Naomi a speech. "We don't do things like that. It might look funny on YouTube, but it's not funny in real life. Many of the pranks you see there are either planned with the person they pull the prank on, or they don't show you that those people were hurt or angry. They just show you it's funny for them. But it's not. Naomi, I know you're smart, and considerate, and kind, and that you would never hurt Hannah on purpose, but what you did was dangerous, and we're lucky it only ended with a broken milk tooth. I don't want to think what would have happened if she had swallowed the marble."

Naomi, who until then had held it together, began crying. "I'm sorry, Mom. I'm sorry, Hannah. I didn't mean to, and I'll never do it again."

"I know you won't," Hope said, feeling torn again on the tightrope of parenthood—having to be the bad guy and the good guy, and the educator and comforter, and everything in-between, especially as she did most of it alone.

It was Hannah who leaned from her side of the back seat toward Naomi's booster and wrapped her arm around her. "It's okay, Naomi. Look how many stickers we got."

By the time she entered Riviera View, the girls were chatting in the back seat, and Naomi was mimicking Hannah's slightly slurred speech, a result of the anesthesia.

She hadn't forgotten the man who was waiting for her. Her blood pressure must have climbed high as she made her way to their street because she began hearing it flowing in her ears as she hoped, and feared, to find him still there.

He wasn't there, and her heart sank in disappointment. A surprising sentiment, given everything that had happened. There was also no sign of the rain when she pulled up next to the house.

As the girls unbuckled, she looked at her phone.

"*I didn't want to impose on you. I'm in Riviera and can be at yours, or anywhere else, if you can meet me. I need to see you. And if you can't, just let me know Hannah is ok.*"

She let the girls inside, put a frozen pizza in the oven, and dialed Aunt Sarah's number.

"*I can meet at the Promenade in an hour. Surfers' Point. Hannah's fine, but I need to get them to bed first,*" she texted after getting a positive reply from Sarah.

"*Thanks.*"

Why did that single word of his hurt so badly? Maybe because he didn't take her for granted, and because she had rarely heard a sincere *thank you* from the man who she had been married to for over ten years.

When Sarah arrived, the girls were already in bed, reading with their bedside lights on. Hope tiptoed out of the house in the dark orange of sundown.

On Madison Drive, the seafront promenade, Surfers' Point, was empty of its usual pack of teenagers, glowing under a sky that became more purple by the minute. The streetlights that illuminated it were already on.

She saw him as she approached with the car, leaning his backside on the low stone wall that ran along the ten-foot cliff, his long legs stretched in front of him. When he noticed her, he straightened up.

His broad shoulders and the strong arms hiding beneath the grey dress shirt that he had on painfully reminded her of how much she would rather be wrapped in them. Hope had to remind herself of the chaos that she had faced that morning before the mini chaos with Hannah had taken precedence. It was time to deal with that, too.

It was chilly, but she felt colder inside. The warmth she knew was waiting in his arms was made harder to resist. She steeled herself.

"Hey, thanks for meeting me," he said when she stopped to stand in front of him.

She just nodded. If she opened her mouth, she didn't know what would come out.

The sound of the ocean, the breaking waves, the salt in the air were there, but all she could see was how tired he looked.

"Hope, you've had enough for one day, but I had to see you. I wanted to explain. I've been wanting to tell you this for a long time, before we even … But I was afraid. Still am."

"That's okay. Just tell me, Jordan."

"I'm not going to beautify it."

"I don't want you to."

"Okay." He took a deep breath. "In May this year, I made a stupid, terrible mistake. I had a one-time ... thing ... with Sharon Rush when she was separated from her husband." He huffed a breath, and his eyes escaped hers for a moment, but then he forced his gaze back to hers.

She could see it—the struggle, the regret. The truth he was telling and how hard it was for him.

His jaw muscle twitched before he spoke again. "One time. She initiated, I shouldn't have gone for it, but I did. It could have ended there, but then she found out she was pregnant and wasn't sure about the dates." He took another deep breath, and that jaw muscle danced again, straining the tendons of his neck. She almost reached out to touch it.

"She went back to her husband, but we had to wait until it could be tested during the Amniocentesis. It's not mine." He pressed his lips up, creasing his chin. "I never loved her, I never touched her before or after. But, for the record, I would have recognized and supported that child if it were mine. And if she wanted me to. But it wasn't, and she was back with her husband, and those few minutes should have remained in the past. Except—"

"Except she's well-known."

He watched her for a moment. "Yes." He then breathed in as if he was steeling himself for more. "But that thing that happened, it wasn't what bothered me the most." He averted his gaze toward the ocean.

The breaking waves frothed, their sound muffled by the distance.

"I want you to know everything, Hope. That's not why I left D.C." Bringing his eyes back to her, he continued, "I left because ... because my initial instinct after she told me was to help her cover it up, prevent a PR issue. I advised her to not disclose she had been separated from her husband. I made sure there was no proof of me being in her hotel room." He stopped when he noticed her averting her gaze as a mental image crossed her mind. "I'm sorry I have to tell you all this, but this was before I ever met you."

She brought her gaze back to his, and he continued, maybe knowing he had to get it all out now. "And I found the clinic that would do the confidential paternity test. And this ... my initial instinct and actions—that's what made me sick of myself, of D.C. That's what made me come here, to try to understand, remember, who I ..." His sentence died out.

She watched him in silence as he was the one to turn his eyes toward the ocean this time. Then he suddenly scoffed. It was a bitter, dry scoff.

"And the funny part was that, when she told me that it wasn't mine, I felt a sort of disappointment. Not because of her. It had nothing to do with her. Because ... I don't know. A punishment maybe?" He rubbed a hand over the right side of his face then turned to her, and his expression was of someone who was waiting for a verdict.

She skimmed her eyes over his face, yearning to remove that pain from his eyes. "I believe you."

He looked at her with a question, and she nodded, pressing her lips together.

"Yeah, I do. I believe you that it was just a mistake and that you regret it. And if she wasn't in the House of Representatives, this would have been … I don't know … one of those things you share on the seventh date or something. Nothing like what those *Whisperers* try to pin on you. Nothing that would … be any of my business." She lifted one shoulder. "No one's a saint. And I don't … You're a good man, Jordan. And you beating yourself over this is just more proof of that."

He huffed a breath that had him slightly recoil back in surprise.

"No, really," she continued, encouraged by the fact that the words came out as she meant them to. "It's … I can understand why you're bothered by it. But we all do, and react, and think things that we're not always proud of or do us credit. And I think you're much better than you think you are. You don't deserve this self-beating. I mean, she has older kids and a husband she eventually … And you tried to prevent … I understand."

"Hope, I—"

"No, wait. I'm not done." It was her turn to take a deep breath. Now, more than ever, she needed the logical scientist in her to be in control, not her rebellious heart or traitorous body that both screamed for him. "But your life, D.C., this distance—not just the physical one, but the … I don't know… stylistic one? … I don't know what to call it—what you're used to, the aspirations, the influence, the power game, your everyday, the … the media, the level

241

you're dealing with, the risks you take or given to … the whole … it's a whole other world. So different. And it's not something I can embed into my life, into my daughters' lives. I don't presume to think you're offering, but I'm preempting."

"Hope, I'm willing—"

"No. Don't tell me that you'd change this constellation for me. No." She shook her head, as if she needed convincing, too. "We just met, and you're good at what you do."

He closed his eyes, as if she had just stabbed him in the chest.

She pointed at his rental car that was parked not far from them. "I can't be your vacation or escape from yourself. Your life is not here. It hasn't been for over twenty years. I don't want you to change your life for me. You'd like it for what? A few months? And then what? You saw what happened today. That's my life, Jordan—that." She pointed with her arm back, in the imaginary direction of her house. "A seven-year-old who saw a prank on YouTube and thought it'd be hilarious to try it at home. A mother-in-law I can't even call unless I want to hear a lecture on why I'm allowing YouTube, or why I go out once a week with friends. An ex-husband who'd … Oh, he'd make a really good case of … all of it." She stopped for a moment to swallow the tears that accumulated in the back of her throat. "Our lives … you and I … are not compatible."

He just watched her, eyes dark, wide.

She then delivered the last blow. For herself, not less than him.

"Better if we remain as Luke's brother and Libby's friend."

Chapter 30

It wasn't a curveball, after all; it was a wrecking ball that knocked him off his axis altogether.

Though she believed him and had said he was beating himself needlessly over what had happened, she still believed that he was so different than her, so unable to be any different than what he was. And she didn't want him in her life. She had children, and he didn't fit into her life. She needed someone who wasn't him.

Her face … Her honest, open, beautiful face told him everything. He could see the determination, that nothing he said now would change it. He could see that she wanted to reach out, he could see that she resisted it, he could see that if he grabbed now and kissed her, she would let him. She would even kiss him back. However, it wouldn't change her mind. And it wouldn't be fair. Because her heart was entangled.

It was all too fragile, and he had known it from the start.

"Say something, Jordan."

He chewed the inside of his lip and looked away before he brought his eyes back to hers. They were a deep forest that he could get lost in.

"You wouldn't want to hear what I really want to say, Hope. You wouldn't like it. It'd go against what you just asked me to do."

"It's the right thing, Jordan, and you know it. *That's* why you didn't contact me after that kiss in your kitchen—because you knew even then that what I say now is true."

Jesus, it stung. It motherfucking hurt so bad that he was glad the wall was there to lean against. She was right, of course. And it seemed that every fear of his, every sin of his, came back to haunt him eventually. He had known from the start that he shouldn't sully her, that she wouldn't come out of it unscathed. Now he had this to carry, too—not only the pain of losing her, of losing the hope, but the knowledge that he had caused her pain.

"It's the right thing," she repeated, half-mumbling it to herself. "I shouldn't have let it …"

The only good thing he could do for her now wasn't to tell her that he loved her, like he was dying to do, but to let her go. Not perpetuate this or the damage.

"I'm sorry for everything, Hope. For the mess, for involving you in this, for letting things get … Tell the girls …" He stopped. He had no right. None. "Just tell them I said hi."

She bit her lower lip, and he could see that tears were clouding her eyes.

He couldn't hold himself back anymore. He reached out and ran his thumb under her eyes. A tear that she didn't let fall wet his fingers.

She closed her eyes, and he leaned in, kissing her forehead. "Bye, Hope. I'm sorry," he said against her skin, breathing in the smell of her hair.

She didn't lean in, just stood there, planted on her stand. He wanted to hug her, but it would only prolong the torture.

He dropped his hands to his sides and moved back.

She opened her eyes and looked at him. "Bye, Jordan."

He nodded once, and she turned to walk back to her car. They glanced at each other once before she got in and drove off.

The melted rock in his chest congealed again as he turned toward his rental.

His phone rang just as he climbed in.

"Luke, meet me at Mom's if you want. I'd better not come over to yours with Liberty there. It's over, and I don't want to cause issues for you and her. Hope will talk to her, you will talk to me, and I don't want this thing to come between you. There's been enough damage."

Chapter 31

Only when she couldn't see him anymore in her rearview mirror did she let herself cry, let the tears that he had tried to absorb spill freely down her cheeks. She dried them with tissues that she kept in the car before going back into the house. Even *that* brought up a memory that crushed her chest.

"They fell asleep fast. Had an adventurous day," Sarah updated, putting her tennis shoes on.

"Thanks so much, Sarah, especially with the short notice."

"Are you okay, dear?" Sarah narrowed her eyes and tilted her head.

"Yes, I'm fine."

"But you've been crying."

She breathed out. "It's been a long day, with Hannah and all."

Sarah nodded and patted her arm. "Yes, it has." She gave her a little smile.

Hope smiled back. At least, she hoped it looked like a smile. Can you smile when you feel like you're walking around with a dagger in your heart? A dagger you put there?

After a long shower, she replied to the group chat where Libby and Roni checked in on her.

"Hannah broke a tooth. Dentist. Long day. Am beat. We spoke. It's just like Libby said. But it's not right for me. Talk to you tomorrow. Love you. Night."

The heart emojis and hug gifs that followed in response from both told her that they understood.

With a numb head and heart, she went to bed. No TV or website could prompt her to look at them. She had the truth from the source, and she couldn't take seeing him being stomped on publicly when she might have just done the same privately.

~~~~~~~~~~~~~~~~~~~

The next day, when she stopped at home after dropping Naomi off at a friend's and Hannah at dance class—"I don't dance with my teeth, Mommy; don't worry"—Hope left the car in the street. Walking toward the house, hands loaded with grocery bags, she pressed the button to lock the car behind her. Instead, she heard a grinding sound. It wasn't until the garage door lifted that she realized where the sound had come from. Surprised, she walked and stopped in front of it.

Placing the groceries on the concrete, she approached the door and looked at its left side. A new hinge. It took her a second.

"Oh, my God," she mumbled.

Jordan Delaney was the only man she knew who didn't need a single word to torch her heart.

~~~~~~~~~~~~~~~~~~~

Libby stirred the hot cocoa mug that Hope had handed her as a knock was heard on the front door.

"Must be Roni," Libby said.

Hope went to open the door. "Hey, hon."

Roni just squeezed her into a hug. "Love it when we meet and it's not even Monday," she said in a half-whisper, entering the kitchen. The girls were asleep, and Libby and Roni had insisted on coming over.

"What's new on the Jordan front?" Roni asked.

"He's driving with Luke to the airport. Luke has a shift, and he found a flight, so they left an hour ago," Libby repeated what she had already told Hope.

With hot mugs, a bowl of cookies, and a throw blanket for each, they went to sit in the backyard.

"Have you looked into *The Whisperers* or the others since yesterday?" Roni asked, munching on a cookie.

"No. It'd feel like betraying him if I did. He told me the truth, and why would I?"

"Yeah, we didn't, either," Libby said. "I've never seen Luke so eager to punch a screen before. They're such low-lifes for messing with people's lives like that."

"Was there anything new there?" Hope asked.

"No. Same shit. But they're down to talking about it for only two minutes, so that's good news. They have nothing new to offer."

"Jordan told Luke that, if no credible, major network or source picks it up, then they'll drop it soon. That's their MO. And that Rush is considering suing them for slander."

The last sentence sent a fist of jealousy into Hope's chest. He was in touch with Rush. Then the rational train followed. Of course he would be. They were in this together, both being hunted down by those jackals. Besides, what he did now was none of her business.

She then told them about their conversation but didn't delve into the details of what he had revealed to her, feeling the need to protect him even from the people who wouldn't use it against him.

"Oh, hon, I can see your rationale—I do—but … why can't things be simple?" Libby said over a sigh.

"Simple? I had to tell Eric today about the marble. He demanded the girls not be allowed to watch YouTube, though I explained that it was YouTube Kids and not the regular version, and that they don't get that much screen time. I know kids and parents. I know some are getting way more screen time and apps than I allow."

"Did it help?" Libby asked.

"No. He continued to push until I snapped."

Roni's eyes lit up. "What did you say?"

"That I'll forbid it if he stopped buying them Barbies that look like his fantasy, and I added that neither of his wives looked anything like it."

"Oh, my God, I love this!" Roni called.

"Nah, it was stupid and just led to an argument. And today, he sent me a list of holiday splits because I also reminded him of how he dropped the Florida vacation on me. I sent it to my lawyer."

"I'm sorry, honey." Libby intertwined her fingers with Hope's.

"Can you imagine how he'd react if he knew about Jordan on top of that?" Hope sighed.

"So, I take it Eric heard the gossip?" Roni asked.

"You bet."

"What did he have to say? He used to like Luke when we were in high school, though can't say that the feeling was mutual," Libby said.

"He tried to squeeze information on 'the scandal your friend's fiancé's brother is involved with,'" Hope sputtered. "He reveled in knowing someone who made the headlines, though he only knew Jordan vaguely, as Luke's big brother, and he hasn't seen either in ages."

Like too many others, Eric enjoyed chewing on the gossip as long as it didn't touch his own life, not realizing that his ex-wife was closer to it than just as Libby's friend.

"He'd freak out if he knew that his daughters know Jordan, that he was in this house. I'd be hearing from his lawyer if he knew. Or worse, from Lucile."

Neither replied. They were quiet for a long moment, wrapped in the silence and scents of the backyard and its soft lights.

"Well, if you change your mind, we can chase Jordan to the airport. You know, like they do in every good movie," Roni said, trying to lighten things up, as usual.

"Sorry to ruin this for you, but we could just call Luke and tell him to wait," Libby said with a little chuckle.

"Party pooper."

"Don't think that I'm not tempted, but it wouldn't be right." Hope leaned her head back and stared at the night sky.

"Maybe you just need time," Libby said. "You just now started coming out of two years' worth of stupor, and then you had this whirlwind of a start, and this mass of emotions. It's confusing. And now he dumped all this info on you, and you need to make sense of it. I know you," Libby said. "You can't assess how you feel when you're like that."

But it wasn't how she felt that she needed to assess. It was everything else. In that, Libby was right. It had taken her a long time to assess, analyze, and figure out things when her marriage had dissolved. Though, in hindsight, it had been as clear as day. And maybe it was in this case, too, but she had to sift through it herself.

"Libby, I'm sorry if you're stuck in the middle of this with him being Luke's brother and all. I should never have—"

"What? No!" Libby cut into her words. "Don't be silly. I'm not taking sides, and there are no sides to take, so I'm not stuck in any middle. The funny thing is that he said the same to Luke."

"Damn, I feel guilty," Roni said all of a sudden. "I shouldn't have said you should let him send you off with a bang. I didn't realize how deep he got into your system."

"Yeah, it's all your fault, Roni," Hope said with a little smile when the other two just sat there and looked at her like she was delicate.

The laughter that followed reminded her that, whatever happened, these two would help her piece her heart together.

Chapter 32

"Who would have thought that, just a few months after our ride from the airport where you asked me about Lilac and Libby, we'd be driving the opposite direction and you'd be telling me about Hope?" Luke's gaze was on the 101.

"You didn't even realize you were in love with Libby," Jordan said. "At least I know my state."

"Shit state."

"Yep," he expelled over a sigh.

"I gotta say, when I warned you about Hope, I didn't think of *you*. I was afraid you'd break *her* heart, not the other way around."

"I hope I didn't break hers. That's the last thing I want."

"I said a few other things I regret saying then. I honestly didn't think you were ready for …" Luke turned his head toward him for a brief moment instead of finishing the sentence.

"Nah, I should have listened to you," he said with a tired smile. It waned as he turned his gaze to the side window and added, "You're not the only one who thought I'm not made of the right stuff."

"What are you going to do about Rush, and the news, and all that?"

"Tell her not to sue if she doesn't want them to dig deeper and find that some of it is true."

"Will you be okay there all alone?"

"Been there for over twenty years, as has been pointed out to me only yesterday. So, yes, I will."

When he landed in D.C. the next morning and drove toward his hotel, Jordan thought he could smell the stench of the river in the cold air of the early morning hours. A striking contrast from the ocean breeze that he had rediscovered and now left behind.

~~~~~~~~~~~~~~~~~~~

"I appreciate you checking with me first, Chidel. You know I'm gonna say 'no comment' if you go with this, right? Because I have nothing to comment on. So, go ahead." Jordan hung up and put his phone facedown on the desk. There were a few journalists whom he considered sort-of-friends and several had called to check with him first before deciding if to publish. By telling them to proceed and publish, he had convinced them to do the reverse.

His news aggregator analysis app indicated a declining interest in the story, which he was glad of. If glad meant numb and working on autopilot.

Outwardly, it was as if nothing had changed— attending meetings, discussions, analyzing strategies, talking all day, not caring what people thought, eating alone by choice in his hotel room, then jogging half the night. Inside, his heart had gone from frozen to charred. The damage and pain were similar, the treatment to both conditions out of reach.

~~~~~~~~~~~~~~~~~~

"Hey, Jord. Called to check in on you but you're not picking up. Been over a week since we last spoke. Don't work so damn hard. Also, wanted to tell you that, if you still want to buy a place in Riviera View, then I have a suggestion. Call me."

He listened to his sister's voicemail while eating a sandwich for his late dinner over his laptop in Warber offices on Independence Avenue. He didn't bother using earphones, since the place was deserted at that hour of the night.

He had been drowning himself in work—anything that would numb the constant ache that pulsated with the rhythm of his heart.

"Didn't know Gen Y knew how to use old-school voice messages," he texted his reply. *"I wasn't looking anymore, but tell me."*

"I do my best to connect with the older generations in their preferred means," Ava texted back almost immediately, adding a winking kissy face emoji. *"There's this large plot, 4K sqf, but sonofabitch will sell it only as one, though it's divided into two houses. Zack and I can't afford the whole thing. Thought you might be interested."*

Jordan ran a hand over his mouth. After months of limbo, he wanted to belong somewhere, to have an address at least. Despite everything, he had no intention of buying in D.C. Renting something close to his previous apartment was as far as his scattered thoughts had reached.

Riviera View still felt like home.

"*Send me the details*," he texted back.

Chapter 33

Hope pushed open the door of Breading Dreams and let Hannah and Naomi enter before her. "Remember, I said just one for each," she reminded them.

"Hi, Connie." She approached the counter.

"Hey, lovelies!" Connie smiled. "You're all looking so pretty, as always. Unicorn cupcakes for all?"

"Just them, thanks."

Connie handed the girls their cupcakes, and while Hope paid, she half-whispered to her, "Your ex-mother-in-law came in the other day. Tried making me feel bad for 'letting my daughter marry into the Delaney scandal,' as she called it."

"Oh, I'm so sorry, Connie." Hope sighed. So many people around her had a stake in this, and every reminder drove the sword deeper into her heart.

"You have nothing to be sorry about, sweetie. She's always been like that. I'm sorry *you* have to deal with her."

Hope could only imagine how Lucile would react and what she would do if she knew her granddaughters were "associated" with the scandal, too. Just the thought sickened her. It was another reminder of how volatile things were.

Connie handed her a box with the bakery's logo. "Here. On the house." Preempting Hope's refusal, she added, "Just a few mini quiches. Take them."

"Thanks," Hope relented. "Is Anne here?"

"Took a few days off. But she's still doing the evening rounds for the food saving."

"Tell her I said hi."

~~~~~~~~~~~~~~~~~

"Is it okay if we talk about Jordan?" Libby asked from her place on the other side of the table in Life's A Beach, two weeks later.

The week before, Hope had killed any attempt to talk about him when she had told her friends that her lawyer had reached an agreement regarding the holidays. "But for this Halloween, Eric's parents will pick the girls up after Trick or Treat and fly to Nevada so Prince Hays can take them trick or treating there, too. The girls were thrilled to hear they'd get to do it twice, so at least I have that for comfort," she had told Roni and Libby.

"What about Jordan?" Hope asked now. Saying his name out loud hurt. She had been trying to avoid mentions of him, hoping life and time would take their course, do their damn thing, until she got over him. So far, she had failed, but she kept hoping.

"What about him?" she repeated when Libby and Roni exchanged glances. That wasn't a good sign.

"He's buying a house in Riviera View. A split-plot with his sister," Roni said carefully, as if she was

259

notifying a death in the family. "He wants me to renovate it for him. Pay me to do both houses. For his sister, too; said it was her wedding present."

Was the floor moving? Because Hope suddenly felt seasick.

"Is he moving here, or …?" Her pulse pounded with anticipation.

Libby chewed on her bottom lip before replying. "He's still on a contract and has more offers. Doesn't talk much about what's next. I'm not sure *he* knows."

"Oh. Okay." The cool ocean air that came in through the large window suddenly wasn't enough to drive away the smell of frying, and coffee, and beer that permeated the large space.

"It's crazy how all that media noise almost died like that." Roni snapped her fingers. "And he has more offers? Maybe it's true what they say that no publicity is bad publicity."

"Ava offered the plot to me and Luke first, but we like it on Ocean so much that we have this idea to buy the apartment next to mine and connect the two into a larger one," Libby said almost apologetically.

"Wow. Okay. Congratulations, Lib," Hope said. "I was a bad friend for not even asking about your house hunt."

"There wasn't much to ask. We didn't hunt. We just … It's a recent idea we had."

"And you're going to work with … for him?" she addressed Roni.

"Yeah. Turns out he wants the best and can afford it," Roni said with a wink and a soft smile, reminding her of that night on his terrace in Wayford.

She was expecting she would have to meet him sometime, like at Libby and Luke's wedding, which didn't even have a date yet, but she wasn't expecting that Roni, too, would be in touch with him. With both her friends somehow connected to him, how could she escape constant reminders? And, what did him buying a house here even mean? Probably nothing if he was still there.

That surge of data, and possible scenarios, and hypotheses required reprocessing. She was still trying to be in scientist mode when it came to him. She couldn't cope, otherwise.

When she did let herself *feel*, which was more often than was good for her, every particle of her ached for him. Every iota of her missed him.

~~~~~~~~~~~~~~~~~~~~

When she organized the house one afternoon, she realized she wasn't the only one.

She was putting things away in Hannah's room, trying to rediscover the surface of the desk that hid under papers, rubber bracelets, fairy miniatures, markers, and textbooks, when she noticed an envelope. It was made of a pink A4 sheet, which Hannah had folded and glued to look like an envelope. It was addressed in Hannah's squiggly handwriting.

Mister Jordan Delaney
Washington D.C.
U.S.A.

Hope covered her mouth. It wasn't sealed, so she opened it. Inside was a sheet of the same pink paper. It was decorated with little drawings of globes, hearts, rainbows, and butterflies, and a sticker of "*I'm a Champion*" that Hannah had received at the dentist's office. She read the letter.

> *Dear Jordan,*
> *I invite you to my contest.*
> *I know what to do, but what if I need more advice urgently? If you come, you can help. And I know you will clap.*
> *Regards,*
> *Hannah Hays*
> *18 Maple Street*
> *Riviera View*
> *California*
> *U.S.A.*
> *Earth*

Hope sucked in a painful breath as tears shot into her eyes and blurred her sight. It was her daughter's raw request of him that had done her in. He had shone a light on her, and she wanted and needed it back. Much like she did.

With trembling fingers, she folded the paper and put it back into the envelope before it could get wet.

Chapter 34

"I told you they'd drop it eventually if we act smart." Jordan got up from his chair and paced the room.

"Smart would have been to prevent it before it happened."

"Well, she's your client now, Brin, so why didn't you prevent it?"

The silence on the other end of the line told him he had gotten his point across.

"Any tangible impact for her?" he asked.

"No. People are glad to pretend this hot potato never existed. They probably expect to receive the same grace when it happens to them."

"Good luck with that," he muttered.

"Anyway, *The Whisperers* are the only ones still giving this attention on their evening session. That Val bitch is practically wetting her panties over this. But I can see them dropping it, too, soon."

"They will." Jordan lifted then immediately put the lid back on the room service tray. The smell of the beef made him sick.

He went over to open the window.

"So, what's going on with your poetic endeavors? With you running off to Cali first thing, I assume the woman who stole your heart is there? Did you get her to see you're a catch after all, or was she appalled by this?"

"Night, Dana. Nice doing business with you again." He pressed the red key on his phone.

He didn't need reminders of the woman who held his heart in her hands, a continent away. She was on his mind all the time.

He moved from the window and back into the room that felt less stuffy now. Pushing the things that were scattered on the desk, including one plastic-covered drawing of a wonky globe, Jordan sunk himself in the type of thing he was good at—work.

Chapter 35

The evening that she had found Hannah's letter, after attending a PTA meeting and knowing that Sarah was babysitting, Hope let herself cry in the car.

Only when she was sure her tears were dry, and that girls were asleep, she went home.

"Hey, hey, what's the matter with you?" Sarah asked almost the moment Hope entered through the front door. She got to her feet and put her palm on Hope's forearm.

The tears, the goddamn tears, brimmed in her eyes again.

Sarah pulled her into a hug, filling her with the smell of gardenias and hair products. "There, there. Who broke your heart?"

"Who told you—"

"That you got your heart broken? Oh, I can see. I'm a pharmacist; I know the different looks of pain."

Hope pulled herself back and sniffed. "*I* broke it."

"You? Why?"

"Because … this man I was … seeing, he wasn't perfect, but who is, right? He made mistakes. He's …

Who hasn't? But I can only account for myself, and I made big mistakes, and I can't make more, especially not with the girls. We're different and live differently, and it's too complicated and risky. And besides, I won't stand in anyone's way when eventually … I had someone who knew the right thing to say to get me, someone who had ambitions, and then … And the three of us had to learn—"

"Wait, wait. You lost me. Are we talking about this man you were seeing, or is this your ex-husband you're telling me about?"

She sniffed. "Both."

"Both? Can I be honest, dear?"

"Please."

"Okay, let's not mix things. You married that boy Lucile Hays raised, whose name you still retain for your girls' sake. He wanted to be some hotshot, go to MIT like his mother always announced he would, but he had to go to Nebraska or something instead."

"Minnesota."

"Minnesota. Whatever. And he found you there, a little gem of a woman who he couldn't even see for who she was. And because nothing in his life was ever good enough for him, because that's how his parents raised him—like nothing was ever good enough for him, not even them, by the way—he wooed you then made you feel like he settled on less than he deserved. Am I right? And he treated you like that for too many years."

"Not all the time, but yes. And I let him."

"You let him, and *that* was your mistake. But like you say, we all make mistakes. But if the man we're talking about now is a Delaney—as I suspect we are—ever since that day you called me after Hannah broke her tooth—if that's the man we're talking about, and if it wasn't him who broke your heart, and if he wants to be with you—then let me tell you something, sweetie. You'll be making another mistake if you let him get away altogether."

"But he's—"

"Yes, he's away, and he's been having issues, and he's in the public eye, and he's best friends with the President, and you're an elementary school teacher," Sarah enumerated in a I-couldn't-care-less tone. "It's all petty cash if there's love. Did *he* ever let you feel that way? That you're a compromise? Jordan?" Sarah asked.

"No."

"No. So, he's not the problem. I heard what they said of him. I don't watch that crap, and I wouldn't believe it, anyway. I saw him grow up, and I saw him at the engagement party, and I heard what Deidre said about him. I know his mother, and I see what his brother is made of. He can talk all right—he wouldn't be in politics if he couldn't—but I don't think he's one of those who tell you what you want to hear only to make you feel like shit later. So, whatever you have on him, take that off his list of symptoms." Sarah giggled at her own medical reference.

"I never said he was like that, but I also can't expect him to … He has a whole life and—"

Sarah placed her palms on Hope's biceps to stop her. "It's not about him. It's *you* who first needs to heal, to get over what that douchebag—yes, I hear how you girls talk. And I sell douchebags in my pharmacy. And let me tell you, they're more useful than some men who are nicknamed after them, for some reason. Anyway, you have to get over the damage he's done first. Without it, you won't be able to fully believe, trust, or be with anyone in any good sort of way." Sarah pursed her lips into a thin line and nodded in a *I know I'm right*.

Hope sniffed again. "But—"

"Do you love him?"

Hope pressed her fingers to the corners of her eyes to stop the tears. "Yes." She had never admitted it with words, not even to Libby and Roni.

"I'm not saying it's easy, especially with your ex and his mother. And no one can promise you anything. It's a risk, especially with those two over there." Sarah jutted her chin toward the bedrooms. "But love's a risk, and life's a risk. Everything's a risk from the moment we're born. You're too emotional right now, sweetie. Take your time. Then reassess yourself."

Hope nodded in rapid succession, taking in Sarah's words, almost hanging on to them.

"Thanks, Sarah. For everything. I wish you were my aunt, too."

"Oh, honey, but I *am*." Sarah smiled.

Hope hugged and squeezed the older woman tightly.

Chapter 36

He read the words again. She was apologizing, like she always did, not realizing that she had just made him happy. Still hopeless, but happy that she had removed at least some of the barricades between them.

"Hey, Jordan, I hope you're doing ok. I'm sorry I'm dumping this on you. I wasn't sure, but Libby said you'd want to see this, and I promised Hannah. She wrote you this letter, and I promised I'd send it to you. I know you care, but I also know how things ended. If you'd like to type in a reply for her, or talk to her, I'll let her have my phone. Really appreciate everything you did for her there. And everything in general. Let me know. Thanks. It's ok if not, btw. Don't feel obligated. I know how things ended."

He smiled to himself while reading it. It was one of the longest messages he had ever received, and it was so *her* that he could picture her saying it. The image hammered down the granite that had settled in his chest.

The picture of the homemade envelope in childish writing, and the letter, warmed his heart further, but Hannah's last sentence crushed it with its brutal simplicity.

"*Thanks for sending it to me. When is it?*" Brief and short was a dam against the flood of feelings that his fingers could have typed.

The words "*Hope is typing*" appeared on the screen on and off for at least two minutes before a short text arrived. She was probably typing and deleting, maybe fighting the same instincts. "*Right before Halloween. I'll send you the details.*"

"*Tell Hannah I'll do my best to attend. And Hope, I'm happy to hear from you. Don't ever hesitate regarding anything. And stop apologizing.*" He yearned to add more, so much more. The numbness he had managed to submerge himself in had been ripped open, and every atom in him throbbed.

The next thing he did was open the airline website on his phone.

~~~~~~~~~~~~~~~~~~~

He didn't promise, unsure if he could face everything that he wanted and couldn't have.

He could cancel the flight. But why should the girl, whose excitement choked the end of her speech when she had recited it to him over the phone, suffer? He should be able to get over himself for her sake.

He had texted Hope a day after her initial message, asking if he could talk to Hannah. A few moments later, his phone had rung, and Hope's name on his screen had tightened his chest. He had picked up to find Hannah on the line.

"Is it good? Do you think I did well?" she had asked after relating one of her arguments.

"You did excellent. That's a good speech you have there, and I love that you know your partner's part, too, in case he forgets it. And remember to count to three with your breathing if you're asked or opposed with something you weren't prepared for."

"Okay. I'll ask my mom to send you pictures of me."

"I'd love that. I'll try to be there," he had said.

He was a grown man; she was a child. She counted on him. And he never let down his clients. Or people he loved. Except her mother.

To avoid further disappointment, for anyone, he hadn't notified of his arrival, just in case he wouldn't be able to make it. Now he disembarked the flight with no luggage and walked the familiar corridors of the San Francisco airport, knowing he would be pacing them again on his way back in a few hours.

He took an Uber to the conference center. The smallest hall had been assigned for the middle school level and below, so Jordan made his way there, his footsteps slower than the crazed horse that raced under his ribcage.

The session hadn't begun yet. People were standing in clusters all over the floor, up to the front where the stage was decorated and ready.

He shouldered his laptop bag and moved slowly from the entrance, using his height as an advantage to scan the room.

When he was near the middle of it, he noticed a flame of copper at the far end. Like a magnet, he was pulled to it, making his way through the chattering crowd, hardly hearing it over the pulse that strummed in his ears.

With just one group between him and the double flame of heads—one tall, one small; one copper, one curly, strawberry-blonde—he halted. For some reason, he had forgotten about the man who stood in their little circle, chatting, smiling, casually touching Hope's arm.

He would have turned on his heel and stepped away after what felt like a semi-truck hitting him, but Hannah's face, the way she bounced nervously on her feet, reminded him why he was here.

He circled the group that screened him from view, and it was Hannah who first noticed his approach. She was facing in his direction, and the way her face lit up when she saw him was worth the way his heart waned right before.

"Jordan! You came!" she called, bolting toward him.

He smiled and slightly bent before she collided with his abdomen, throwing her arms around his midsection.

"Hi there, I didn't want to miss it," he said, wrapping one arm around her back. "That tooth of yours looks fine," he added as she happily grinned up at him.

He lifted his eyes and saw Hope's and Chris's surprised looks. His eyes instantly locked with Hope's as Hannah escorted him the last few feet to the group.

"Hey," he said, eyes still magnetized to Hope's, unsure if to shake her hand, hug her, or just stand there like an idiot.

"Hey," she said, but it was a half-whisper. "Thanks."

He nodded and closed his eyes once in a *you bet*, then turned his gaze to the less painful spectacle. "Chris," he said, reaching out his hand. "Nice meeting you again."

"Yeah, you, too." Chris cleared his throat. "Is … everything okay after all the …? You were on the news." He then cleared his throat again.

He almost forgot that, outside D.C., this would be most people's reaction to him.

"Yes, I was. But everything's fine. I appreciate your concern, but I wouldn't call everything I see news." He smiled, hoping he didn't sound too sarcastic.

Chris cleared his throat again. "Anyway, it's nice of you to come. Avery's not here, though." He sounded sincere.

Jordan almost laughed at the enormously wrong conclusion that Chris had reached.

"I'm here to support the best team out of my old school." He smiled at Hannah, who beamed at him.

He could feel Hope's eyes on him. He turned, expecting to find green daggers. Instead, he was met with soft green moss. She was in the blue dress from his brother's engagement party and, from the looks of it, there was no armored shaper below it. He could die just at that thought.

"You're all set?" he asked no one in specific. *Work.* He should treat it like work.

"Yes, we're all set," Chris replied. "Hannah and her partner … Where is he?" He turned his head, looking for the other kid. "Oh, there. With his parents.

They're all set, and we've been assigned the committee we've been preparing for."

"Ladies and gentlemen, we're about to begin. Please, take your seats," an announcement called.

Jordan turned to Hannah. "Good luck. Show them what you've got. I'll see you at the break."

She nodded with a small smile, gave her mother a quick hug, and then walked with Chris and the other kid toward the stage.

He now faced Hope alone. Until now, they had exchanged just two words.

She pointed at the rows of chairs. "We have seats there. I didn't know if you would come."

"I didn't know, either. That's why I didn't say anything. I hope it's okay?"

"It's more than okay." She held his gaze, and he saw her throat move as she swallowed.

The crowd of excited teachers, participants, and family members was swirling around them, but he didn't even notice it. All he saw was her. He could swear that all she saw was him, too, because she was startled when Chris reappeared and said, "Come on; we should get to our seats."

They both went with him, and Chris seated himself between them. Not purposefully; it just happened. To some extent, Jordan was thankful. He wanted to concentrate on the excited kid who sat at her representation desk, her legs waving back and forth under the table.

She was excellent. Her partner was, too. There were other good teams there, but they were the youngest, as the others were mostly in the sixth grade. Jordan made sure that, whenever she would look at them, she would see that his attention was all hers. He had even switched his phone off, because even a senator wouldn't come before this client of his.

He smiled at her while clapping hard after their turn to present their stance. And when the moderator announced a break, he broke conduct, put two fingers in his mouth, and whistled.

Hannah giggled in her seat on the stage, and Chris looked at him funny.

"How very undiplomatic," Hope said with a grin as they went to talk to Hannah.

"Can't completely uproot the small town in me." He grinned back.

"You're doing great. Keep it up," Chris said to the two kids.

"I'm so proud of you, baby," Hope said. "I sent pictures to your dad. He's excited."

Jordan side-eyed her and noticed the muscle that flexed in her jaw after she had said that.

"You're focused and calm, and that's how you do it. They're clapping like crazy for you," he said in a low voice to Hannah.

"And you whistled," she replied, her green eyes shining brightly.

"And I whistled." He laughed and ruffled her curls.

He gave her team a standing ovation, which made others stand, too, when they were announced as the second-place winners.

"They're the youngest here, and that says something," the moderator indicated.

"When you reach their age, you'll easily win the gold." Jordan put his hand on Hannah's shoulder and smiled. "You, too." He turned to the boy.

"Maybe you'll coach us," Hannah said, looking like the dictionary definition of happiness.

"Maybe."

He then moved aside and let Hope take pictures with her daughter, and Chris, and other contestants.

He didn't even reach the seats when Hope touched his shoulder. "Jordan."

He turned, and the room evaporated.

"Thank you. I know I've said it, but really, it means so much to her, to me. It's … Her dad didn't even come."

"I'm sorry. It's his loss."

"We're going for dinner. Will you come? I forgot to even ask … I was so surprised and so … Have you booked a hotel—"

"I have a flight back in two hours. I need to get to the airport."

"Oh. So, you just came for this?"

"Yes."

"I don't know what to say."

"So don't. I'm here for Hannah, Hope, not to confuse you."

"You're not … I asked you. I even hoped …"

"You hoped?" he encouraged, wanting to hear the rest of it. Fearing it wouldn't be what *he* was hoping for.

"To see you."

"Why?"

"Because I … To know you were okay after … that media circus."

"That circus is over. I'm fine." That wasn't what he was hoping for.

"Good." She expelled a breath, and her gaze escaped to the side.

It was torture. He was glad he had booked that flight out.

"You bought a house," she suddenly said, turning her eyes back to him.

"Yes."

"I passed by it on my way to … It's a nice street." Her cheeks flushed the way they had when she had told him that she had been following Rush's career because of him. She cleared her throat.

"Yeah. I need to see it for myself. I only saw it in Ava's pictures and Google Earth."

"So, you'll be in Riviera soon?"

"I should."

"Oh." After a beat, she added, "Good."

"It is?"

"Yeah." One syllable, but he had hope again.

"Is Chris staying overnight, too?"

"He is, but there's nothing … nothing."

"Hope, if there's any—"

"Jordan! Did you know that my sister and I are going trick-or-treating twice?" Hannah, bless her, burst in on them excitedly. "Not once. Twice! First with our mom at home, and then Grandma will take us to trick or treat in Nevada!"

He couldn't help but chuckle, although his fate was still hanging. "That's amazing. I've never heard of anyone who got to treat or treat in two states. That has to be some world record."

"I read the Guinness World Record book of last year and 1999. That's old!"

"It *is* very old." He smiled then bent a little toward her. "Hannah, thank you so much for that invitation letter. I had a blast. Even Gandhi would have had fun here."

Her laughter rolled. "Mom, take a picture of us."

Hope bit her lip, tapped her phone, and directed it at them. "Ready?"

He wrapped an arm around Hannah's shoulders as she leaned her head against his side.

"Cheese!" Hannah called, holding her silver medal in front of her.

He smiled, and Hope snapped the picture.

"I'll send it to you," she said.

"I have to get going," he said, looking at the time on his phone.

"Thanks, Jordan." Hope sucked in her lips and bit them, and he was pretty sure she wanted to say something else.

"Bye, Jordan," Hannah said. "When you visit us again, I'll show you my new Lego Friends."

"Deal," he said, smiling, though he felt like a fucking liar.

"Bye, Jordan," Hannah said again in that easy manner only kids are capable of.

"Bye," he said to both.

Hannah ran to join a bunch of kids that stood close by. This was her crowd. She seemed to thrive among them.

He turned to leave and took one step. But he couldn't. Not like that.

He turned on his heels, and Hope was still there, looking at him. He wrapped his arms around her, nestled her against him, and buried his face in her hair. He didn't care if people recognized him, didn't care about making a scene. He wasn't even aware there was anyone else there. She was all that he could see, all that he wanted to smell, touch, feel.

She clung to him, her arms around his shoulders, her face buried in his chest.

He had no idea how long it lasted, no idea who was watching. When she took a step back, he let go of her. His heart was too full to allow her to say something that might tear it apart. He just rubbed his palm over her arm, turned, and left, leaving unspoken words hanging between them.

Chapter 37

Nice try.

That was what the voice in her head said the whole evening, the whole damn night, and it would have said it the whole damn morning after if she didn't shut it up so she could concentrate on enjoying the morning with her daughter in the big city.

Nice try hoping she could get over him.

Nice try pretending she hadn't gone to Bay Street, especially to see the house he had bought, because it was an extension of him in her warped-with-longing mind.

Nice try acting as if seeing him at the conference hadn't made every logic fly out the window.

Nice try wishing her heart wasn't already completely taken by the man who she had reached out to a few days before with trembling heart and fingers.

Nice try imagining she could unlove him, or that she could compromise on someone who would make her heart flutter less than Jordan did, or treat her daughters better than he did. Or on someone who was less than Jordan, period.

Nice try.

Her mind finally acknowledged that her heart had been right. It was still a risk, a chance, but one she was willing to take because *he* was worth it. If he was willing to risk replacing his life of power and influence for her picket fence existence, with her draining ex and ex-in-laws, then she was willing to take a chance on him, too. She was willing to tell Eric to shove it, tell Lucile that her grown-ass son didn't need her as much as her grandkids did, tell the world that she loved Jordan Delaney.

She knew him enough to trust him to take *his* risk, only if he could meet it. If she tried to say it all with words, she would fail. Still, she had to somehow let him know.

Chapter 38

If anyone was capable of sending a life-altering text while someone was ten-thousand feet up in the sky with no ability to see it, it was Hope.

He could have seen it, if he were connected to the flight's Wi-Fi, but since political advisors' phones were extra protected, he never connected to those networks. Yet another reason to shed the title that was bearing on his soul for too long.

Nevertheless, there was nothing like deplaning from a red-eye flight, only to be sparked back to life again.

Hannah's smiling face next to him in the picture preceded a text message.

"She missed you. I did, too. Would anybody take a bite out of the Capitol Dome if it was wrapped as candy?"

He understood perfectly well what she had done. She had let him know that she was willing to try and left him to make his decision under the condition he could stick to it. The funny thing was that there was a doubt in her mind, while there was none in his.

"*You know I miss you, too. You just have no idea how much. And if anyone can make anything look like candy, it's Naomi.*"

He knew they weren't talking only of the girls but understood why she had put them front and center.

Because he was sometimes paid to put words together in a compelling way, he knew how changeable words were, how fluid, how they could be manipulated. He didn't put much stock into words. He preferred actions. There was no point in saying pretty things if he wasn't there with her to back them up.

He texted three more words then began taking the necessary steps that would make her understand that she was his end game.

"*I'll be there.*"

Chapter 39

She sat on the single step that led to her front door, watching other families, who were still trick or treating, crossing the street from side to side and going from house to house. Her lane was mildly decorated with strings of orange lights and two pumpkins lit from within. Without Hannah and Naomi, it seemed bare and un-festive, especially in comparison to some of the neighboring houses, who had gone overboard with their front yard displays.

She sent pictures of the girls in their costumes to her mother and sister and received pictures of her nephews back. She smiled as she thought of the candies that the girls had collected when she had taken them trick or treating earlier. When Lucile had arrived to pick them up for the airport, she had allowed them to take some, if they stored it in their trolleys. They had left, still in their costumes, excitedly dragging their sugar-filled luggage behind them.

Now and then, parents and kids passed her house, walked up the lane, and she welcomed them, especially those who were in her class, asking about their costumes and chatting with their parents as she extended a large bowl of candy.

She was group-chatting with Libby and Roni in-between, sharing kids' pictures and joking about Libby and Luke's couple costume as pilot and flight attendant. She had always wanted to do a couple's costumes, but Eric had never cooperated and instead always had something to say or someone to compare her to, because she hadn't gone for a sexy nurse, cop, angel, demon, or sexy whatever costume.

She was just typing something about it to her friends when she sensed someone approaching up the lane. She was about to reach out for the bowl without even looking up when a familiar gravel catapulted her heart into her throat.

"Hey, Libby's friend. That's a smart costume."

She lifted her head, feeling her pulse rising with it, and her eyes met with those of Jordan's.

He stood there, towering like a column, with those wide shoulders and chest, and that soft smile that he always had for her, and that warm gaze of his. She missed him so much that, if she wasn't afraid her knees wouldn't cooperate, she would lift herself off that stoop, run, and wrap herself in him.

Her throat went dry. "Yes, it's so smart that no one guesses what it is." She chuckled nervously. "I think my daughters were a bit embarrassed for me. I should have gone for Wonder Woman."

"But then it wouldn't be a costume."

She sucked in and bit her upper lip. Damn, he knew his way with words. Yet, she knew he was so much more than that.

When he had replied to her text, ending it with, "*I'll be there*," she hadn't asked, "*When?*" She wanted him to do it if and when he would be ready. She just hadn't expected it to be this soon.

"What did they dress up as?" he asked.

"Naomi was a unicorn, and Hannah, a jellyfish."

He nodded in appreciation. "People underestimate the jellyfish."

She looked at him with such surprise that he tilted his head in a *didn't you know?* and added, "She had it in her argument for global cooperation on marine microplastic pollution cleansing."

"I didn't know. It wasn't in the regionals." What she did know, without a shred of doubt, was that her heart was forever his, whether she agreed to it or not.

"Can I take a guess?" he asked, pointing his chin toward her.

"Sure."

"You're Neon and Helium, which don't combine with other elements, or even with each other."

"How did you know?" She couldn't help but smile at his added explanation.

"You mean, except for the fact that you're wearing neon-colored shirt, pants, and sneakers, and that you have helium balloons tied to your wrists and hairband?"

He, on the other hand, wasn't in his right-out-of-D.C. clothes that had made her knees mellow at the conference, but in a pair of jeans and a black button-down shirt that had the same effect on her. His smirk mellowed her knees so much that she would have definitely fallen on her ass, if she wasn't already sitting.

She laughed. "Yes, except that."

"Because I memorized the periodic table."

With a puddle where her heart used to be, she huffed an audible breath. "Why?"

"You really have to ask?"

She shook her head.

"I'll tell you, anyway. I memorized it because, Hope Hays … How can I put it in a way you'd understand?" He squatted in front of her, bringing his face at level with hers and holding her gaze. "You're the noblest element I ever came across, the rarest component, the most beautiful explosion I've ever seen, and I want to compound with you."

Her chuckle came out choked, rattling the balloons. "And what does *that* mean?"

"I just told you."

"Not in English." Her throat clogged with memories.

"Okay. I'd love to do this in English. Some say I'm very good at it." He shifted and sat down on the stoop next to her, his denim-covered, strong legs reaching farther out. Their shoulders brushed, and his scent filled her. If there was ever an ad for the scent of a sexy, ruggedly handsome man, he could star in it.

They looked at each other, and her eyes took in every angle and feature of his face before they locked with his amber eyes.

"I'm in love with you, Hope. Hopelessly so."

She was lost. She knew she was, even before he had come, but she had to make sure one last time before she gave in, so she wouldn't have to tell herself *told you so* later. "You wanted to swallow the world, Jordan. There's no action or glamour here. Do you honestly think you can replace that with *this*?" She jutted her chin toward the street and rolled her eyes up to hint at the five sheer pink balloons that hovered above, linked with a short string to the rubber bracelets that she had borrowed from Hannah, and the black hairband.

He shifted his eyes between hers before he spoke. "You're not a replacement, Hope. You're the real thing. Yours is the only world I want. I want *you*! Jesus, I *want* you! All of it! I won't compromise on a life without you. And if you want me, if you love me, don't *you* compromise on us."

When she reached out, instead of answering, and placed her hand on the stubbled ridge of his jaw, the balloons rattled again. She leaned in and did what she had been craving to do for weeks—press her lips to his.

Jordan pivoted toward her, cupped her face and neck with both hands, and welded her mouth to his.

She clung to his strength and the solid mass of his warm, hard body. It was lucky that he supported her back, or she would have lain back right there on the stoop and pulled him on top of her, although they were outside and people passed by on the sidewalk, just a few feet away.

They broke the kiss, and he looked at her with her face still held in his palms.

"Now, I want to hear you say it," he rasped, his gaze linked with hers. There was that flame again in the honey eyes.

"What?" That kiss had taken away her capacity to compute thoughts. She was a blaze of a beating heart and skin that burned for his touch.

"What I see in your eyes," he said in a low timbre, holding her gaze. "Say it."

God, just that rasp could kill her.

"I love you, Jordan. I tried not to, was afraid to, but you're so ... good, and kind, and your heart ... and ... and I love you. I love you. I love that you're ... that each time ... "

When Jordan's mouth landed on hers mid-sentence, she didn't mind. She didn't mind at all.

Chapter 40

"Fuck, I've fantasized about you and this door," he said the moment he rammed it shut behind them and pressed Hope up against him, her back to the door. He kissed her again on the mouth and throat, and she grabbed his shoulders before linking her hands around his neck. But those balloons, those five ridiculous balloons, kept shaking and making that annoying sound of air-filled rubber clanking against itself.

He shifted his head back and looked at her. Eyes wide, lips raw and red from the force of their kiss, bangs loosening from the hairband and falling to her forehead, she was heaving, her chest rising against his, and so fucking beautiful.

Without taking his eyes off hers, he gently caught the hairband at both sides behind her ears and slid it off, causing the three balloons to clash even more, then tossed it behind him.

Hope brought her hands between them, presenting her wrists, eyes on his, and *this* ... this could be the end of him.

Without removing his eyes from hers, he slid off one rubber bracelet, then the other, and tossed them aside forcefully to countereffect the float of the helium. He then crashed his mouth on hers and, with his hands under her thighs, lifted her so she could wrap her legs around him. She huffed a breath into their kiss as her center pushed against his hardness.

Jordan chafed his hands up her body, and when they were at her waist, he lifted her yellow neon shirt over her head and threw it. The way her hair fell back from within the shirt to her shoulders, landing on the black bra straps, took his breath away.

They watched each other, eyes skimming, caressing, devouring, taking in the way the other reflected their need. He smoothed his palms over her exposed skin, and Hope tugged at his shirt and fumbled with the buttons. She then tore her eyes from his and undid them one by one. He enjoyed watching her as she slid her hands into the open shirt.

He began kissing her neck and groaned into her ear as she trekked her hands up from his abs to his chest and shoulders until she took the shirt off him completely.

Pressing her with his pelvis to the door, he undid her bra. There was enough light coming from the living room behind them for him to enjoy the sight of her naked breasts before he brought his palms and mouth to touch and kiss, caress and lick.

She moaned into his ear and tried to push eager hands into the front of his pants, making him huff a breath when she touched the tip of him.

When she ground against him, Jordan pushed them off the door and carried her to the bedroom with her legs still wrapped around him. He wanted access to all of her, he wanted to take his time with her, he wanted this to be more than a fuck against a door. They would have time for that later.

He stripped her of the rest of the neon clothes, sliding the black panties down her thighs. She stripped him, too, and they kissed, breathed, and tasted every inch of each other's skin they exposed.

With no more layers separating them, Jordan kissed and licked his way down her body. He smiled when he noticed she had sorted out what she had considered an issue last time.

This time, she didn't pull him up. Threading her fingers in his hair, she bucked against his mouth, instead.

When she was getting close, he lifted her and flipped them over so she would be on top of him. Her green eyes, cloudy and wide with arousal, didn't leave his eyes until she threw her head back and closed them as she moaned his name at her climax and brought him to his.

He tightened his hands on her thighs that straddled him, and when she collapsed on top of him, he enveloped her in his arms, found her mouth with his, and kissed her for as long as their rugged breaths enabled.

Chapter 41

"So, you memorized the periodic table?"

"It wasn't easy, but you can test me."

"Maybe I will. Maybe I'll grade your test hard against a wall."

"I'd love that. Just give me a few minutes."

She laughed then traveled her eyes and fingers over his light brown hair, his face, down to his neck and shoulders, then along his arm, tracing the veins on the strong forearm as she had craved to do. She then brushed her fingers up and stopped at his corded bicep, caressing his surging wave tattoo. "Why this?"

He hadn't removed his gaze from her face the whole time, and it felt like he was caressing her, too. "I was freezing my ass off in Ithaca during my second winter there. It was gorgeous, but so far from home, and this ocean, and what I was used to. I even missed the smell of sunscreen. When a friend offered we get tattoos, I went along. The moment I saw this one, I knew."

"And you spent all these years on the other coast."

"The prodigal son is ready to come home, especially when there's you."

"You're hardly a prodigal son."

He scoffed. "You won't let me enjoy at least some notoriety?" He slipped a hand over her cheek and threaded his fingers in her hair.

"But, seriously, what will you do here?"

"Do you know how many offers I have here, not just in politics? One of the largest economies in the world? Silicon Valley? Ava and I talked about this a while ago. She's a content creator, and there are multiple opportunities to cooperate and branch out together."

She puckered her lips, still tracing the wave with her fingers. "Won't you miss politics?"

"Like chemistry, there's politics in everything." He smiled, reminding her of their conversation that night at the beach house kitchen. "Whether I like it or not, I'll always have to deal with it. We all do. You do, too."

"The teachers' lounge *can* be cut-throat."

He laughed. "I bet it is."

"Especially when Avery finds out where you are." She couldn't even fathom the lectures she would get from her.

"I'd say leave her to me, but you can handle her better."

She sighed. "I have Eric to handle first." She would have to tell him before the girls. With the girls, she would have to take it extra careful.

Jordan bit his lip. "I didn't feel I had the right to say anything until now, but you know what I learned about people like Eric? They act like nothing is ever good enough for them, but deep, deep, deep down, they don't think they're ever good enough for nothing. They're not even aware of it, but if you know that about him, you can play that to get him to play fair."

"God, you *are* good at politics." She chuckled. "I hope you're not playing *me*."

"I can't play you."

"Why not?"

"You're unpredictable." He smirked and drew his thumb along her hairline. "And disarmingly beautiful. And the only person who can look sexy with balloons hanging from them."

She laughed, but damn him, he made her sweat again.

"And I love you," he rasped. "I never wanted or tried playing you. I hope you know that."

She looked into his eyes. "I do."

"You're the only person I can't find the words with."

She leaned closer to him, breathing in his skin, then kissed him, absorbing his taste, never wanting to let go. "I love you, too," she whispered against his lips.

~~~~~~~~~~~~~~~~

It wasn't the door they ended up using. It was her shower wall. After making use of the bed again the night before, they had fallen asleep. When Jordan used her shower in the morning, she went in there to put out a clean towel for him. Instead, she found herself up against the wall, clothes and all, so fast that she became almost dizzy. She *did* become dizzy with excess of oxygen when he made her hold on to him for dear life, gasping his name against his wet skin as he thrust hard into her against the wall.

Later, with a towel around his waist, Jordan picked up the wet clothes that he had taken off her in the shower. She wanted to clap—Eric wouldn't ever dream of picking anything up—wondering inside when she would stop comparing.

"Where's your luggage?" she asked when they went back to the bedroom and he put on the clothes that he'd had on the night before. "I didn't even ask where you're staying. When did you arrive?"

"I kept your mouth busy." He smirked at her, and she felt ridiculous to blush, yet she did. "I arrived yesterday, left my stuff at my parents', then drove here. I was supposed to go see the house, too. Thought about leaving my stuff there, but …"

"You came to see the house?"

"You're the only reason I board planes these days, Hope. Do you want to come with me to see it, or did you have enough eyeful when you passed by?" That smirk again … and those dimples. She could never get enough.

"I'll go with you."

"We can drive my new car." He pointed out the window, at a black Volvo SUV that was parked on the other side of the street.

"You bought a car?"

"I'm not here on vacation, so I need one." His smile was lopsided.

She realized what he was doing.

She rose to her toes and kissed him. "It's a ten-minute walk. Speaking of, I never got to thank you for fixing the garage door."

"I think you pretty much did." He ran a finger over her jawline then planted a kiss on her lips.

They walked there. The place was more a construction site than when she had seen it before. Roni and her crew had begun working on it, though Roni wasn't there the day after Halloween.

"Will you move here? To suburbia?" she asked, still incredulous. They were standing on the lawn that needed some TLC and gazing at the house from the outside.

"I'll move to fucking Siberia, if you're there." He held her hand and pulled her to him, wrapping his arms around her waist, and her hands landed on his shoulders. "We have work to do if you're still wondering about my wanting to be here and nowhere else."

"Just a little work." She blushed. Yes, she still had work to do with herself, but they were both worth it.

He tightened his hold on her waist. "You know, there's a saying—never let a good crisis go to waste. When that thing with Rush happened, it forced me to face things, to make a change. That was the good outcome of that crisis. Because I got to know you, and you changed my perspective on possibilities, on what I wanted to be, to do, to have, even on who I am."

"How did I do *that*?"

"Just by being you."

She stared at him, her mind indexing, her heart registering, flailing.

She reached up to his nape and brought his lips down to hers. Kissing him was her way of telling him, until she could find words, that he had done the same for her.

Chapter 42

She could get used to this—waking up in Jordan's arms, getting ready for work knowing he was in her kitchen, making coffee, kissing him whenever she wanted. However, she had only two days to do that before her daughters returned, and they had agreed to make things less public for them. Then he would have to go back to D.C. for a few days.

"It's a marathon, not a sprint," he said the night after their checking on his house, when she had told him that she had to go to work the next day.

Now she tucked her purple blouse into her black slacks and shoved her feet into a pair of black ballerina flats.

"Fuck, Miss Hays, good thing you teach elementary," Jordan said when she appeared in the kitchen. "I know I'll fantasize about you in this outfit all day."

She caught the two sides of his open shirt and tucked them together. "That will make two of us."

He kissed up her neck then stopped next to her ear. "I haven't forgotten that I wanted to take you out somewhere fancy when I was back. We have until tomorrow when the girls return. Wanna go out with me tonight?"

"Are you asking me on a date?" she said into his neck.

He pulled himself back and looked at her. "An official one."

"Then, yes." She smiled.

"Great. Pick you up at seven."

They left the house together, kissing before they split—she to work, and he to his car to see his brother first, then to Wayford to see Ava and work at his parents'.

After an afternoon video chat with her daughters, who showed her a horrifying amount of candy, she got ready for her date with Jordan.

She wore a green dress, no shaper—let it cling to whatever it had to cling to—and with enough cleavage to focus the attention not just on how the color matched her eyes.

"You look amazing," he said when he picked her up. "Though I'm more partial to Tweetie."

"Thanks. You don't look too bad yourself." She chuckled, but in his business-casual dark chinos and pale blue dress shirt, he looked amazing and, at that moment, dinner was just in the way of her peeling those clothes off him.

The restaurant and wine cellar that he took her to in another town were worth waiting with the clothes peeling until after dinner. She knew she wouldn't remember what they ate or drank, but she would recollect the drive there, holding his hand, talking, laughing, satisfying his interest in her family, childhood, the town she had come from.

"One sister, older, married, three kids, living near my parents, working as the accountant in their auto shop business, harsh winters, church on Sundays."

"Any more bullet points?" He laughed. "Do you miss them?"

"I do. We saw them in the summer, and I promised to bring the girls for Christmas."

She knew she would also remember the way her heart expanded until she was almost breathless with happiness. She would recall walking toward the entrance with him by her side, his palm on the small of her back, and his whisper, "You look absolutely amazing, and I hope I can last through dinner," right before they went in.

In the months that she had known him, she had collected more happy moments of love, care, kindness, and attention than she had in the decade that had preceded him.

Chapter 43

If the amount of time to pack, and the weight of belongings collected, was any indication of a life, then his life in D.C. had been a vacant one. Most of the things that ended up in his suitcase were things he could buy anywhere—clothes, a few books, and his laptop, which was all work. No plants, no pets, no memorabilia of emotional significance, nothing to regret leaving behind. A few meetings, another visit or two to close things off, and he could kiss this city goodbye before Christmas.

Yet everything he carried on him—his tattoo, a plastic-covered drawing, and his heart—were all directing at the point he was shipping his luggage to.

Home was there. Home was her.

Epilogue

"So, if you two become sisters-in-law, that leaves me as just a friend." Roni pouted, looking at the glass she was holding.

"Just a friend, will you help me choose a wedding cake?" Libby asked. "Anne showed me a few designs, and I can't decide." Luke and Libby's wedding was planned for the spring.

"Liberty Latimer," Roni said, using Libby's full name in rebuttal. "Thanks for trying to make me feel included, but you could have come up with something better than choosing a wedding cake. I know you couldn't care less about what wedding cake you'll have. It could be a Betty Crocker mix for all you care, even though you pretty much grew up in a bakery."

Libby laughed and exchanged a look with Hope. "I can't with her. She knows me too well. What do you think? Should we add her to the family?"

"I'm not marrying Jordan … yet. You're jumping way ahead," Hope said, placing a hand on Roni's arm, though she knew Roni was joking. "We only just made it public with my family, and he's closing things off in D.C."

"And living half the time in my construction site," Roni said. "Only men can live in a house that is basically a construction site. I mean, there's no glass on some of the windows, dust everywhere." She threw her hands up in a theatrical gesture of *I don't get it*.

"Well, he's not exactly living there," Hope said with a faux coy expression. "He's spending most nights at mine and leaves before the girls wake up, which is really early. But, for now, we want to ease them into us."

"Yeah, that's why he's been bringing us breakfast three times a week when he's here," Libby said, chuckling. "He then stays at ours while we're at work, then goes back to Hope's."

"Ah, families," Roni said with a sigh. "I don't feel left out at all."

"Left out? You talk to him three times a day with all the house stuff."

"Nah, I mostly talk to Ava," Roni said, dropping the fake mad act she had going on. "He's not big on design, your boyfriend. Has no idea what the difference is between sage and olive green."

Hope felt the stupid smile spreading on her face before Libby said, "Look at that smile!"

She shrugged, still unable to wipe it off. "It just feels strange—boyfriend. I feel nineteen again. I haven't been in love in ages, and I don't think I've ever been *this* in love, either."

"So, what did the girls have to say? They probably suspected, seeing him around a lot these past few weeks."

"They see him. Just not early in the morning. We spend some afternoons and evenings together and told

304

them Jordan was my very good friend, and that we love each other, and that we're spending time together."

"And …?" Roni prompted. "You probably already told this story to your future sister-in-law here, so now tell me, too."

Hope chuckled at Roni's sarcasm. "Hannah said, 'Mom, that's what Dad said about Jenna, and they got married. We're kids, not stupid. He's your boyfriend. But that's okay because we really like him.' And Naomi said, 'And he's very tall,' which I think means she approves of him."

"And Eric?" Roni asked.

She huffed a loud breath. "I think I learned a new way to handle him. I name-dropped a lot—it always makes an impression on him. Told him the name of the senator that Jordan works with, and that he's sort of a celebrity in D.C., and that's why the media was keen to invent things about him. As a cherry on top, I added that he's the most famous person to come out of Riviera View."

"Oh, smart! That *had* to sting Eric." Roni tilted her ouzo shot toward Hope then took a sip. She scrunched her nose. "It hasn't grown on me yet."

"And now he'll be more careful and respectful with you because, to him, having this connection to big names means that you're so much better than he assumed. What an idiot!" Libby hissed.

"Now he really wants to meet Jordan and not just to inspect him for the girls. Lucile knows, too, of course. I told her right after Eric so he wouldn't get to tell her first. With her living here, I had to. I also kinda hinted that it'd save them a lot of travel money and time if they moved to Nevada."

"Hope!" Libby exclaimed.

Hope laughed. "I'm done giving a"—she lowered her voice—"fuck."

"It's about time," Roni said.

"By the way, we're thinking about doing something together for Thanksgiving. I don't know if Ava told you, Libby, but if the houses are ready by then, Ava wants to invite everyone. And you're coming, too, Roni. How that's for a family?"

"She hasn't told me yet," Libby said, just when Roni went with, "It should be ready."

"I know you guys might think it's too soon for mutual holidays and everything, but when you know, you know. You know?"

Again, they spoke in tandem. Roni with, "Oh, Hope, I missed you. No one can make sense like you do," just as Libby said, "We know."

They laughed at their synch.

"I don't think it's too soon," Libby completed.

"You guys are so right for each other, it's obvious. And thank you. We'll be happy to," Roni said.

They clinked their glasses and took a sip.

"Oh, look. No, don't look," Roni suddenly said. "I'll tell you when you can look. Seems like we're not the only ones who thought to check out the taverna." When a new place opened in town, everyone came for a test drive. And a Greek taverna sounded promising. "Avery just came in, and I think she's on a hot date. She's all dressed up on a Monday, as is the guy she's with. Okay, carefully, you can look now, but quickly. Any idea who that is?"

Hope and Libby snuck a glance at the table that was on the other side of the floor from them.

"He looks vaguely familiar," Libby said.

"Does Avery know about you and Jordan?" Libby asked.

"Yes." Hope drew her mouth to the side. "Rumors travel fast here, and there's a limit to the number of times we can be seen together in town, or kissing on my doorstep, without it reaching her. But she hasn't said a thing, and that's unusual for Avery. So, I take it as a good sign."

"She found someone else to keep her busy," Roni muttered.

"By the way, with everything that went on, I didn't get a chance, but I'm still up for inviting Anne to join us." Hope looked at her friends for approval.

"Worth a try," Libby said. "She's so different than her cousin over there. They don't even seem related."

~~~~~~~~~~~~~~~~~~~

The evening at Ava's was great. Everyone brought something, and the table that was set in an L shape, to accommodate everyone, was full to the point of collapse. Joe Delaney brought the biggest turkey that Hope had ever seen and kept bragging about it all evening, while Libby brought salads and kept apologizing that this was all the cooking she was capable of.

Hope couldn't have been more thankful than to see her daughters playing with Roni's kids, as she sat at the same table with her two best friends, and have the man her heart belonged to raising a toast of the special cocktails that he had prepared and say, "To family, and to all the elements lining up to create the best compound."

When they went next door to his house, to put boxes of leftovers in his fridge, the girls went outside to the backyard that was just a plot of crushed lawn. It was next on Jordan's list.

The house still smelled of new paint, and as he closed the door of his fridge, and Hannah's drawing, magnetized to it, flitted with the motion, Hope came in through the door that led to the backyard. In synch, they both reached for the other, and Jordan encircled her in his arms and kissed her.

"By your fridge, like the first time," she said, smiling.

"We've had many firsts in the past few weeks, and seconds, and thirds, and ... I want to have all those moments with you an infinite number of times."

"Me, too."

"Hope?"

Something in the way he said it made her heart skip a beat. "Yes?"

"I know it's just my kitchen and fridge, and nothing romantic like you deserve, but ... Will you marry me? I don't have a ring on me, though I know which one I wanna get you, and I would drop on one knee if Hannah wasn't facing me from the yard, and you might think it's too soon, and we need to prepare everyone, and you can take all the time you need to think, decide, and—"

She crashed her mouth on his and kissed him until her head floated in a daze. He gripped her hard, and only the playful voices of Hannah and Naomi outside prevented them from going further.

"Yes," she said, panting, when they broke the kiss.

"Yes?" His smile was so wide that the dimples became caverns.

"Yes."

They were both lost for any other words, and no other words were needed when love was deeper, vaster, and fiercer than any logic, science, or language could explain.

He kissed her again, gently this time, then leaned his forehead against hers. "When will we tell the girls?"

"By Christmas, because I want you to come with us to Minnesota."

He rubbed his nose against hers. "Will give me a chance to get you that ring."

She felt like she was hovering above herself, above that moment, as if her body was too small to contain all this happiness.

"Jordan." Naomi and Hannah announced their presence as they came running in, giving them just enough time to pull back a bit. The girls had seen them kiss and hug before, but they made sure not to overdo it.

"Jordan, can you build a pool like Casey Davis has? We don't have room in our backyard." Naomi stopped next to them, putting her hands on his leg, still treating him like a column whenever she stood next to him.

"Casey Davis's parents are wasting water," Hannah reproached. "Jordan, tell Naomi you don't want a pool. It's a waste of water. And having a lawn does, too. I read about it in *National Geographic*."

Jordan looked at Hope with a smile and raised brows, and Hope returned it, holding his gaze.

He then let go of her and crouched so he could be at level with the girls. "You know what? You both have great points. Let's think together about a solution that will make both you and the environment happy. You'll help me decide, okay?"

Even when he was crouching, Naomi had to rise to her toes to put her palms around his ear so she could whisper something straight into it.

"That's not fair, Naomi," Hannah called. "There's a thing that's called concession."

"I only told him that Casey has a hot tub, too," Naomi replied defensively.

"We'll find a solution together, I promise," Jordan said, looking from one to the other. "Deal?" He raised both his palms for them to high-five.

"Deal," Hannah said first, then Naomi, both sticking their small palms to his. He then wrapped an arm around each for a little hug, patted their heads, and straightened up.

"Okay, girls, time to go home," Hope announced, smiling at him and yearning for the day when going home would be done with him.

"Can Jordan come, too? I want to read him and Naomi the article in my *National Geographic*."

They exchanged another look over the girls' heads.

"I'll be happy to," he replied with a smile.

"Okay, but then straight to bed," Hope said and nearly chuckled when she realized what it sounded like.

"Straight to bed," he whispered into her ear while locking the front door, sending a heat wave straight into her bloodstream.

~~~~~~~~~~~~~~~~~~

"Naomi snored before Hannah finished the first paragraph, and when *she* yawned, I read to her until she fell asleep," Jordan said as he entered her bedroom, closing the door behind him.

She was sitting on the bed, still in the red dress that she had worn for dinner. "You handled it well. Even Casey Davis's parents wouldn't have dealt with it that well."

He laughed as he pulled her up into his arms. "Good thing I have negotiation and mediation experience. Trust me, some of the people I dealt with weren't as smart or caring as Naomi and Hannah."

She laughed and started opening the buttons of his shirt. "They'll teach you new skills."

"They already do." He kissed her then, leaning his weight in until they fell on the bed and began stripping each other.

"I was told once we're not compatible. I don't know about you, but I feel we're *very* compatible," he rasped when he was inside her.

"Experimenting proved my hypothesis wrong," she whispered then pressed her lips to his in a deep, scorching kiss.

Read the other books in the 'Riviera View' series:

Visit Lily's website for a bonus epilogue:
www.lilybaines.com
Don't miss an update. Follow her on Facebook
and Instagram:
www.facebook.com/lilybainesauthor
www.instagram.com/lily_baines_author/

Binge the 'Of All Hearts' Series – finding love in
an unexpected place, time, and person:

Acknowledgments

Thank you to every reader who takes a chance on my stories! Writing is part of my escapism (says the woman who wrote romance books about small towns in Italy, Greece, and Montenegro), so I hope I was able to provide a small, fun escape from reality for you, too.

I want to give a special shout-out to the readers on my ARC team who have been there since my first book. Moran, Demi, Lene, Malcolm, Ana, Julie, Jacquelyn, Darian, and Denise. Your support means the world!

Thank you to those who read the draft of this book and whose comments and highlights made me swoon, giggle, correct, or all of those combined. Brooke Burton alpha-read this book and dragged me up the last mile of writing. Beta readers, Leigh Ann Jordan, who's a wonderful supporter; Louise Murchie, who's an awesome author herself; Demi Abrahamson, who's both a beta and an ARC reader and has the task of reading each book twice.

Writing can be a lonely experience, but thanks to friends I've been lucky to make in the bookish community, it feels much less so. Special thanks to authors Brenda Margriet, Mellanie Szereto, and Stephanie Morris who, together with me, run the Worth The Wait Seasoned Romance Facebook readers group that celebrates romance books with mature heroines. And to authors Devin Sloane and Sionna Trenz, Debbie Cromack and Nalani Titcomb, who are also awesome authors, people, and friends.

There are many bloggers and bookstagrammers whose support and kindness are beyond amazing and I thank each one of you. Thank you to those I reached out to when I had pretty much 0 followers and who made me feel welcome, connected, and have been supportive since: Anita, Marla, Michelle, Samantha, and Susanne. Extra thanks to Kau @koosreviews who became an encouraging voice in my head.

Thank you to my editor, Kristin Campbell from C&D Editing, for helping me grow as an author. Sorry, Kristin, for all the past perfect imperfections.

And last, but certainly not least, thank you to my kids for being who they are and for their pride in me. Their combined personalities and antics inspired some of Hannah and Naomi's in this book. My eldest daughter lends her opinions on my covers and teaches me (without hiding her amusement) how to use Instagram; my son always asks how my day goes and tries to be patient when I daydream; and my youngest is the cute, proud owner of the Gandhi and marble references.

A loving thanks to my everyday romance hero, my husband, who supports me in a million ways and has promised he'd read my books as soon as I write a spy thriller involving the MI6, Mossad, and CIA.